THE *ENTERPRISE* DROPPED OUT OF WARP SPEED IN A DAZZLING DISPLAY OF LIGHT AND COASTED TOWARD THE BATTLE SITE . . .

"Raise shields," ordered Picard.

"Rendezvous in three point four minutes," announced Data.

"Impulse Power." Picard still sat unmoving in his chair.

La Forge held his hands poised over the helm panel. "Switching to impulse power."

Ever so gently, the pilot's fingers touched down onto the board. On the viewer, the pinpoint sparkle of distant stars sprang into relief against a featureless black backdrop. In the center of this static image a blur of movement cast shadows over the fixed lights. Two vessels tumbled through space, locked in a deadly dance of combat. A glowing blue fog enveloped them both.

Picard leaned forward. "Go to Red Alert."

The waiting was over.

D0974558

Look for STAR TREK Fiction from Pocket Books

Star Trek: The Original Series

Final Frontier
Strangers from the Sky
Enterprise
Star Trek IV:
   The Voyage Home
Star Trek V:
   The Final Frontier
Spock's World
The Lost Years
Prime Directive
#1 Star Trek:
   The Motion Picture
#2 The Entropy Effect
#3 The Klingon Gambit
#4 The Covenant of the Crown
#5 The Prometheus Design
#6 The Abode of Life
#7 Star Trek II:
   The Wrath of Khan
#8 Black Fire
#9 Triangle
#10 Web of the Romulans
#11 Yesterday's Son
#12 Mutiny on the Enterprise
#13 The Wounded Sky
#14 The Trellisane Confrontation
#15 Corona
#16 The Final Reflection
#17 Star Trek III:
   The Search for Spock
#18 My Enemy, My Ally
#19 The Tears of the Singers
#20 The Vulcan Academy Murders
#21 Uhura's Song
#22 Shadow Lord

#23 Ishmael
#24 Killing Time
#25 Dwellers in the Crucible
#26 Pawns and Symbols
#27 Mindshadow
#28 Crisis on Centaurus
#29 Dreadnought!
#30 Demons
#31 Battlestations!
#32 Chain of Attack
#33 Deep Domain
#34 Dreams of the Raven
#35 The Romulan Way
#36 How Much for Just the Planet?
#37 Bloodthirst
#38 The IDIC Epidemic
#39 Time for Yesterday
#40 Timetrap
#41 The Three-Minute Universe
#42 Memory Prime
#43 The Final Nexus
#44 Vulcan's Glory
#45 Double, Double
#46 The Cry of the Onlies
#47 The Kobayashi Maru
#48 Rules of Engagement
#49 The Pandora Principle
#50 Doctor's Orders
#51 Enemy Unseen
#52 Home Is the Hunter
#53 Ghost Walker
#54 A Flag Full of Stars
#55 Renegade
#56 Legacy
#57 The Rift

Star Trek: The Next Generation

Metamorphosis
Vendetta
Encounter at Farpoint
#1 Ghost Ship
#2 The Peacekeepers
#3 The Children of Hamlin
#4 Survivors
#5 Strike Zone
#6 Power Hungry
#7 Masks
#8 The Captains' Honor

#9 A Call to Darkness
#10 A Rock and a Hard Place
#11 Gulliver's Fugitives
#12 Doomsday World
#13 The Eyes of the Beholders
#14 Exiles
#15 Fortune's Light
#16 Contamination
#17 Boogeymen
#18 Q-in-Law
#19 Perchance to Dream

STAR TREK ®

#3

THE NEXT GENERATION ™

THE CHILDREN OF HAMLIN

CARMEN CARTER

POCKET BOOKS

New York   London   Toronto   Sydney   Tokyo   Singapore

An *Original* Publication of POCKET BOOKS

POCKET BOOKS, a division of Simon & Schuster Inc.
1230 Avenue of the Americas, New York, NY 10020

ISBN: 0-671-73555-1

First Pocket Books printing November 1988

10 9 8 7 6 5 4 3

POCKET and colophon are registered trademarks of
Simon & Schuster Inc.

Printed in the U.S.A.

Dedicated to MDK,
who has put up with this madness of mine
for the past twelve years and is resigned
to the fact that it may never go away.

Acknowledgments

I wrote *Dreams of the Raven* over the course of two years, with no thought of publication until the manuscript was finished. In a moment of absolute insanity, I volunteered to write *The Children of Hamlin* in three months. Writing to the demands of a deadline was an entirely new experience, and I could never have succeeded without the help of the following people:

Daphne Kutzer, who knew I could do it and exhibited great patience as I continually told her why I couldn't. She read every word and kept asking for more.

Pat Hoffmann, who held my hand long-distance and got me over the rough spots.

Dave Stern, who asked me to write a *Star Trek: The Next Generation* novel and let me change my mind after I said no.

Denise Tathwell, who knows the crew of the NCC-1701D better than I do and made sure I got them right.

And special thanks to Apple Computer for developing the Macintosh. (If you have to ask, you wouldn't understand.)

Chapter One

Day is a concept born of planets spinning captive about a sun. In deep space, far removed from the light and heat of flaming stars, the kingdom of perpetual night reigns . . .

"CAPTAIN, WHAT ARE you doing awake at this hour?"

The words pricked the fragile bubble of thought that carried Jean-Luc Picard through space. He pulled back from the void, back inside the protective shell of the ship's hull. His gaze focused on the clear glass of the port window and met his own reflection: dark, piercing eyes set in a lean face, its strong features heightened by a high forehead and closely cropped fringe of gray hair. The fingers of his hands, resting lightly on the clear glass of the port window, were stiff with cold, their warmth drained into space. He lifted his palms from the chill surface, and turned to face the woman who had entered the observation room.

"I might ask the same of you, Dr. Crusher," he said.

Beverly Crusher walked up beside him and peered out the window. The captain continued to look at her.

"It's all in the title. I'm a doctor; we're always awake when everyone else—almost everyone else—is asleep." She yawned and ran a smoothing hand back over her long and somewhat tousled red hair. "What's your excuse, insomnia or ship's duty?"

"Philosophy." But the formless, almost mystical emotion that had welled within him had slipped away, and he had no desire to call it back now that she was here. "How serious was the medical call?"

"Not serious enough to warrant a report to the ship's captain, if that's what you're asking." She shivered and wrapped the blue medical jacket more tightly around her slender frame.

Picard stepped away from the chilled air lining the port wall, and out of the lounge into the corridor beyond. Crusher, her easy stride matching his own, kept pace beside him. The curving passageway was empty and still; the soft glow of deck lights tracked a path for their boots. "Nevertheless," he said, "I'm always concerned about the welfare of the crew."

"Then you'll be relieved to know that Lieutenant T'sala's firstborn is resting quietly after a somewhat nasty bout of colic."

"Ah, colic." Picard arranged his features to convey what he hoped was sympathetic interest. "I didn't think Vulcan infants were prone to colic."

"Well, strictly speaking, Surell's condition involves a circulatory rather than gastric distress, but the result is a baby that cries very loudly for hours on end. It might as well be colic." Crusher threw him a quick glance and smiled. "But these aren't the usual concerns of a ship's captain, are they?"

"Perhaps not," he conceded with an answering smile. Even in the subdued light of the corridor he

12

could detect the glint of amusement in her eyes. Such very blue eyes.

Picard cleared his throat with a self-conscious cough. "How have our new passengers taken to life aboard the *Enterprise?*"

"The Oregon Farmers?" The doctor sighed. "Well, of course, Starfleet certifies that all emigrant populations are medically fit. And it's to be expected that there will be some emotional adjustments when faced with such a different environment as a starship . . ."

"Dr. Crusher," broke in the captain. "What seems to be the problem?"

"No problem yet," she said. "But Troi reports that one of the young Farmers seems to be unusually fascinated by starship technology. He's been severely reprimanded by the community for exploring the ship."

"I see." Picard pondered the implications. "Poor young man. I gather the Oregonians are rather suspicious of modern technology. Still, I dare say it's not too serious. In another day they'll all be on their new planet, safe from the corrupting influence of—" He stopped suddenly in the corridor, his prediction unfinished.

"What's wrong?"

"Can't you feel it?" Picard balanced the weight of his body on both feet, reading the subtle movements of the deck. "The *Enterprise* just changed course . . . and increased warp speed." His right hand flew up to the silver emblem pinned to his chest, activating his communications link with the ship. "Picard to bridge . . ."

"Riker here, Captain. We've received a priority distress call from a Federation starship. They're under attack."

"Who is attacking them?" demanded the captain. "The Ferengi?"

"Unknown. It's an automatic signal, probably from an ejected buoy. We're still trying to raise a response from the ship itself."

"Very well, Number One. I'm on my way." Picard broke contact and erupted into a fast-paced walk.

"Good night, Captain," Crusher called after him.

"Oh, yes," Picard paused in mid-stride and looked back over his shoulder.

"Don't wait for me," she said without changing the pace of her leisurely stroll. "The *Enterprise* is your patient, not mine."

Picard managed a parting wave, then walked on, duty wiping all thought of Beverly Crusher from his mind.

Wesley Crusher had been creeping silently through the cabin day area when the beep of an emergency medical call pulled his mother out of her bed. Ducking back into his room, he listened to the muffled sounds of her conversation with T'sala and the accompanying shrieks of a Vulcan infant who was too young to control pain or distress. His mother left their quarters a few minutes later.

After counting to thirty, Wesley peered out of the cabin and checked to see if she was still in the vicinity. To his relief, she was gone—nevertheless, his heart was beating faster than normal when he stepped out into the corridor and headed toward the turbolift. He surely *felt* old enough to manage his own time without having to account to his mother, but she might not agree. So the easiest course was to keep her from finding out he was leaving their quarters.

The ship was quiet this late at night, but there were still people moving from one section to another. No one he passed was bothered to see him—despite his youth, Wesley was as tall as many of the adults and his striped cadet shirt emphasized his connection with the crew. His reputation as an earnest, precocious student helped lull any remaining suspicions.

Dnnys was waiting at the appointed place, a deserted crew lounge on Deck 21. "I thought you weren't coming."

"I was delayed," said Wesley.

A knowing grin broke out over the other boy's face. "Yeah, I almost got caught, too. But after the last whipping Tomas gave me, nobody believes I'd try to leave the passengers' quarters again." He snapped to mock attention. "So where do we start, Mr. Crusher?"

"Engineering," said Wesley. He had mapped out their course while lying in bed, passing the time until the rendezvous. "I can get you into certain nonrestricted areas, but you've got to be on your best behavior because you're going to be noticed."

"Who me?" asked Dnnys with wide-eyed innocence. He looked down at his traditional Farmer clothing of faded blue pants of roughly sewn cotton and a wool overshirt with a red and black patchwork pattern.

"I would have brought a change of clothes, but I don't think it would have made much difference." Wesley pointed to the Farmer boy's shaggy brown hair. "You'd need a haircut, too."

Dnnys shrugged off his appearance. "Can we visit the bridge?"

"No way," said Wesley emphatically. "The captain has declared it off limits to all kids. Before I was an acting ensign, he yelled at me for even looking at the bridge from the turbolift." He paused, then continued. "I didn't mean to boast. About being an ensign, I mean."

"You didn't," said Dnnys. "Not much, anyway. If I could work on a starship's control center, I'd crow like

15

a morning cock." He paced to the threshold of the lounge. "Come on, let's get going. I haven't got much time before I'm missed."

Wesley lagged behind. "Are you sure you want to go through with this? You could get into a lot of trouble."

"Oh, I'm always in trouble for one thing or another," sighed Dnnys. "I've gotten used to it."

Wesley shrugged—and, since Dnnys showed no signs of backing down, led the way to the outer perimeter of the engineering section. The night crew was certainly not going to challenge Ensign Crusher's entrance, and they gave his companion little more than a curious glance before returning to their duties.

"The central shaft is more interesting," apologized Wesley as they walked through a wide, squat room filled with system control panels.

"Maybe, but this is all pretty exciting to me," countered Dnnys. He pointed to one panel, "What's that do?" Dutifully, Wesley began to describe the panel's function, his words underscored by the constant basso hum of the nearby matter/antimatter blender. Dnnys nodded, his eyes glazing over as he struggled to absorb a whole new world of information, as alien to him as farming would have been to Wesley.

Dnnys started at an unfamiliar sound and his eyes skipped from one end of the room to another. "What was that?"

"We've increased warp speed," exclaimed Wesley, startled by the sudden shift in tempo and strength of the vibrations of the quivering deck. He turned away from the circuit monitor to ask why, but the duty technician had slipped away into another area.

He would have to figure it out for himself.

The main bridge of the *Enterprise* was its nerve center, a spacious room with a vaulted ceiling and curving walls that added an aesthetic dimension to its functional structure. The chairs of the duty stations were cushioned, the deck carpeted: warm pastels predominated, but a diffuse light revealed flat black control panels with displays of bright, flowing colors.

William Riker, first officer of the *USS Enterprise,* stood at attention on the bridge, his tall muscular frame tensed beneath his uniform, eyes fixed on the viewscreen that filled the front wall of the circular room.

"Steady as she goes," Riker told the helm crew. He heard Lieutenant Worf's heavy tread on the elevated deck behind him, and almost asked for another report from the long-range sensor scans, but stopped himself; the request would be redundant. He'd already done what he could for now.

Riker's response to the distress call had been automatic: a quick assessment of the message, a rapid spate of orders that brought the starship onto a new course and increased its speed. His next action should have been to contact the captain, but even as his hand moved to issue the call, Picard's voice had rung out demanding an explanation. Riker did not doubt the appropriateness of the orders he had issued, or the pressing need to act instantly, but he did regret not having reached Picard first. A first officer who usurped a captain's authority, even when that captain was supposedly sound asleep, should account for his actions without being asked.

The hiss of the opening turbolift doors was immediately followed by the distinctive voice of Captain Picard. "Status report, Number One," he ordered in clipped, sharply enunciated words as he strode down the ramp to the command level of the bridge.

Riker quickly recited the speech he had prepared while waiting for Picard's arrival. "The *USS Ferrel,* a Constitution-class starship, is broadcasting an automatic distress signal." He took a deep breath and continued. "I ordered an immediate course diversion to their source coordinates and increased our speed to warp six."

"Yes, so I noticed," said Picard dryly.

Riker met Picard's steely gaze without flinching. The first officer towered a half head above his captain, yet somehow Picard always seemed to be at eye level.

"Quite right, Number One."

The rise and fall of Riker's chest was the only sign of the relief that echoed in his own mind. He was still feeling his way with this new captain, but Picard consistently kept his ego divorced from the concerns of command. Riker relaxed his ramrod posture and finished his report. "Estimated time of rendezvous with the *Ferrel* is twenty-two minutes."

"Security, go to Yellow Alert," ordered Picard. "And notify Starbase Ten of our diversion." The steady pulse of alert lights sprang into life across the bridge. The captain dropped down onto his command chair. He tugged sharply at the waistline of his uniform, snapping the fabric into place. "Sit down, Will. There's nothing we can do now but wait."

Riker envied the captain's composure and wondered if his relaxed attitude was genuine or merely a pose. Perhaps the difference was irrelevant. The first officer sat down as bidden and concentrated on emulating the appearance, if not the substance, of Picard's example.

Natasha Yar was on her feet by the second flash of the alert lights. By the third her blue eyes had opened wide and her mind was fully awake. Her hand groped in the dark for a communications link. "Security chief to bridge," she called out as her fingers closed in on the cold metal of her insignia.

A full five seconds passed before she received a

reply, time she put to use scrambling into her uniform. Yellow Alert meant she could afford to get dressed properly, but there was no time for a shower. She ran her fingers through short locks of blond hair and considered her grooming done.

"Bridge here, Lieutenant."

She measured the tension in Riker's voice and accurately judged the severity of the alert. The ship was not in danger. Yet.

"I'm on my way." Yar didn't bother turning on the lights as she ran to the door. She had memorized the layout of her cabin for just such emergencies.

Her sprint to the bridge was several seconds short of her best time, but neither Riker nor the captain uttered a reprimand when Lieutenant Yar erupted out of the turbodoors. Taking her position at the tactical console, she surveyed the activity on the upper and lower decks, then studied the main viewer. Nothing of interest was on the screen, so she turned her attention to the distress signal that ran across the communications board in an unvarying pattern.

"No response to hailing calls," said Worf, standing by her side.

"Why didn't you call me as soon as you received the transmission?" hissed Yar.

"I was busy," said Worf.

"I should have been here to initiate Yellow Alert." Wary of drawing the captain's attention, Yar kept her voice low, which weakened her display of anger. Not that a full-volume explosion of temper would have made any greater impression on the Klingon; the emotional storms of the human race were little more than a mild summer rain to him.

"I was busy."

Yar was suddenly too preoccupied to pursue the one-sided argument. Scan readings had changed. The orange tracing of a fluctuating energy profile was faint but unmistakable.

Geordi La Forge dashed out of his cabin only to stumble over a pair of feet that blocked the portal. A strong arm shot out across his chest, breaking his fall.

"What are you doing here?"

"Waiting for you," replied Data. He pushed Geordi upright effortlessly, then fell into step beside him. They raced in concert down the corridor, a study in contrasts. Lieutenant La Forge was shorter and more solid of build with a deep brown skin that accentuated the unnatural pallor of his companion. Lieutenant Commander Data's eyes were a golden color that matched the metallic gleam of the visor on Geordi's face.

"So what's going on?" gasped Geordi as they jumped through the opening doors of a turbolift.

"We are on Yellow Alert," offered Data after calling out their destination. Unlike La Forge, he was unwinded.

"Yes, but why are we on Yellow Alert?" persisted La Forge. The positronic components that gave the android his strength and endurance were also responsible for certain lapses in his understanding of human speech. Geordi knew which direction the conversation was taking and patiently played out the game; he had undertaken an informal role in Data's social education and there was always time for a quick lesson.

"Presumably, we have encountered a situation that necessitates an increased state of vigilance that—"

Geordi cut him off. "Just say, 'I don't, know, Geordi.'"

"I don't know, Geordi," repeated Data. He puzzled over the verbal exchange. "I see. I was being too literal again."

"That's right, Data."

"I shall endeavor to be less literal next time."

"That's what you always say," sighed Geordi as the lift eased to a halt.

Yar logged their arrival on the bridge with a curt nod of her head. "Bridge crew complete, Captain."

With practiced motions, La Forge and Data exchanged positions with the nightshift helm. The maneuver was seamless in execution, one set of hands lifting from the controls as another settled into place.

Deanna Troi sensed the heightened anxieties on the ship's bridge even before the alert signal sounded. Stirring in sleep, her mind drifted upward through the layered textures of unconsciousness, lazily waiting for a summons from the bridge to complete the journey.

When the call did not come, she pulled herself through the final barrier.

"Troi to bridge."

"You're off duty, Counselor. And your services won't be needed for a while."

Riker's reply should have been a relief; instead, the matter-of-fact statement called forth a stab of annoyance. He knew her too well, could anticipate her thoughts.

"If I can be of any use . . ."

"Captain Picard applauds your initiative; we'll call if the situation changes."

"Don't do me any favors," she replied, but only to herself. On a moment's reflection Troi admitted her ill temper was due to being awakened from a sound sleep and could not with justice be blamed on Will Riker. She would take him at his word, that the ship's counselor was probably not needed, and indulge herself in a shower before dressing. Checking her reflection in the cabin mirror, Troi frowned disconsolately at the tangled mass of dark hair that crowned her head. Someone like Tasha Yar might be able to respond to emergencies within seconds, but Troi preferred a few extra minutes to pull herself together.

The dormant engineering section had been transformed into a storm of activity as off-duty crew tumbled into the room, racing to their reactivated posts. Wesley and Dnnys exchanged looks of pure joy at their good fortune.

"Do you report to the bridge now?" asked the young Farmer.

Heady excitement, and perhaps a lack of sleep, made the question sound reasonable. Without thinking, Wesley opened a link to the bridge.

"Ensign Crusher here—" He got no further than that.

"Get back to bed, young man," snapped Captain Picard's voice.

Both boys bolted from Engineering.

As the *Enterprise* sped nearer and nearer to the *USS Ferrel,* Picard held himself in check, fighting against any physical movement that could distract him from the reports of his bridge crew.

"Captain," said Yar. "Sensors detect energy emissions at source coordinates for the distress transmission. The pattern is unfamiliar, but very powerful to be detected this far away."

"Raise shields," ordered Picard.

"Rendezvous in three point four minutes," announced Data.

La Forge held his hands poised over the helm panel. "Ready to leave warp speed."

"Impulse power." Picard still sat unmoving in his chair.

Ever so gently, the pilot's fingers touched down onto the board. With an almost imperceptible shudder the ship's engines shifted to sublight drive. The universe contracted.

On the viewer, the pinpoint sparkle of distant stars sprang into relief against a featureless black backdrop. In the center of this static image a blur of movement cast shadows over the fixed lights. Two vessels tumbled through space, locked in a deadly dance of combat. A glowing blue fog enveloped them both.

Picard leaned forward. "Go to Red Alert."

The waiting was over.

Chapter Two

ANDREW DEELOR ESTIMATED that the *USS Ferrel* would
last another six minutes before the bridge dome
collapsed, crushing him and Ruthe and the ship's
crew within. Which meant that he had five minutes
and a handful of very unpleasant seconds left of life.
Realization of his approaching death occupied only a
small corner of his mind; his attention was fixed on
the translucent blue haze that rippled and flowed
across the surface of the main viewscreen. The starship was held in the grip of an energy matrix. Minute
by minute the matrix contracted like a fist closing
tighter, crumpling the hull of the main saucer between
its fingers.

The starship shuddered. The bridge screen went
black.

Over the last hour the ship's sensors had failed, one
after another, until the viewscreen was Deelor's sole

remaining source of information. He had whispered a description of everything appearing within its frame into the palm-size vocoder cupped in his hand. Every brief glimpse of the alien ship, every detail of its structure, every impression of its tactics, was on record, but without the viewer he was blind to what was happening outside the hull.

Deelor switched his attention to the interior of the *Ferrel*. From his seat at the center of the circular bridge he could scan the entire room. He described the dropping temperature and dimming emergency lights as the ship's energy reserves were funneled into the defense shields in a losing battle against the alien force field. He described the glittering flakes of white paint that drifted through the air like snow, and the metal wall panel that blew out from under the inoperative communications station, knocking Lieutenant Morrissey hard against a railing, bending him double.

The man sagged to his knees, then coughed a bright spot of blood onto the deck. Dr. Lewin jumped to his side with an open field kit. It was a futile gesture to Deelor's mind and he did not include it in his report. If there were to be posthumous commendations for the crew, they would be based on the captain's log.

The screams of compressing metal plates grew louder, threatening to drown out Deelor's comments. He pressed the grill closer against his mouth, but his voice had grown too hoarse to rise above the background noise. He snapped the protective cover down over the vocoder before slipping the unit into an inner pocket of his jacket. If the record were recovered, his successor would have a detailed description of the penalty for failure.

His failure. Deelor regretted that epitaph more than his death. He turned to the woman sitting beside him. Ruthe was hunched into a tight ball, her legs drawn up

25

beneath her chin, a gray cloak wrapped tightly around her body. She had buried her face in the coarse fabric. Loose locks of straight black hair fell down over her knees.

He leaned over, bringing his mouth up against her ear. "We're about to die," he told her, not certain if she had realized that yet. "I'm sorry."

Ruthe looked up. Her skin was pale, but that was its natural color. "I'm cold. I hate being cold."

"Yes, I know."

A sudden cessation of activity around them triggered an alarm in Deelor's mind. The crew had frozen in place, oblivious to the groans and labored breathing of the saucer hull as it flexed in and out. Their faces were turned in one direction, to the rear of the bridge, and he twisted about to follow their gazes. They were watching the captain and his first officer. The two men stood side by side at the weapons console, their backs blocking sight of their actions, but Deelor knew immediately what they were about to do. And why they mustn't.

Deelor shouted at Manin to stop, but his voice could not carry above the pervasive din of disintegrating metal. He scrambled out of his chair, but the buckling deck surface pitched him down onto his knees. He would never reach them in time. Plunging a hand into the folds of his jacket, he fumbled at the inner pocket. His fingers shoved aside the familiar cylindrical vocoder and closed in on the blunt casing of a hand phaser.

He fired at both men, but the tremblings of the hull threw off his aim. D'Amelio dropped in place under the impact of the stun beam; the captain was only grazed. Manin whirled about in confusion. When he caught sight of the weapon in Deelor's hand, bewilderment quickly transformed into a burst of rage.

"Kill him!" The scream was inaudible, but the

shape of the words was clear. And the order was instantly obeyed.

Andrew Deelor never saw who fired.

Three centuries of engineering knowledge, the product of the combined efforts of the brightest minds in the United Federation of Planets, culminated in the galaxy-class starship known as *Enterprise*. The finest metals and alloys, the strongest polymers, the newest computer technology, had been expertly crafted into a vessel designed to travel to the farthest reaches of the galaxy. She was manned by officers and scientists of the highest caliber, dedicated to an extended exploration of that new territory which beckoned so seductively.

Sometimes the search turned deadly.

With shields raised and weapons primed, *Enterprise* dropped out of warp speed in a dazzling screech of light and coasted toward the battle site.

"Mr. Data, what do you make of that blue aura?" demanded the captain, studying the clouded figure of the *USS Ferrel* and its attacker.

"Blue?" exclaimed Geordi. "Looks more like a riot of color to me."

The comment reminded Picard of how radically the pilot's visor transformed Geordi's vision to cover the entire electromagnetic spectrum.

"It's some kind of fluctuating energy field," said Data as the ship's computers displayed a readout on his ops console. "Purpose unknown, but its effects appear to be of limited range."

"Captain, I still can't raise either ship," announced Yar. "All communications channels are silent."

"The *Ferrel* may be unable to respond," said Data. "Its control systems appear to be inoperative or barely functional."

"Mr. La Forge, set a direct course for the hostile,"

ordered Picard tersely. He had only a few seconds in which to decide his course of action against the unfamiliar alien vessel. The explorer in him was exhilarated by the thought of a possible first contact, but as a Starfleet commander his first duty was to defend a fellow starship and the *Ferrel* was definitely on the losing side of its struggle. "Prepare to fire phasers at my next command. Perhaps a change in the odds will deter the *Ferrel's* assailant from continuing its attack."

Tasha Yar signaled Worf from the aft stations to the tactical console and the two officers divided defense and assault responsibilities with short telegraphic gestures.

Picard tensed. "Fire phasers," he said.

Lieutenant Worf splayed broad hands over the surface of the weapons console. Each twitch of a finger triggered a phaser blast from the underbelly of the *Enterprise*. Most of the pulses dispersed harmlessly into space, but two hit squarely on target.

The effect was immediate. The blurred haze enveloping the two battling ships vanished, revealing the ravages of their conflict. The large saucer section of the Constellation-class starship was distorted, its frame twisted and warped. Hovering close beside the *Ferrel,* apparently undamaged, was a densely packed cluster of spheres, translucent orange in color. The ships were of an equal size, but the *Enterprise* dwarfed them both.

"Open hailing frequencies, Lieutenant Yar." Picard rose from his command chair. "This is Jean-Luc Picard, captain of the *USS Enterprise*. Identify your vessel." He waited patiently as the seconds passed. Riker moved silently to his side as the silence continued.

"No response," concluded Yar at last.

"No verbal response," said Data. "But they are

28

reacting." He was the first to detect movement from the cluster.

The irregular mass of the alien ship had no discernible features that marked one end of the structure from another, but the entire group of spheres had started to revolve slowly on an internal axis. As the back side of the ship rolled into view, one spot of deep purple appeared nestled amid the orange. The rotation accelerated, whipping the odd-colored bubble out of sight, then back again.

Still spinning, the ship began to float toward the *Enterprise.*

Picard signaled another communications broadcast. "Alien vessel, if you do not respond, your approach will be considered a hostile action."

The cluster did not slow its progress.

"I would have preferred a nonviolent conclusion to this conflict," admitted Picard in a whispered aside to his first officer. "But it seems this life form doesn't share my view. So be it." His dropping hand signaled Lieutenant Worf to release another round of phaser fire.

A cascade of disrupting beams raked over the approaching ship. The surface of the spheres crackled and sparked, but only for the split second of actual contact. When the glow of the phasers had faded, the bubbles were intact. Worf loosed another volley, to no greater visible effect.

"Evasive action," ordered Picard tersely.

Geordi La Forge sent his hands dancing over the console and the *Enterprise* swerved in its course. "They're gaining on us, sir"

"Maintain phaser fire."

Throughout the barrage, Data announced the rapidly closing distance between the two ships. "Ten kilometers, five kilometers, one kilometer." His chant stopped. "One kilometer."

"Too close for our photon torpedoes," declared Yar. "At this range the explosions could damage the *Enterprise* as well as the target."

If we move any farther away, the *Ferrel* will be vulnerable to a renewed attack," said Picard bitterly as he studied the alien ship. Time for counteraction was quickly running out.

And then it was gone. Having finally met some unknown parameter, the purple sphere whipped away from the spinning main cluster.

"It's coming directly toward us," warned Data. "Prepare for impact."

An explosion of violet light seared the crew's eyes, but there was no accompanying jolt, only a faint trembling that could be felt on the consoles and in the deck beneath their feet. Rivers of pale blue crackled over the main viewer.

Data relayed the information from his sensors. "The energy field covers the entire outer surface of the saucer section."

"It's a net," exclaimed Geordi, and Picard knew he was describing his unique view of the field. "A matrix that's been woven out of charged filaments; I can see the separate strands. And one thin umbilical current is still attached to the mother ship."

Yar studied the tactical console closely. "Shields holding without strain. The power output of this net is not very high."

Picard frowned. "Then why is the *Ferrel* so badly damaged?"

A low-pitched hum was added to the vibration.

"The field is contracting, increasing pressure on hull defenses," announced Data. He blinked, making a quick mental calculation. "Assuming a constant rate of contraction, we can withstand the effects for two point six days before ship's power reserves are exhausted. At that time, without shields, we will be vulnerable to structural damage."

Riker stepped up to the aft deck environment console to monitor incoming signals from each section of the starship. "Captain, current status reports from all stations indicate minor short circuits in electrical systems near the outer hull. No major damage."

"But our passengers are undergoing major trauma," said Lieutenant Yar. "I've logged a dozen calls to my communications board from the Farmers' quarters since the start of Red Alert."

"Contact Counselor Troi," suggested Riker. "Have her calm them down. We may be here for quite a while."

"But not for two days," said Picard, falling back into the captain's chair. "Not for two hours if it can be helped. There must be a way to penetrate their defenses."

Hands braced on the railing of the aft deck, Riker studied the alien ship's unusual construction. Blue haze blurred the image of the bubble ship on the viewer. "Those spheres look just like a bunch of balloons. All we need is a needle to pop them with."

"An interesting analogy, Number One," said the captain approvingly. "Let's give it a try, shall we?"

Worf eagerly reprogrammed the weapons console to Riker's specifications. The spread of phaser fire was reduced to the minimum recommended by Starfleet guidelines. With a little extra work and creative juggling of the controlling parameters, the beam was narrowed even farther. When Riker pronounced himself satisfied, Worf triggered a test shot.

Despite its reduced intensity, the resulting pinpoint ray drilled straight through its target. A single sphere on the outermost layer of the cluster exploded, releasing a viscous glob of matter into space. Tattered remains of the exterior shell dangled limply from the core group.

"Way to go, Worf," exclaimed Geordi.

"Try another," Picard ordered. "If necessary, we'll take that ship apart section by section." He was determined to continue the assault until his ship was out of danger.

The second explosion was the last.

"Energy field dissipating," announced Data as the viewscreen cleared. "And the enemy is pulling away."

Picard responded immediately. "Tractor beam, Lieutenant Worf. Let's give them a taste of their own medicine." He suspected that the Klingon would have preferred to keep firing until the enemy had been annihilated, but the order was obeyed without comment.

"We've got them, Captain," said Worf when the moving bubble cluster halted abruptly. "But they're draining power at an incredible rate."

Picard tried once more to establish radio contact. "I order you to surrender your vessel." He did not really expect an answer. There was none. But as before, the alien ship began to change. Its spheres contracted in size; the clumped mass shifted, rearranging its connections. A single bubble was extruded out from the cluster. Another followed directly behind the first. Then another.

The angle of the starship's tractor beam widened to cover the changing shape. Bridge lights flickered as more power was diverted to Worf's console. Overload indicators rippled across instrument panels as the bubbles stretched into one long strand.

Riker rejoined the captain on the command deck. His brow was furrowed with anger and frustration. "At this rate, we'll be forced to tap into our emergency power reserves. Even then I don't think we can hold them for long."

"This enemy is certainly full of tricks." Picard couldn't keep the admiration out of his voice. His praise raised a surprised double take from Riker. "There's no shame in recognizing a worthy opponent, Number One." The shame lay in losing. Picard considered what effect another phaser attack would have on the alien ship's struggle for escape.

"Captain," called out Data. "Sensors show that the *Ferrel's* primary hull is badly damaged and the atmosphere-containment liner shows signs of rapid weakening at stress points. It could rupture at any moment."

A wave of the captain's hand signaled Worf to cut loose the tractor beam. Picard's voice hoarsened with urgency. "Yar, all power to the transporter stations. Commence immediate transport of the *Ferrel's* crew with wide beam coordinates. Bring over anything that moves. Hurry."

Turning back to the viewscreen, Picard watched the alien ship glide away with increasing speed, like a beaded necklace slipping from the grasp of its owner.

Old Ziedorf was deaf and slept through the commotion, but the other Farmers awakened in their strange beds amid the lights and noise of a nightmare. The shouts and cries of mothers and uncles clutching on to their sleep-dazed children drowned out the calm instructions given by the ship's computer. The Farmers would not have listened to the disembodied voice anyway, especially since it asked them to stay in their cabins.

Men and women poured out of the passenger suites into the connecting corridor, crying out in their confusion. One man among them, who had learned something of the ship's operation, turned down the volume of the nearby intercom speaker, the better to hear his neighbor. Nobody answered the entreaties of the security officer's voice, which was now reduced to a faint whisper.

Children who absorbed the undercurrent of excitement in the crowd struggled free of any constraining grip and darted away, eager to play at this unaccustomed hour. Others who were less hardy of temperament responded to the words of fear and added their own wails to the clamor.

Dnnys threaded his way among the adults with difficulty. One after another they grabbed him by the elbow or the shoulder and demanded an explanation for the ship's strange behavior: to them, his notorious familiarity with the *Enterprise* made the situation his responsibility. Still, he was only a child, so there was no sense in listening to his answers, especially when he urged them to return to their cabins.

Again a hand caught hold of him, and Dnnys threw it off. Then he saw who had reached out and he wriggled over to his cousin's side. Her light brown hair was too curly to show signs of an abrupt awakening, but the tails of her blue workshirt were hanging loose outside her jeans.

"I can't get into your mother's room," said Mry. "She, of course, stayed put just as she should. But when she didn't come out, everyone else went in after her." Of the hundred and twenty Farmers, nearly fifty had crowded into the suite. The rest milled aimlessly in the corridors.

"You should have stayed in place, too," scolded Dnnys.

"Tomas made me come. He said we had to protect both our own mother and yours since she was all alone." Mry frowned suddenly. "I reminded him that you were with Patrisha, but I can see I was wrong."

Dnnys ignored the reprimand. He knew that his

34

cousin wouldn't tell anyone about his absence. "Wesley says a Yellow Alert isn't too serious, but we should . . ."

The young ensign's advice was never heard. Flashing amber lights turned red, and the Farmers' raised their voices to shout over the sound of the klaxon.

A piercing scream thickened the knot of people peering out the clear windows that lined the outer wall. Those who could see called out a muddled description that passed from person to person through the crowd, growing less comprehensible with each retelling. A single damaged starship was transformed into a derelict plague ship, a drifting graveyard of ghost ships or a rampaging pirate fleet, depending on who was asked.

When blue fire cascaded over the transparent surface of the ports, the crowd that had surged forward reversed its direction. Mry and Dnnys were swept apart by the stampede of people finally convinced of the wisdom of returning to their cabins.

To anyone sensitive enough, the panic emanating from the passenger section of the starship was like a dense fog. And panic was contagious. As she drew nearer to the Farmers' quarters, Counselor Troi fought down her instinctive empathy, repressing the desire to flee back to the safety of her own cabin. She cast about for a familiar mind and set in that direction.

Dnnys was alone in a corridor, face pressed against the crackling glass. Troi ran up to him and pulled him back. "Come away from there."

"It doesn't hurt. It just sort of tickles." Dnnys demonstrated by placing a hand against the humming panel. "Where's the blue light coming from?"

"We don't know what it is," said Troi sharply, diverting the thrust of his question. "And it may be dangerous." He was only a boy, with a boy's fascination with the unknown. An adult Farmer should have taken charge of him, but the adults all seemed to be cowering in their rooms. Perhaps, in their fright, they would speak to her now. So far the reclusive colonists had rebuffed her attempts to make them welcome. As a result, she knew few of their number by name and little of their customs. "I must speak to the leaders of your community."

Dnnys laughed at the request. "We haven't got any leaders."

"But I spoke to a woman in charge when your people first came onboard." Troi hadn't asked the woman's title, respecting the Farmers' reticence on such a personal matter, yet she possessed an unmistakable air of authority. "Her name was Patrisha."

"Oh, you mean my mother." The boy's smile dissolved into a frown. "But she isn't a leader. Nobody has to obey her."

Troi sensed his defensiveness. "I'm sorry, I didn't mean to offend." She gingerly felt her way to a less emotionally charged definition of what she sought. "I meant only that people seemed to listen to what she says."

"Oh, that's different. People always listen to my mother," said Dnnys proudly. He pointed to a door farther down the corridor. "Go on in, she's got plenty of company right now."

When she had reached the threshold of the cabin, but before she had stepped inside, Troi felt a stab of disappointment coming from Dnnys. She glanced back to the far end of the passageway where he stood.

The blue light had disappeared from the port window.

Chapter Three

CAPTAIN MANIN SCRAMBLED over the shifting rubble that had once been the *USS Ferrel*'s bridge. He heard the moans and dry coughs of his dying crew, but he couldn't see them through the smoke and swirling dust. Less than a minute remained of his last command, but the seconds stretched ahead of him like an eternity. He had tried to spare everyone the pain of a prolonged destruction. Deelor had stopped him. Manin pushed aside his anger; it was a waste of what time he had left.

Reaching out blindly for another hold, the captain's hand brushed against a body; the skin was cold to the touch. His fingers groped the outlines of the slumped figure and finally traced the slender shaft of an antenna. Only one Andorian had been on the bridge, which established the identity of the dead officer. Wishing Godspeed to his pilot, to whatever afterlife she was bound, Manin edged away from the helm in search of his command chair. When death came, he would meet it there. He took another step and his boot struck something soft.

The something kicked back. "Go away. I don't want company," said Ruthe, then broke out in a fit of coughing.

Her annoyance was ludicrous under the circumstances, and Manin was still alert enough to appreciate the humor of the situation. His laugh brought a gush of blood to his mouth. He wiped away the trickle that escaped his lips. If the translator was here, then Deelor's body was not far away.

"A phaser death is clean, Deelor," said the captain softly. "You got off too easy."

Stars blurred and shifted their position on the viewer as Data enlarged the image of the *USS Ferrel* to fill the screen. Picard and his first officer stood side by side on the bridge, watching the death throes of the *Ferrel*. Removing the energy matrix had come too late to prevent the starship's final destruction. Riker stirred uneasily as the metal hull jerked and quivered, its supporting structures collapsing from within.

The captain was the first to speak. *"Merde.* We'll never make it in time. It'll take at least twenty minutes to beam the entire—"

"There she blows," announced La Forge from the helm.

A plume of white vapor spewed out from the underside of the saucer, dispersing instantly in the vacuum of space. Debris from the interior, wrapped with the frost of crystallized water, glittered and twirled outside the hull of the ship.

"Worf, launch every shuttlecraft we've got," called out Picard. He knew such a rescue attempt would be useless, but it must be tried. "Data, focus a short-range scan sweep around the *Ferrel*. There may be survivors among the wreckage."

"Not necessary, Captain," announced Tasha Yar. "The transporter chief reports the entire crew is aboard." She paused, stunned by the count. "All thirty of them."

Picard felt the shock of her words like a physical blow. Thirty lives out of a crew complement of hundreds. He had lost the *Stargazer* nine years before —he knew that pain—but his crew had not perished along with the ship. He turned to Riker and saw his own alarm mirrored in the first officer's eyes; anyone who accepted the responsibility of command was aware of all that could go wrong at that level. Picard knew better than to dwell on the disaster. Dread could turn to paralyzing fear. "Number One, check the transporter stations. Find the captain, or the most senior officer among the survivors, and have that person report here immediately." The errand would end the first officer's role as a helpless observer.

"Right away, Captain," said Riker, moving quickly toward an exit.

The rescue mission was far from over, but Picard could feel that the height of the crisis had passed. During the battle, his attention had been tightly focused; his mind had filtered out all distractions. No longer. The staccato beat of Red Alert grew more irritating by the second. It was also a reminder of an unresolved conflict. "Lieutenant Yar, how far has the hostile traveled?"

"According to my sensors, the alien ship appears to be gone, Captain, passed beyond scan range."

Her statement brought a protest from La Forge at the helm. "But, Tasha, it can't have left the sector already, not in that short a time."

"The matrix did leave an ionized cloud of residual

energy," noted Data with interest. "It is decomposing rapidly, but scan readings may have been affected."

"What do you make of the energy matrix they threw over us?" asked Picard. This trap had been foiled, but the next one might not be escaped so easily. He had an uneasy feeling that another encounter was likely.

"The field did not operate like a standard tractor device, but given the unusual structure of the alien ship, it is not unreasonable to presume that this adversary possesses a much more advanced, or radically different technological base."

"A better mousetrap," mused Picard.

"No, sir, a better tractor beam."

Picard chose not to respond to the comment. He also chose to stifle his smile as he caught Geordi's exasperated sigh. Data's face creased in puzzlement at the subtle criticism, but he appeared unable to pinpoint his offense.

"Yar, return the ship to general quarters," ordered Picard. Even if the alien ship's absence proved to be the calm before a gathering storm, he would take advantage of the lull.

The security chief gently tapped the surface of her console. The flashing red lights faded, but the troubled look on her face remained.

The captain stood to address his crew. "Thank you all for your comments. Given the possibility of a renewed attack, I am certain you will remain especially vigilant despite our peaceful status." If they were attacked again, he had scant knowledge with which to build an effective defense. Picard allowed the bridge officers wide latitude for discussion, but he also recognized the limits of their speculation. He needed facts now, not theories.

Deanna Troi scanned the impassive faces of the Oregon Farmers gathered in the suite. Clamoring voices had fallen silent as soon as she crossed the threshold. If nothing else, her entrance had shifted the emotional spectrum of the room's inhabitants. Their agitation was now giving way to suspicion.

"I'm Counselor Troi." She smiled in a desperate attempt to slow the gathering wave of resentment. "The bridge reported that you have been alarmed by—"

"Warmonger!" Several of the standing Farmers moved aside to reveal a stout man with a shortly cropped beard. He looked much the same as the other men in the room, but he was far more pompous. "The fighting must stop at once. I demand it."

"We're not at war," protested Troi. "This is only—"

"Liar!" shouted a woman by the man's side. She was skinny and much older, but despite the difference in stature and age the two bore a family resemblance. "Your own self-serving machines have revealed the infamy of your actions. Listen!"

In the silence that followed the woman's imperious order, the even drone of the computer alert instructions could finally be heard by everyone.

"We are currently engaged in combat with a hostile agent. Please remain in your cabin until the Red Alert signal has ended."

Troi made a mental note to review with Data the computer system's passenger interface. His insistence on accuracy was not necessarily in the best interests of the passengers. Surely a more diplomatic and less informative phrasing would have lessened their fears.

"The message is just a precaution," said Troi. "We have encountered an unknown vessel. An inability to communicate with them has resulted in a misunderstanding that will be settled soon." To her relief, the Red Alert signal faded as if on cue. The next words from the computer were more reassuring.

"Red Alert is now over. You may resume your normal activities."

Another Farmer stepped forward from the crowd, one Troi recognized as Dnnys's mother. Patrisha's features were too strong to be called pretty, too arresting to be called plain. Her graying hair was braided into a single plait which trailed down her waist. Years of hard work had roughened her hands and thickened her frame, but she carried herself with poise.

"Thank you for your visit, Counselor Troi."

The speaker had issued an obvious dismissal. Though Troi could detect no personal animosity from this woman, the hostility from the other Farmers had not lessened. Sensing that her continued presence would only aggravate the passengers further, Troi quietly took her leave.

"We should never have left Grzydc!" said Tomas as soon as the outsider was gone. He tugged furiously at the tufts of his beard.

"We weren't given the option of staying," Patrisha reminded him, but she knew Tomas had no interest in discussing their exodus from that planet. Too many in this room were aware that his continual disagreements with the Grzydc government had contributed to the friction between the Farmers and their adopted world.

"Somebody must speak to the captain concerning this outrage." The man's emphatic statement was greeted with a murmur of consent from several of the other Farmers. "He must be made aware of our position."

An outsider might have assumed that Tomas was volunteering for that task, but Patrisha knew better. Somehow, by the time a group consensus was reached, she would be the chosen delegate. She could refuse, of course, but in her own way Patrisha was just as predictable as the other Farmers. Rather than let Tomas antagonize yet another authority, she would take on the responsibility herself.

Andrew Deelor had lain flat on his back, staring up at a featureless sky for what seemed like a hundred years before gathering enough strength to turn his head. "Heaven is a transporter room. How quaint," he said weakly.

"Speak up, I can't hear you."

With great effort he turned in the other direction and saw the blurred outlines of Ruthe sitting cross-legged beside him. He tried to fit her into his new world. "And you're an angel now." She made a beautiful angel, though a severe one; high cheekbones set in an angular face emphasized her large, dark eyes above.

"What are you talking about?" Ruthe asked sharply.

"I should be dead, but this place looks very much like a transporter room." One which reeled and swayed from side to side, but Deelor suspected he was merely dizzy. He closed his eyes and felt the deck beneath him steady its wild movement.

"I heard someone say we're on board a ship called the *Enterprise*."

"Ah, that explains it." He must have drifted out of consciousness for a time because when he next opened his eyes, his vision had cleared. He could see the huddled figures of other casualties on the deck. Then an unfamiliar voice drew Deelor's attention to the starship officer standing beside Dr. Lewin.

"I'm looking for the commanding officer of the *Ferrel*," announced the stranger. He stepped aside as Lewin directed the removal of a loaded stretcher out through the doors of the transporter room.

"Isn't that you?" Ruthe asked Deelor, drowning out the doctor's reply. Fortunately, Ruthe never raised her voice so the officer didn't hear her. "Weren't you in charge?"

"This isn't the time to mention that," Deelor whispered back. He fought against a wave of nausea. The side effect was typical of anticoagulants; he must have received medical treatment at some point. "Later, when I'm feeling better, I'll let them know." He would need a clear head to explain his presence on the *Ferrel* and to establish his authority on the *Enterprise*.

"Captain Manin has been sent to sickbay."
Picard listened to Riker's intercom report with unexpressed relief. Given thirty survivors out of the full crew complement of a constellation-class starship, there was no reason to expect any high-ranking officer had been saved. "Report back as soon as you've spoken to him." Picard burned with the desire to conduct the questioning himself, yet he couldn't leave the bridge so soon after an attack. The captain waited for his first officer's return with impatience, masking the unruly emotion behind his usual facade of studied calm.

Ten minutes later Riker stepped out of the forward turbo, then quickly turned to urge another man in a dusty fleet uniform to step through the doors. The stranger was tall and lanky, with an untidy shock of salt and pepper hair.

"Captain Manin is in surgery," explained Riker. "This is First Officer D'Amelio."

"Welcome aboard the *Enterprise*," said the captain, approaching the two men. Picard's greeting brought a smile to D'Amelio's face, but several seconds passed before he noticed the captain's outstretched arm. Moving in slow motion, the officer reached out and limply shook hands. He stood in place until Riker pulled gently at the man's elbow, ushering him into the adjacent Ready Room.

The captain followed. He waited until the door had closed before giving voice to his misgivings. "Number One, this man is in shock. He should be in sickbay."

Riker pushed the first officer down into one of the chairs facing the captain's desk. "He's already been treated. I'm sure Dr. Crusher would have released him if I'd asked, but I didn't want to disturb her."

"In other words, we'd better talk fast before she finds out he's gone," said Picard, taking a seat across from them.

The session did not run smoothly. D'Amelio appeared unable, at times unwilling, to answer any questions about the alien ship that had attacked the *Ferrel*. The few answers he supplied gave rise to more questions.

Picard took a deep breath, suppressing the hard edge that had crept into his voice. "Mr. D'Amelio, you maintain that the *Ferrel* was operated by a skeleton crew. That's welcome news, indeed. We had thought your fatalities were much higher. However, I'm sure you can understand our confusion—forty-six people is an unusually small crew for a starship."

"It's all we needed."

"Needed for what?" asked Riker.

As before, D'Amelio did not answer. His gaze drifted vacantly across the room. Picard and Riker exchanged looks of frustration and growing skepticism. A predictable pattern had formed. Any question concerned with the starship's mission resulted in a lapse of attention. Picard did not need Deanna Troi's empathic abilities to realize D'Amelio was withholding information, but perhaps the counselor should be brought into the meeting if there was no change in the man's response.

The trill of a communications contact stopped the

captain from a direct challenge to D'Amelio's evasions. *"Crusher to Captain."*

Picard had been expecting the call. "Don't worry, Dr. Crusher, we're taking good care of Mr. D'Amelio." He studied the first officer's profile with dissatisfaction. "But we still need to ask more—"

The doctor overrode him. *"Captain, one of the Ferrel's casualties was wounded by a blast from a hand phaser."*

All three men in the room were startled by her statement. "Are you certain?" asked Picard. "Perhaps contact with the alien force field—"

"No, not the force field. The cellular disruption pattern is quite characteristic of phaser burns, and he's the only one brought aboard with injuries of that nature. Everyone else is suffering from shock, vacuum exposure, impact with debris. This man was shot."

Picard turned to the first officer. This time he did not mask his anger. "Mr. D'Amelio, what the hell was happening on that ship?"

"I don't know anything about it." In his confusion, D'Amelio dropped out of his dreamy stare. He turned from Picard to Riker in turn. "Honest, I don't! The bridge was collapsing . . . we didn't have much time left. No hope of rescue, or so we thought. Captain Manin and I were preparing to initiate a self-destruct sequence."

"But you didn't finish it," said Picard.

"No." D'Amelio shook his head as if to clear it. "I was about to confirm my rank identification when I blacked out."

"What is that man doing out of sickbay?" demanded Crusher. Too late, the captain realized she was still listening. *"Return him at—"*

Her voice broke off abruptly, although the link remained open. Picard heard a crash, followed by the faint sound of shouting in the background. Crusher's voice resumed. *"Stop! Captain Manin, I will not stand for this . . . security to sickbay."*

The words sent Picard and Riker racing out the door.

If sickbay was an unlikely arena for violent confrontation, the combatants were even less convincing. Dr. Crusher had dragged Captain Manin away from his assault on her other patient, but she was more concerned with the harm he was doing himself as he struggled to escape her grasp and resume the fight. His strength was deceptive—she knew him to be badly injured. Only the force of a considerable anger had overcome his body's weakness.

"Damn you, Deelor!" shouted Manin as he wrestled against Crusher's restraint. "You destroyed my ship, my crew!"

Crusher cast a glance over her shoulder to the target of this accusation and assessed the second man's condition. He sagged weakly against a wall, and his face was bathed in sweat. Manin had landed several blows to an area of scorched skin and muscle on Deelor's chest, but there were no spreading stains on the protective bandage. The doctor attributed Deelor's pallor to renewed pain rather than blood loss.

The doors to sickbay flew open. Security Chief Yar sped through the portal with Riker and Captain Picard on her heels. At the sight of the man grappling with Crusher, Yar pulled out her phaser.

"No." Dr. Crusher moved to block Yar's line of sight. "He's badly hurt. Even a stun blast could kill him."

Captain Manin took advantage of the doctor's distraction and lunged toward Deelor. Picard jumped between the two men, forearm raised to ward off a swinging fist, but the blow never came. Manin staggered to a halt after one step. Picard caught him as he collapsed, then gently lowered him to the floor.

"Lie still. You'll only hurt yourself," urged Picard, but the sound of his voice increased the man's agitation.

"It wasn't my fault," gasped Manin with labored breath. "I followed his orders. Starfleet made me."

"Quiet!" Deelor warned. "I order you to be quiet."

Crusher knelt down beside Picard and examined the man cradled in the captain's arms. "Help me get him under the scanner." They moved quickly, lifting the limp body onto the bed of the diagnostic machine, but the doctor could see Manin weakening by the second. The panel that closed down over his chest emitted a frantic electronic chatter. "He's started to hemorrhage again."

Calling out for medical assistance, Crusher tracked a path of widespread tissue damage in the liver, spleen, and kidneys. "Tissue factor," she demanded, and the nurse slipped a hypo into Crusher's palm. The doctor administered the clotting agent to a vein in his neck, but the bleeding continued. A second dose thickened the blood, but it continued to fill his chest cavity. There would be no third dose. An additional injection would coagulate his entire circulatory system.

Oblivious to Crusher's efforts, the captain of the *Ferrel* clutched at Picard's arm. The grip lacked force, but Picard let himself be pulled closer. "Full mission control . . . to a damn bureaucrat."

"Shut up, Manin!" Deelor pushed himself away from the wall and staggered toward the table, but Lieutenant Yar still had her phaser drawn. She swung the weapon toward him. Deelor stopped, swaying unsteadily in place. "You're violating Starfleet security."

Crusher knew her patient was too weak to withstand surgical invasion. She would have tried anyway except his vital organs had been reduced to pulp and there was nothing left to operate on. Instead, she requested a drug that would ease his pain.

Manin's voice had dropped to a whisper. Picard leaned closer, straining to hear. Only one word was clear.

"Hamlin?" Picard echoed. "What about Hamlin?" There was no reply. The hand fell away from Picard's sleeve.

"You fool!" Oblivious to Yar's warning cry, Deelor closed the distance to Manin's bedside. "I'll have you stripped of your command for this breach."

"He can't hear you." Dr. Crusher switched off the medical unit above the still body. "He's dead."

Chapter Four

Captain's Log, supplemental: The events surrounding the destruction of the USS Ferrel *are still shrouded in mystery. We beamed aboard thirty people from a ship that should have carried hundreds. And not one of those thirty will tell us why their ship was attacked.*

THE BRIDGE LOUNGE had been designed to provide a sense of well-being to those who used it. Cushioned chairs circled an oval table of generous proportions; wide, gently curving windows lined the outside wall, presenting a breathtaking panorama of jeweled stars. A dozen people could sit around the table without feeling confined, but only four entered now.

"Counselor, are you feeling all right?" asked Picard. Troi had sunk into the comforting embrace of a wide chair and immediately closed her eyes.

Her dark lashes fluttered, and she opened her eyes again. "I'm a little tired," she admitted reluctantly. "My contacts with the Farmers and the survivors of the *Ferrel* have been draining."

"And not very informative," said Riker as he and Data circled the table. "They all act as if we're the enemy."

Picard saw Troi tense as the first officer passed behind her chair. The reaction confirmed his suspicion that she was unusually sensitive to Riker's moods. The force of the man's present frustration must be battering against her emotional defenses.

"Let's begin the briefing," suggested Picard, moving away from Troi to sit at the head of the table. He realized his own impatience was probably adding further turbulence to her emotional surroundings.

"I don't understand what's going on," fumed Riker as he settled in place. "According to the first officer, Deelor is an efficiency consultant assigned to improve operations and maintenance procedures of the *Ferrel,* but according to Starfleet personnel records he's not a member of the crew. He's not even listed as being aboard the ship."

"I ran a full computer identity check on his name," confirmed Data. "And came up with nothing. There is no record of an Andrew Deelor in Starfleet or in any Federation civilian population in this sector."

"And the *Ferrel* crew won't talk about who tried to kill him or why. It seems they were all looking in another direction when he was shot," said Riker with obvious disgust. "Deanna, tell the captain what you felt."

Troi hesitated, struggling to put the impressions she had gathered into words. "Such a tangle of conflicting emotion. Sorrow for their captain's death; anger, almost hatred, at the mention of Deelor's name; and

51

always the need for secrecy. If they know anything, they will not admit it, not without considerable duress."

"This is not an inquisition," said Picard with an admonishing wave of his hand. "Yet I can't allow this incident to remain unresolved. I must know what happened to the *Ferrel*, to protect the *Enterprise* if nothing else." He frowned at the unbidden image of his own ship torn and mangled, its crew and passengers floating amid the wreckage. "What about the other civilian, the woman?"

"Her name is Ruthe," said Riker. He uttered a sigh of exasperation. "She won't give us a last name and she won't answer any other questions. She just repeats 'ask Deelor.'"

"Who isn't feeling strong enough to provide any answers." With the announcement of Manin's death, Deelor had developed a convenient fainting spell. "His injuries are real enough, but the timing has a familiar ring. He's faking weakness," said the captain grimly. "Just as D'Amelio was faking shock. But why? What are they all hiding?"

Yar's intercom message brought a temporary halt to the briefing. *"Farmer Patrisha has called the bridge. Again."* The lieutenant's voice was hardened by her annoyance. *"She insists on speaking to you personally, Captain."*

"Tell her—" But Picard thought twice before completing the statement. He began again. "Tell her everything is under control and I will meet with her just as soon as my duties allow."

He severed the link with a flick of his finger. "Passengers, like children, should be seen and not heard," he said to no one in particular. Dismissing the Oregon Farmers from his mind, he returned to the puzzle. "Hamlin. To me, that means only one thing—

the Hamlin Massacre. I was only a small boy at the time, but I remember the incident well."

"I read the historical accounts at the academy." Riker caught Troi's questioning look and provided an explanation. "Hamlin was a mining colony located on the Federation frontier. Fifty years ago they reported first contact with a new alien race, then suddenly all communications from them stopped. The next supply ship to reach the planet found that everyone in the colony had been killed."

"Not everyone," corrected Data. "Just the adults. The colony's children were missing, presumably also dead."

"Some say eaten." Picard murmured the dark words as if echoing a long-forgotten phrase.

"Inquiry: eaten, as in consumed? As in food source?"

"Yes, well, the more sensational reports mentioned the possibility." Picard regretted his comment immediately and tried to dismiss it from the conversation. He turned to Riker. "Could the aliens who attacked the *Ferrel* be the same ones responsible for the Hamlin Massacre?"

But Data was not to be deflected from a new line of conjecture. "Perhaps the missing crew of the starship were eaten as well. Though several hundred bodies would presume a considerable hunger."

Another call from Lieutenant Yar saved the captain from having to respond. "Not the Farmers again?" asked Picard.

"No, sir. I'm receiving a transmission from Zendi Starbase Ten."

Riker rocked back in his chair, arms crossed over his chest. "They've taken a long time in getting back to us, sir. The communications lag is only a few hours, not a full day."

"Late or not, at least we'll get some answers from Admiral Zagráth," said Picard. "Pipe it in here, Lieutenant."

Advise you to take the message in your office, sir. Scrambled transmission, Code 47—for your eyes only.

"The message was only three minutes long," protested Yar. She leaned over the aft deck railing, staring at the curving wall that separated the bridge from the captain's Ready Room. "But he's been in there for ages."

Data swung the ops console around to face the other bridge officers. "Ten minutes, twelve seconds. Not an unreasonable duration for contemplation of a classified transmission. If one is human, that is."

"I call twenty minutes unreasonable," said Geordi a while later. "After all, how many times can you listen to a three-minute message?"

"Six point six, six, six, six . . ."

"Data," said Yar, breaking into the android's computation. "Has there been any computer activity from the captain's terminal?"

"Not according to my . . ."

Riker shook his head firmly. "That's enough, Data. We're getting close to an invasion of privacy. We'll know what's going on soon enough." After waiting another ten minutes, the first officer turned to Troi. "You haven't said very much about the captain's absence. Aren't you curious?"

"That's a leading statement and you know it," responded Troi tartly. "What happened to your concern for his privacy?"

Geordi and Data both turned from their posts and stared silently at the counselor. She glanced above her head and saw both Yar and Worf looking at her as well. Troi sighed heavily. "If you must know, I sense he is experiencing great anger. He is trying to bring his temper under control."

Any further explanation was forestalled by the sound of the Ready Room doors opening and closing. Face stripped of all emotion, Picard marched stiffly to the front of the bridge. He stood at attention, back to the viewer, and coughed loudly, as if calling an unruly class to order. In a flat, uninflected voice, he addressed a point in the center of the room.

"On instructions from Starfleet Command, there is to be no further discussion among the crew concerning the events we have witnessed in response to the distress call from the *Ferrel*. All log entries and sensor data involving the *USS Ferrel* and its attacker will be sealed. I trust each and every one of you will follow these instructions to the letter."

The trill of an incoming call broke the uneasy silence that followed the captain's announcement. Yar cut off the shrill sound with a swift jab at her communications console. "It's from the Oregon Farmers, Captain."

"Inform Farmer Patrisha that I will see her now," answered Picard evenly. He had already reached the doors of the turboelevators before he turned and spoke again. "Data, you have the conn. Number One, I'll need your assistance."

Riker asked no questions as their compartment dropped deck by deck through the center of the saucer. Eyes front, he matched the captain's severe demeanor with his own martial stance.

"Hold." Picard's sudden order brought the turbolift to a standstill. A flashing alarm signaled their location between decks. "As first officer, you deserve to know at least some of what that transmission contained."

"Off the record, I assume," said Riker. He glanced around the small compartment. "The setting for the briefing is a little unorthodox."

The tight line of Picard's mouth curved ever so slightly. "It appears that the mysterious Andrew Deelor does indeed exist. And at a very rarified height. Admiral Zagráth called him a diplomatic ambassador." A dry cough betrayed his skepticism. "Possible, but Fleet Intelligence is more likely."

"That could explain the *Ferrel*'s small crew. Top security, high risk."

"Yes, but we'll probably never know what they were doing out here. The entire *Ferrel* incident has just been pulled behind a veil of secrecy." Picard restarted the elevator. "In the interests of Federation security."

The simple phrase startled Riker into protest. "But, Captain, that's the highest security classification in use."

"Exactly."

The doors of the turbo compartment slid open. The discussion was over.

When the door chime sounded, Patrisha took a deep breath and faced the threshold of the passenger suite. "Come in," she called, and the doors parted of their own accord. Such a silly waste of power, she thought, then shoved aside her scorn to greet the two men who stepped inside.

"Thank you for coming to see me, Captain," said Patrisha to the older of the outsiders. She had never been introduced to Picard, and she had yet to sort out the signs of rank that studded the collars of Starfleet uniforms, but she had learned to recognize the air of command. These officers walked with a characteristic grace and arrogance, and this man was more lordly than any other she had seen on board the starship. She turned to the one who was not a stranger. "Well met again, Mr. Riker."

"After too long, Farmer Patrisha."

The younger man's smile was much warmer than that of his companion, and Riker had answered her with a Farmer idiom. She would have preferred to continue the conversation with him, but that was not the way of these people. Their rigid hierarchies must be honored.

"I understand you were disturbed by our alert?" said the captain.

"The entire community is most concerned by recent events," acknowledged Patrisha. The captain broached the substance of this meeting most abruptly, but she had no desire to prolong the encounter either. "I speak as one of many."

"Yes, so I gather," said Picard with a quick glance toward the other room of the suite.

Patrisha flushed at the wry comment. He had heard the stealthy rustle of moving bodies and whispering voices coming from behind the wall and was aware that listeners hovered just out of sight. She covered her embarrassment with a declaration of Farmer principles. "Captain Picard, we are a peaceful people."

"I'm sorry if our recent encounter upset anyone," said Picard, though she detected no apology in his manner. "Please assure your people they were never in danger and that the attacking ship has left this sector."

"That is not the point, Captain. We will not take part in military actions."

"I quite understand your concern. However, the *Enterprise* is required to assist ships in distress. In this particular instance assistance required a show of force. Regrettable, yes, but necessary. We will resume our journey to New Oregon soon, very soon."

"But why the continued delay?" persisted Patrisha. If she must safeguard the community, and certainly none of the other Farmers were willing to confront the captain, then she would ask the necessary questions.

Riker answered her. "We're providing maintenance support to the crew of the damaged ship so they can return to Starbase Ten."

Patrisha could tell Picard's patience was wearing thin by the way he shifted his weight from one foot to another. He looked just like Dnnys, ready to bolt out the door as soon as minimal courtesy had been satisfied. In any event, she could think of no more questions. "Don't let me keep you from your work any longer."

This was a traditional Farmer closing, but Picard froze, as if suddenly aware of his display of impatience. He managed a sincere smile before leaving. "Please call Counselor Troi if you have need of any further assistance."

"I will be pleased to do so," said Patrisha politely as she ushered the two men to the exit. She sighed with weary relief when the cabin door shut and the outsiders had returned to their rightful place outside. Seconds later a door behind her whisked open.

"They left the stink of their technology in the air," said Dolora, sniffing loudly as she walked across the floor.

"Oh, please," groaned Patrisha, but she was drowned out by the approaching babble of querulous voices. More Farmers poured out of their hiding place and into the day area.

"You were entirely too accommodating," said Tomas with his usual bombast. "We can't be held here against our will."

"On the contrary. We have no choice in the matter," countered Patrisha. "However, Captain Picard

58

was tactful enough not to point that out." Only Tomas could anger her sufficiently to defend an outsider.

Dolora shook her finger in the direction of the corridor. "It's an outrage, and the Grzydc government must be informed of the treatment accorded its citizens."

"They never treated us any better," grumbled another woman.

A man on the other side of the room cried, "Outsiders don't know the meaning of respect. You can't expect common decency from any of them."

Shouting the Farmers down with rational arguments would only waste her breath. Patrisha threw herself down onto a sofa and shut her mind to the various recitals of real and imagined grievances. The scenario had been repeated over and over, with minor variations, since the yearlong trek to New Oregon had begun and was no less tedious for all its familiarity.

"The Farmers accepted the delay rather more calmly than I expected," remarked Picard after he and Riker had left the passengers' quarters. His first officer was not given to complaint, but rumors of temperamental storms by the colonists had reached the captain through other channels.

"That particular Farmer took the news well," said Riker grudgingly as they walked through the corridor. "But then, they must be resigned to delays by now. The group waited for nearly a month on Starbase Ten before we were assigned to carry them the rest of the way. Their home world used its diplomatic influence to get the community aboard the *Enterprise.*"

"I didn't think Grzydc had any influence," said the captain as they entered a turboelevator.

Riker directed the compartment to the bridge. "According to Wesley, the Grzydc government has actually paid for the Farmers' new territory."

"Terraformed land is very expensive," said Picard thoughtfully. "I'm surprised a resource-poor world like Grzydc would be so eager to help a group of naturalized citizens."

Riker grinned ruefully. "It may have been a small price to get them off the planet."

The turbo slowed to a halt. Picard and his first officer stepped out onto the bridge and into the middle of a heated confrontation between Security Chief Yar and Andrew Deelor. Yar broke off from shouting at the captain's entrance and stiffened to attention; Deelor shoved his clenched fists into the pockets of his blue medical jacket. The robed woman known only as Ruthe stood by his side, unmoved by the commotion.

"What seems to be the problem?" asked Picard. He addressed Lieutenant Yar, but his attention was really on Deelor. Details of the man's appearance had blurred since their brief encounter in sickbay. The ambassador had an undistinguished face, neither handsome nor ugly, and easily forgotten. He was of medium height and medium build—all in all, an unremarkable man.

"*Ambassador* Deelor will not leave the bridge as requested." Yar used the man's title, but her suspicion of its authenticity was obvious. "I was about to call for a security team to escort him to his quarters."

"You acted correctly, Lieutenant Yar." Picard turned to Deelor and his companion. "Passengers are not allowed on the bridge without my express permission."

"I am not an ordinary passenger," stressed Deelor.

"Evidently not." Picard's smile was not reflected in his eyes. "You've made a remarkable recovery from your wounds, Ambassador."

"Dr. Crusher is a very able physician. I'm feeling much better." He eased his hands out of the jacket pockets and let his arms rest by his side, but the tension in his shoulders remained.

"Good. Then you'll be able to answer some of my questions." Picard ushered the two down the curving bridge ramp to the threshold of his office. He and Riker followed them into the room, but Deelor shook his head at the first officer's presence.

"It's best if we speak alone, Captain." He made no pretense of making a request. This was an order.

"As you wish, Ambassador." Picard signaled Riker to obey.

Ruthe, seemingly oblivious to the undercurrent of tension in the room, stared with fascination at the lionfish swimming in the wall aquarium. Riker stepped briskly around her and left. When the door had closed, Picard walked past his guests to take his place behind the office desk, star window at his back. He remained standing, the fingers of his hands resting lightly on the polished surface of the tabletop.

"Admiral Zagráth has made it very clear that I am to refrain from all inquiry into the attack on the *USS Ferrel*. Does that also mean I'm to drop my investigation into the attack upon you?"

"There was no attack, Captain," said Deelor steadily. "My injury was an accident."

"I'm pleased to hear that. Then you'll be quite safe aboard the *Ferrel* on its return journey to Zendi Starbase Ten. Of course, the accommodations will be somewhat primitive with thirty people crammed into the service areas of Engineering, but the trip should take only eight or nine weeks."

A wry smile tugged at the corner of Deelor's mouth. "Touché, Captain. But let's put an end to our fencing. You know too much already, and yet not enough."

The ambassador pulled a chair alongside the desk and sat down. He rocked back to a comfortable angle. Picard lowered himself into his own chair, but kept himself carefully upright. He wasn't fooled by the pretense of informality.

"I have no intention of returning to the *Ferrel,*" admitted Deelor. "As you pointed out, the trip would be quite uncomfortable and tedious. Tempers can fray under the stress of confinement."

"The crew of the *Ferrel* hate you. Why?"

"Because I had command of the mission over their captain. And because I underestimated the strength of our adversary. As you've probably surmised, the aliens who attacked us are also responsible for a rather unfortunate incident on the planet Hamlin."

"The Hamlin Massacre," said Picard flatly. Those words still touched a chord of shock in him. "Three hundred people were killed without reason. Such butchery usually counts as more than an 'incident.'"

Deelor's brows crept upward. "I can see I won't have to brief you on the details."

"What do you know of these aliens?"

"They call themselves the Choraii."

"The Choraii," repeated Picard slowly. So now the enemy had a name. "And this was not a chance encounter."

"Oh, no. It's taken months of radio contact to arrange the rendezvous between the *Ferrel* and a Choraii ship." Deelor paused uncertainly. When he spoke again, the arrogance of his manner was muted. "I was prepared for hostile action from the Choraii, for a testing of our defenses. It was essential that the *Ferrel* display a military force equal to their own, one strong enough to earn their respect yet not so strong as to scare them away."

"What went wrong?" prompted Picard.

"I miscalculated, held back too long. The Choraii saw this as weakness and closed in for the kill. Their energy net was a surprise. Our power reserves weren't able to withstand the pressure of the field for more than a few hours. A hard lesson, but a valuable one. Next time, with the *Enterprise,* I'll succeed."

Picard's open palm crashed down on the desktop. "Not with *my* ship!"

"I have the authority to override your command. Or didn't the admiral tell you that?" Deelor's arrogance was back.

Picard drew on thirty years of Fleet discipline to suppress the urge to leap across the distance separating them and physically teach the ambassador his place. "Yes, I was so informed," he said at last. That particular portion of the transmission had set off a rage that he could still feel burning within him. "And what, if I may ask, is the purpose of your contact with the Choraii?"

This capitulation to authority added a trace of smugness to Deelor's face. Picard could feel his own jaw clench in response. Oh, to be able to wipe away that smile.

"The Choraii are in search of a variety of metals: zinc, gold, platinum, lead. Evidently they lack the ability to refine the ores found in asteroids. If convenient, they will kill to obtain what they need, but it is my mission to persuade them to enter into trade negotiations instead."

"Trade!" cried Picard in outrage. "Trade for what? What do they have that we could possibly want?"

Ruthe stepped out of the background. "The children of Hamlin."

Chapter Five

THE *USS FERREL* dangled in space. The soft glow from its four slim engine nacelles bathed over the crumpled outlines of the main saucer with its row upon row of darkened, lifeless port windows.

Picard studied the scene from the comfort and safety of the captain's chair on the *Enterprise* bridge. He was flanked on either side by his first officer and the ship's counselor. "Are you sure, Number One?" Picard asked dubiously as he reexamined the image on the viewscreen.

Riker shrugged. "I can hardly believe it myself, but Logan swears the *Ferrel*'s engines can sustain full impulse power long enough to reach Starbase Ten." With an outstretched hand he traced the line of damage. "The contracting energy field netted around the main hull and pulled the saucer in on itself, but the nacelles were left intact. Our maintenance crews sealed off the connecting necks leading to the damaged section and concentrated on returning basic ship's services to the remaining areas. No gravity, no food synthesis, no comforts to speak of, but it will keep them alive."

"Not my idea of a good time." Geordi spoke under his breath, but the captain overheard his remark.

"Agreed, Mr. La Forge. Now that the *Ferrel's* crew has seen their new accommodations, they may think better of their decision. Lieutenant Yar, open an audio link with the starship." Despite Engineer Logan's best repair efforts, the communications section of the saucer was still too badly damaged to provide visual contact.

"Channel open, Captain."

"Are you still determined to go through with this, Mr. D'Amelio?"

"Captain Manin is returning home on his own ship. We won't have it any other way," replied the voice of the first officer floating down from above.

Counselor Troi leaned closer to the captain and whispered an aside. "They are determined to remain on their own ship, but not just to honor their captain. They are eager to sever their association with Ambassador Deelor."

Picard understood that sentiment only too well. "As you wish, Commander. The *Ferrel* is free to go. And the best of luck on your journey."

The crackle of static gave the answering laugh an unnatural harshness. *"Don't waste your luck on us, Captain Picard. You'll need it more than we will."*

The USS *Ferrel* departed without ceremony. A brief shudder rocked the distorted structure, then it lurched into a slow crawl across the viewscreen. Picard watched the image pass out of the viewer frame with a growing sense of unease, uncertain whether his concern was for the crippled *Ferrel* or his own ship. D'Amelio's parting words echoed in his mind like an alert siren.

The *Enterprise* had proved her worth as a fighting ship on several occasions, but her basic mission was peaceful. Unlike his previous Fleet commands, this starship carried families on board. It had taken Picard weeks to get used to the sight of children walking through the corridors. They were the most prominent symbol of the expanded population, and their presence disturbed him. They were a constant reminder that the nature of his responsibilities had been altered in new and uncomfortable ways. With a ship like the *Stargazer,* Picard wouldn't hesitate to attempt the rescue of the Hamlin captives, but the *Enterprise* was different. Where did his duty lie now? Could he in good conscience risk the thousand lives aboard this vessel for those long-forgotten children? More disturbing, did the captain of the *Enterprise* have any say in the matter?

"Captain," said Data from the helm. "I've computed the Choraii ship's trajectory from our sensor readings. Course laid in." He waited expectantly for further orders. If he felt any surprise at Picard's hesitation, he did not show it.

"Ahead warp factor four, Mr. La Forge," said the captain at last. He had waited until the decision was truly his, and not the ambassador's. The result was ultimately the same. Yet not quite the same. "Mr. Riker, assemble the bridge crew in the observation deck. Lieutenant Yar, inform Ambassador Deelor that we are ready to begin the briefing."

The visitor's quarters were spacious, even luxurious after the smaller accommodations on board the *Ferrel,* but the ambassador was too preoccupied to make a comparison and Ruthe did not care.

Deelor studied his reflection in the bedroom area mirror, critically assessing the line of his black uniform. He was pleased to see that the synthetic skin covering his burns was too thin to show beneath the form-fitting fabric. Deelor was not a vain man, but he understood the subliminal underpinnings of authority. Any flaw could weaken his position.

Satisfied with his own apparel, he shifted his attention to the reflection of the woman behind him. "You need new clothes, too."

"No," said Ruthe, and curled up on the bed, pulling her cloak tightly around her. The garment had been newly cleaned, but the material was worn and the original dark color had faded to a lighter, uneven shade of gray.

Deelor knew her well enough to drop the issue. He returned to a previous topic. "And let me do all the talking at the briefing."

Her face peeked out from under the folds of cloth. "I always do. Well, most of the time."

"Yes, but it's the times you don't that worry me. Picard is not a stupid man; the slightest slip and he'll pounce. So it's very important . . ." He walked over to Ruthe, who had once more retreated into a formless ball. Sitting down on the bed beside her, certain that she could hear him, he continued. "It's very important, for both our sakes, that he doesn't learn any more than I want him to know."

"Then why talk to him?" she asked with a muffled voice.

"I wouldn't if I didn't have to." He tugged gently at her elbow. "Come on. They're waiting for us."

From his position by the doorway, Picard watched as the conference lounge was filled to capacity by the members of the bridge crew. Lieutenant Worf reached the room early and was the first to file past the captain.

He secured a seat with a wall at his back. The Klingon was followed by Data and Geordi; the android took control of the computer access panel and Geordi sat beside him.

"You're early," remarked Picard when Dr. Crusher crossed the threshold.

"It happens."

"Here, read this while we wait for the briefing to start." He handed her the Hamlin medical report which Deelor had provided. The doctor accepted the package and carried it to the table.

After a short lag, the second group arrived. Dr. Crusher glanced up from the pages of her printout in time to see her son enter with Tasha Yar and Deanna Troi. One hand rose in the air to beckon Wesley to her side, but she stopped in time. Picard was amused to see her cover the motion by scratching the tip of her nose.

"Where's the ambassador?" asked Riker when he arrived. He was exactly on time. "And Ruthe."

"Yes, they always travel as a pair," noted Picard. "So who is she? An assistant, attaché, aide-de-camp?" Meaningless, interchangeable terms, but without them Ruthe's presence was unexplained.

"Lover?" offered Riker. "They've turned down separate quarters."

Picard shrugged. "For all we know, she's his wife." The doors parted at his final statement, revealing Deelor and Ruthe at the threshold. Picard wondered just how much of the exchange the ambassador had overheard.

"This is unacceptable, Captain," said Deelor when he saw the large number of people grouped in the room. "Especially the boy."

"I will not send my bridge crew on this or any other mission without a full understanding of the situation. That includes Ensign Crusher." Picard moved to his place at the head of the table. "I have the utmost confidence in their discretion."

Deelor expressed his dissatisfaction with a frown but said nothing more as he took an empty seat next to the captain. Out of the corner of his eye Picard saw Ruthe skitter away from Riker's offer of a chair. She stood at the back of the room, fading into the gray shadows.

"Well, let's get started," demanded Deelor as if the crew had kept him waiting.

Picard signaled Data to activate the computer display in the center of the table. A miniature bubble ship wavered into existence, hovering just above the desktop.

"Fifteen years ago," began Deelor without preamble, "a Ferengi merchant encountered a crippled Choraii ship marooned in space. Their supply of zinc had been exhausted, rendering the ship immobile. The Ferengi, with an eye to future profit, exchanged a few pounds of that metal for the only salable merchandise the Choraii had to offer: five human captives. In turn, the Ferengi offered those humans to the Federation, at a significant price per head. That was when we finally learned the fate of the Hamlin children. They had been taken aboard Choraii ships and kept there for over forty years."

The man's uninflected voice could not rob the narrative of its horror. "Five survivors," said Picard. "Forty-two children were reported missing from the colony. How many more have been recovered since then?"

"Eight more."

A very low growl erupted from the general vicinity of Lieutenant Worf. The rest of the crew released their anger less directly with the rustle of shifting bodies and the exchange of somber glances.

"You must understand the difficulty we faced," said

Deelor. "The Choraii have no home other than their ships, and though they travel in loose groups, each vessel is autonomous; they do not form a cohesive political entity. Furthermore, the Choraii are nomads and travel over broad areas of uninhabited space so the Federation has lost track of their ships for years at a time. Even after we learned of their reappearance in this sector, it took months to track down the local cluster and weeks of sporadic radio contact before we could persuade one ship to meet with us to exchange a few pounds of lead for their captive."

Yar broke into the explanation. "But at that rate it could take another four decades to recover the rest of the children."

"They're hardly children anymore," said Data. "Given the age range at the time of abduction, even the youngest would be Captain Picard's age."

A smile flitted across Dr. Crusher's face, and Picard wondered if she was amused by Data's unerring instinct for social bricks, or by his own reaction to the unflattering statement.

Tapping thoughtfully at the sheets in her hand, Crusher expanded on the android's comment. "The Hamlin colony medical records indicate the older captives would be in their mid-sixties now. That's assuming they're still alive after fifty years of imprisonment under who knows what conditions."

A voice from the back of the room drew the group's attention. "The Choraii have treated them well."

Picard responded with considerable fire to Ruthe's remark. "Captivity, by its very nature, is barbarous!"

"Yes, well, that's certainly true," said Deelor quickly. "However, we must all remember to contain our natural hostility during the second round of negotiations or we risk severing our tenuous diplomatic ties. And the remaining captives will be lost forever."

The intensity of his own reaction had surprised

Picard, and he saw those same strong emotions mirrored in the eyes of his crew. Discussion of the Hamlin Massacre still touched a raw nerve among Fleet officers, and it seemed the captain was no exception. He struggled to provide a more dispassionate example. "Understood, Ambassador Deelor. I, and my crew, have no wish to jeopardize the outcome of this mission. You can depend upon our full cooperation during contact with the Choraii."

Ruthe spoke again. "Thank you, Captain."

Picard took a second, closer, look at the woman. Until now she had been overshadowed by Deelor's strong personality, but her response implied she was involved in the mission.

"I should have introduced Translator Ruthe earlier in this meeting," said Deelor. "She will handle all direct communications with the Choraii." He stood up abruptly. "So, Captain, if you and the crew will simply mind the store, this venture will proceed smoothly and without incident." Ruthe followed him out of the observation room without any prompting.

The departure of the ambassador and the translator set off another round of uneasy rustling from the assembled crew. Picard sensed their suppressed tension and waited for the inevitable explosion of emotion.

"I can't believe we're going to bargain with the aliens who massacred the Hamlin miners!" cried Yar.

Even Geordi was moved to an outburst. "And they're actually going to make a profit from the attack. That's wrong. Dead wrong."

"Is revenge the right answer?" asked the captain. He was pleased to see Lieutenant Yar rein in her anger. The other members of the crew had also stopped to reflect on the mission.

The security chief sighed heavily. "Getting the children back is more important."

"I still have a number of questions, Captain," said Data. His composure contrasted strongly with the human crew.

"Yes, Data, so do I," said Picard. "However, it appears Ambassador Deelor is not ready to answer them yet." He rose to address the assembly. "We know the Choraii are capable of destroying a constellation-class starship and they came very close to disabling the *Enterprise*. Our first priority must be to create a better defense for the next encounter. For the moment, you will have to make the effort with what little information we already possess."

The briefing was over. The group dissolved into smaller clusters as the officers headed toward their duty posts.

Captain Picard walked out of the conference room with the vague intention of returning to his quarters, but instead he found himself walking alongside Beverly Crusher. He dismissed the possibility that this action was anything other than random. After all, the doctor was the closest to his equal in age, so it was only natural to seek her out at times.

The ship's corridors were well traveled, so the captain and Crusher could talk only of general shipboard matters, but once inside the relative privacy of her office, Picard broached the subject of Hamlin with a personal revelation.

"Nightmares?" exclaimed the doctor.

"Oh, yes, for years," said Picard. "I had a rather active imagination and conjured up quite vivid images of the bloody deaths of the missing children. And it didn't help that a neighborhood bully would threaten to ship me off to Hamlin, where hungry monsters were waiting to gobble up bothersome little boys." He accepted Crusher's amusement at his expense with only a twinge of embarrassment. "After all, I was only five years old at the time and somewhat gullible."

Dropping the loose sheets of the Hamlin medical records beside her, Dr. Crusher threw one hip over the edge of her desk. "And yet, despite those fears, you went into space."

Picard adopted her informal posture. Leaning against the entrance frame, he cast his mind back through the years. "Despite, or possibly because of those fears. I grew tired of being afraid, and tired of the boy's tyranny. I chose to confront my nightmares."

"How ironic. The children weren't killed, but because you thought they were, you now have a chance to rescue them."

Picard resumed his more rigid stance. "Not me. I'm just the storekeeper. My responsibility is to move the trading post into position. A Ferengi merchant would be more useful; at least he could drive another hard bargain with the Choraii."

"A few pounds of lead is a small price to pay. The metal is practically worthless, toxic to human life. We could easily spare a hundred times that amount."

"Yes, and if the Choraii had bothered to ask for what they needed fifty years ago, the Hamlin colonists would still be alive. Over a hundred people killed, slaughtered like animals. Hardly a worthless metal, Dr. Crusher—it has a blood price beyond measure."

The lightness of their earlier mood had faded completely. Crusher took up the papers she had tossed aside. "I didn't have a chance to mention this at the briefing, but the medical records Deelor provided are little more than historical documents. They make no mention of which individuals were returned or their physical condition at that time. If we're going to bring more survivors on board, I'll need as much current information as I can get."

"A legitimate request," agreed Picard. "But somehow I suspect it won't be that simple. Getting answers out of Ambassador Deelor is like breaking open an Aldebaran shellmouth. The result is hardly worth the effort."

"But he wants this mission to succeed. He must realize we're only trying to help in that effort."

"Yes," said Picard. "That would seem obvious. Perhaps he's only a petty-minded bureaucrat clinging obsessively to the status that comes with controlling access to top secrets." The captain compared this assessment with what little he had seen of Deelor in action and judged the fit. No, not a good match. "Either that, or he has something to hide."

In the privacy of their suite, with Ruthe safely asleep in the next room, Deelor embarked on a computer-guided inspection of the *Enterprise*. His ambassadorial rank allowed him to review the ship's engineering specs without any difficulty, but the computer system balked when he requested the crew personnel files. Deelor responded with a five-digit code that silenced all opposition to his access and erased all tracks of the intrusion.

Jean-Luc Picard was his first target. Deelor rifled through the record of the captain's previous postings, but the list of distinctions grew tedious so Deelor switched to more recent information. Gaining access to the Captain's Log required a seven-digit code. The study gave him a good feel for Picard's style and some clue as to how the man might react to the demands of the current situation. Picard was a seasoned officer, but then, Deelor had expected no less from the captain of a galaxy-class vessel.

He spent less time on First Officer William Riker and Lieutenant Commander Data, but his search through their files was thorough. An acquaintance with the other bridge crew members could wait until later.

Ruthe did not wake when Deelor picked up the small chest resting on the dresser by the bed. The box was the only item he had retrieved from the *Ferrel* before its departure. He disliked possessions and he was eager to be rid of its contents. The computer established that Riker and Data were working together in the science section and politely offered to furnish directions, but Deelor declined the information.

Finding his own way to the science lab proved to be a convenient test of his memorization of the ship's layout. Deelor reached the proper location without a false turn. On the *Ferrel* he had walked an equivalent distance in the dark to reach the bridge, a journey that had saved both his life and Ruthe's. The need to duplicate that feat could arise if the Choraii won the next round. Deelor noted the surprise on the officers' faces when he entered the room. Their reaction pleased him. Predictability was boring. And dangerous.

"Mr. Riker, I leave this in your charge." Deelor dropped the small chest onto a lab table. The crack of impact betrayed its weight. He pulled the vocoder out from a jacket pocket and tossed it to Data. The android's reaction time was excellent. "And that's for you, Mr. Data."

Riker examined the box carefully before opening it. Deelor gave him extra credit for his caution. "Lead," said the first officer as he counted the bars inside. "About fifteen pounds."

"I brought extra in case the Choraii raise the price of their captive."

"Why so little?" asked Riker. "Even highly refined metal is fairly cheap."

"They never ask for more than they need," said Deelor. "After laying waste to all of Hamlin, the Choraii probably took only twenty pounds of metal."

"And now we're giving them more."

"Not giving, trading."

Riker frowned with disgust, but Data merely looked inquisitive. "Given their obvious technological sophistication, why haven't the Choraii developed their own processing techniques? Asteroids are an abundant source for the metals they seek."

"Some sort of political squabble," explained Deelor. "It seems the ships with mining capabilities have withdrawn from the local cluster. Choraii social structure is rather complicated and we know very few details of its workings." He proceeded with his instructions before Data could delay him further. Deelor had other more pressing duties than to satisfy an android's curiosity. "Mr. Riker, keep the chest in a secure location near the transporter chamber so the bars can be pulled out at a moment's notice."

"What do I do with this?" asked Data, lifting up the instrument he had caught.

"The vocoder contains a record of the *Ferrel*'s sensor readings on the Choraii. Examine it for any information that can explain their unusual weapons technology. I'll expect a full report as soon as possible."

Riker stiffened in place. "Is Captain Picard aware of these assignments?"

"Feel free to inform him," said Deelor, executing his second abrupt departure of the day.

Chapter Six

"THE BOY NEEDS an uncle," declared Dolora as she folded another shirt and tucked it inside the open trunk on the cabin floor.

"Well, he doesn't have one," answered Patrisha. From the depths of a cushioned chair, she watched the older woman's efforts. Under different circumstances she could have enjoyed her accommodations aboard the *Enterprise*. Farmer principles had never ruled against plush furniture and airy spaces, but the community could rarely afford such amenities. However, a week of sharing quarters with her aunt had made the trip nearly unbearable, despite the physical comforts. "Another example of my mother's thoughtlessness in dying young."

Dolora pursed her thin lips. She found Patrisha's sense of humor to be quite distorted at times. "Tomas would serve as his uncle if only you would ask."

"Tomas already tries to act the part of my brother without being asked."

"He's your cousin."

"He's—" Patrisha bit back her reply. Tomas was a pigheaded ass, but he was also Dolora's son. He came by his aggravating nature honestly. "He's kind, to be so interested in our welfare, but I can deal with Dnnys on my own."

Dolora probed fitfully at the contents of the trunk, considering whether to pull everything out and start over again. "Being an only child has made you very headstrong."

"Thank God." The curse slipped out before Patrisha could stop herself. "I'm sorry, Auntie Dolo." She shamelessly plied the old endearment, so little used now. "It's just that the news Dnnys brought has upset me."

Two bright spots still colored her aunt's cheeks, but the woman accepted the apology. "Do you believe what the boy says?"

"Oh, yes," said Patrisha. "He's quite certain the ship has changed course away from New Oregon."

"Which shows Dnnys hasn't learned a lesson from his last censure," sniffed Dolora. "He's still sneaking away from the community."

And they were back to their first argument all over again. Patrisha took her son's part as before, carefully linking her defense to the Farmers' best interests. "We need his knowledge of the *Enterprise* to protect ourselves. And our cargo."

The practical aspects of that argument could not be denied, even by someone as irrational as Dolora, but she easily found another focus for criticism. "I'd feel much better if he were a girl. Boys are too susceptible to the false attractions of the nonliving environment."

"If he were a girl, then Krn wouldn't have a brother," pointed out Patrisha.

"About Krn," began Dolora with an ominous look. She had lost all interest in the packing.

The fight would have escalated on the next round if not for the arrival of Dnnys. Patrisha tried to send the boy back out of the room with a warning glare, but he saved them both from a direct attack from Dolora.

"Captain Picard is here to see you, Mother."

Patrisha rose from her seat and Dolora quickly announced she had left her best sweater in the other room. She scurried away to retrieve it. Patrisha knew better than to expect her to return while the captain was present.

"Well met, Farmer Patrisha," said the officer upon entering. He carried himself with all the confidence she had noted in their first meeting but none of the impatience.

"After too long, Captain Picard." Patrisha decided to come to the point immediately, which was not a Farmer custom, but she clouded the source of her information in a way typical of her people. "A very disturbing rumor has arisen in our community. Some among us believe the *Enterprise* is no longer journeying toward New Oregon."

Picard looked immediately to her son. "You've become good friends with Wesley Crusher, haven't you?" His demeanor was calculated to inspire terror in the heart of a young boy.

"He didn't tell me, if that's what you mean," said Dnnys with a scowl. "I may be a Farmer, but I'm smart enough to notice a major course change. All I have to do is look out a port window."

"Yes, quite so," admitted Picard. He turned back to Patrisha. "Your son is to be commended on his powers of observation."

The compliment did not distract her. "Then it's true we're no longer heading for New Oregon."

"The diversion is minor," said Picard. "Starbase

Ten has requested that we rendezvous with another ship in this sector to exchange some necessary trade goods. As you can see, the *Enterprise* has many functions besides exploration; we serve as a passenger transport, merchant ship, and rescue vessel."

His litany was a subtle reminder of their own imposition on his command. The captain of their last transport had been less restrained. A four-month voyage with the Farmers had tasked the last of Bucher's patience. She had dropped the entire community off at the nearest Federation starbase and no amount of pleading could win a way back on board the *Forox* freighter. Remembering the shame of that abandonment weakened Patrisha's resolve. "Thank you for taking the time to explain."

"Not at all," he said genially. "That's what captains are for."

After Picard had left, and before Dolora could creep back in, Patrisha asked her son, "Was he telling the truth?"

"I don't know," Dnnys answered sullenly. "And Wesley won't tell me what's going on."

Riker and Data crowded in on either side of Lieutenant Yar, peering intently at the sensor readout on her bridge monitor.

"Got it!" cried Yar in triumph. "Heading thirty-four mark twelve."

Data nodded a confirmation to the first officer. "The residue can be traced fairly easily now that the element profile has been determined."

Picard stepped off the turbolift and saw the cluster of officers. "What's all the excitement?"

"The chase is afoot, sir!" announced Data with great enthusiasm. "We have found a trail of blood."

"Blood? On my ship?"

Riker grinned at the captain's confusion. "Data was speaking metaphorically, Captain. We've determined a way to track the Choraii ship."

"Excellent," said Picard, heading down to the captain's chair.

"Actually, the use of the word *blood* was not strictly metaphorical." Data followed after the captain. "An examination of fragments gathered from the battle site shows that the Choraii ship is constructed of an extraordinary blend of both organic and inorganic matter. By destroying several of its spheres, we actually wounded the ship. Our sensors have now been calibrated to detect the particular combination of elements released from the site of the injury."

Riker had come down the ramp on the far side of the bridge. He met the captain at the command center. "We've tied the data input directly to navigation. Geordi will follow the signal feed rather than compute a straight trajectory that could miss the trail."

La Forge flexed his fingers with a theatrical flourish. "I'm ready whenever you are." Flying free, without computer controls or a set course, was a pilot's dream. Everything else was filler to be endured until the next chance to take over the helm.

"Proceed at warp six," ordered the captain.

"What's wrong with you?" asked Beverly Crusher when her son drooped into sickbay. "Are you feeling sick?"

"I'm okay," he protested, but she laid a hand against his forehead anyway.

"No fever," she said. "So why do you look as if you've lost your best friend?"

"Because I have."

The doctor dropped her hand from his face and

gave him a quick hug. Wesley didn't even squirm away.

"Dnnys knows there's something strange going on and he wants to know what. It's not just curiosity, he's worried for his family's sake. And I can't tell him anything because of the security restriction on talking about Hamlin."

His mother sighed. A fever would be easier to deal with than this problem. "Wesley, if you're serious about a Starfleet career,"—she waved down his automatic protest—"then you'll have to find a balance between the demands of duty and the demands of your personal life. They can't always be reconciled."

In just the few months they had spent aboard the *Enterprise,* Dr. Crusher had seen her son mature in mind and body, yet he was still too young to fully understand how painful the conflict of those two commitments would be. He wouldn't appreciate hearing that from his mother, though, so she kept silent.

"I took an oath," said Wesley with great seriousness. "I have to stand by it, no matter what."

People often remarked that Wesley favored her in looks, but at this moment Crusher saw how much he resembled his father. The comparison brought equal measures of pride and fear. Her husband's devotion to Starfleet had been too great a part of his character to be regretted, but she did regret his early death.

She reached a hand out to ruffle Wesley's hair, but this time he ducked away from the caress, which meant he was feeling better already. Glancing through the glass partition behind his back, the doctor saw Andrew Deelor entering sickbay.

"Speaking of oaths," she sighed as the ambassador approached, "it's time for me to concentrate on the Hippocratic. I've got an appointment scheduled, so get out of here, Ensign Crusher, on the double, or I'll run a few tests on you, too." She was relieved to see her son grin as he raced away. Wesley was too even-tempered to brood for long.

Pushing aside the concerns of her personal life, the doctor turned all attention to her patient. Deelor had been released from sickbay a few days before, but the severity of his phaser wound warranted daily inspection.

"Excellent. The burn is nearly healed," noted Dr. Crusher as Deelor stripped off his uniform, revealing the synthetic skin covering his wound. The artificial material was almost wholly absorbed by new cell growth. She lifted the top of the med scanner and motioned him onto the table. The instrument results confirmed her first prognosis.

"Your body has remarkable recuperative powers." Peering more closely at the scanner readout, she focused on a ghostly image below the epidermal layer. A touch to the probe controls magnified the area. "Which is quite fortunate considering the number of injuries you seem to have sustained in the past. Deep-tissue scars near the heart and liver"—she moved the scope again—"closed puncture wound to the left lung, and numerous break lines on the ribs."

Her scan at an end, she swung the hinged panel up off the man's chest. "I had no idea the diplomatic service was so dangerous."

"I'm accident prone," was Deelor's only reply as he rolled off the bed.

"Like falling in front of a stray phaser blast?"

Deelor eased his way back into his clothes. He was beyond the stage at which dressing was painful, but some stiffness remained.

Dr. Crusher spoke again. "Why aren't those old injuries listed on your medical profile?"

"Aren't they?" he asked with raised eyebrows. The

feigned surprise was ordinarily very convincing, but
this doctor was on her guard.

"Perhaps you're absentminded as well as clumsy.
I'm missing current medical records on the Hamlin
survivors."

"All in due time, Dr. Crusher." He closed the front
seam of the uniform as if sealing in a secret. "All in
due time."

Artificial gravity and inertia dampers maintained
the illusion of level flight for the thousand people who
lived aboard the *Enterprise.* Walking serenely through
its long corridors, at ease in dining rooms or soundly
asleep in their cabins, they were oblivious to the
starship's looping and swerving flight as Geordi La
Forge followed the trail of discarded particles that
marked the passage of the Choraii. However, any port
window revealed the true path of the *Enterprise,* and
people quickly learned to avert their gaze from the
reeling cosmos. On the bridge, the prolonged pitch
and yaw of stars on the main viewer frame was harder
to avoid, and more than one of the bridge crew had
staggered off to sickbay. The rest kept their eyes
trained on their duty station.

This was difficult for Captain Picard because Lieutenant Data was delivering his report while standing
squarely in front of the viewer. Again and again the
captain's gaze drifted away from a neutral spot to
Data's face. And behind his face the stars whirled.
Picard ignored the faint sensation of nausea for as
long as possible, willing it to go away, but the feeling
only grew stronger.

"Enough." Picard stopped for an involuntary swallow. The last few sentences of Data's report had left
no impression. "Let's meet in the Ready Room."

"Good idea, sir," said Riker.

"Will, you're as pale as Data," observed the captain

when they had reached the safety of the enclosed office.

Riker smiled weakly. He positioned his chair so that the one window in the room was at his back.

The android, however, seemed unaffected by the dissonance between visual motion and the inner ear's perception of a stable physical world. He continued his report without a break. "Unfortunately, most of our sensor scans were compromised by the disruptive effects of the energy net. Ambassador Deelor provided a record of the encounter with the *Ferrel,* but those instrument readings were similarly affected."

Picard frowned at the implications. "Does that mean we can't construct an effective defense to the Choraii weaponry?"

"No, sir," said Data. "The task is difficult, but not impossible. Given sufficient time for study, a solution can be reached." He anticipated the captain's next question. "But I cannot specify how much longer the process will take."

"The shorter the better, Mr. Data," sighed Picard. "I would prefer to meet the Choraii with a greater advantage than last time."

"Understood." Data laid a small metal cylinder down on the desk. As an afterthought, he added, "Interesting. This particular vocoder technology is quite advanced, unlike any I've seen in general use by Starfleet personnel. Actually, I would consider it more appropriate for certain intelligence-gathering operations."

"Is that opinion or fact, Mr. Data?" asked Riker.

"Opinion, sir," admitted Data. "But in my case, the two are often very closely allied."

"Well, keep your opinion to yourself, my friend. You're traveling on quicksand."

After a startled look at the deck beneath his feet, Data nodded in understanding. "Oh, I see. You are using a metaphor that connotes danger. Perhaps that would explain the gaps in the tape: security censorship. Should I keep that to myself as well?"

"You can tell us," said Picard, leaning forward. His body's discomfort was forgotten the moment his mind seized hold of a puzzle.

"The vocoder record covers only the latter part of the encounter, after the Choraii ship caught the *Ferrel* in its energy matrix. Several earlier tracks have been erased from the file, but I was able to recover a few bytes of the missing data."

"And what did you find?"

"A single frame detailing the ship's power status just before the energy net was cast. It seems the *Ferrel*'s power reserves were unusually low, making them especially vulnerable to the contracting field."

"Data, does the record explain how the *Ferrel*'s power was drained?" asked the captain.

"No, sir, it does not. If that information was ever present, it has been successfully deleted."

"So the ambassador is still playing his little security games." Picard rubbed thoughtfully at his chin. From out of nowhere, he recalled D'Amelio's last warning. *Don't waste your luck on us, Captain Picard. You'll need it more than we will.* Did the danger lie with the Choraii or with Andrew Deelor?

Wesley's footsteps echoed down the length of the narrow access tunnel and disappeared into the deep shadows ahead. The shadows remained just out of reach no matter how far the boy walked. Every ten steps forward a recessed wall light sprang to life in front of him just as another died behind him. His pace accelerated as his imagination called up half-forgotten horror tales to draw forms in the darkness.

A sudden hiss wrung a yelp of fright from his throat, even as his mind recognized the sound of doors parting. Laughing at his self-induced terror, Wesley sprinted through the opening into the cavernous room beyond. Dnnys had showed him this way to the cargo bay, and it had rapidly turned into a favorite shortcut.

Before the Farmers' arrival, Wesley had never explored the cargo sections of the *Enterprise*. He was naturally drawn to the more intricate technology of the warp-drive engine and the bridge control systems. Only a chance comment from one of the engineers had alerted Wesley to the stasis system the colonists had brought on board. Curiosity led to a visit and the meeting with the Farmer boy in charge of the equipment led to friendship.

Wesley sighed as he remembered that the friendship might be over now. He threaded his way between the towering stacks of faceted shipping containers, automatically counting the left and right turns. Even before he reached the final corner, he could hear the bubbling rush of the cryo-liquid as it cycled through its tubing.

"Dnnys?" Wesley could usually find the Farmer somewhere nearby during the ship's day cycle. This was the only area outside the passenger quarter where Dnnys was allowed and he spent as much time in the cargo hold as possible.

A tousled head popped out from behind the honeycombed structure of the stasis chambers, then ducked back out of sight. Wesley had dreaded this confrontation, and now his fears were confirmed by the silent rebuff. He stood, undecided as to his next move.

"Well, hurry up!" cried Dnnys, his voice muffled inside the bank of equipment. "It's about time you came. I've got a problem."

"You could have called," said Wesley as he bent down on hands and knees and scrambled into the control niche. The space was just big enough for the two of them to hunch side by side.

Dnnys ignored this statement. "There's something wrong." He tapped the face of a dial. The indicator needle quivered in place. "All the readings are normal, but something is wrong."

Wesley accepted his friend's assessment without surprise. The stasis machinery was antiquated, a cast-off relic that only a poor planet like Grzydc would have kept; a strict regimen of daily maintenance was necessary to insure its continued operation. Drawing on Wesley's theoretical knowledge and his own familiarity with the mechanics involved, Dnnys finally tracked the source of the problem. Flat on his back, squeezed into a space made for alien technicians of a different size and shape, he stretched a hand deep into the entrails of a control box and pulled out a darkened chip of metal.

"Fused solid," said Wesley, examining the square circuit. "It must have been shorted out when we were caught in the energy net." The fail-safe checks of the *Enterprise* computers had pinpointed all such failures on the starship, but the stasis machinery was too old for such sophisticated damage control. He slipped Dnnys a replacement chip and watched as the readings on the wall panels fluttered to new settings.

One section on a cluttered board drew their immediate attention. The two boys stared at the chronometer. The numbers on its face were ticking off, one by one, higher and higher.

"The decant cycle has started," cried Dnnys. "It's only a few days from the first unloading." The boy wriggled out of the niche and pressed his face against the nearest stasis window. A dim red glow barely revealed the tiny curled form of an embryo floating inside; it had grown since his last inspection. He moved to the next chamber and inspected the image behind the ruby-colored glass. This embryo was larger, its features more distinct. A tiny hoof moved.

"Can't you stop the cycle again?" asked Wesley.

"Not without a high fatality rate," said Dnnys. "Wes, I've got to know. Is there any chance we'll reach New Oregon before we start decanting?"

Wesley shook his head. He couldn't explain the cause for the detour, but the schedule delay would be obvious to the colonists soon enough.

"Well," said the Farmer. "You're going to be hip-deep in pigs and sheep, not to mention dogs and chickens. I hope your captain likes animals."

"I think I'd better call the bridge," answered Wesley. With luck, he could explain the problem to Commander Riker first.

Chapter Seven

"WILL THE LIVESTOCK be jettisoned into space?" asked Patrisha with dismay.

"Definitely not," said Riker. Surely she couldn't have expected such a drastic reaction. "We have no intention of harming the decanted animals."

"But then where will we put them all?"

Picard had asked the same question with considerable more force and the inclusion of an expletive. As befitted a competent first officer, Riker had prepared an answer before letting either the captain or the Farmer know of the problem brewing in the cargo bay. "The ship's holodecks can be reprogrammed for pasture and farmland, including barns and corrals. Wesley Crusher is working out the computer instructions now."

The captain had insisted on the assignment, as if blaming the messenger for bad news. However, the young ensign was delighted at the chance to alter the simulation parameters. With Dnnys serving as a consultant for the Farmers' requirements, the task was closer to play than work.

Patrisha's face was still taut with anxiety. "A holodeck. Oh, dear."

"Is something wrong?" asked Riker. Dnnys had accepted the solution with relief, but his mother looked even more worried than before.

"It's the only way, really. I can see that," said the Farmer. "However, holodecks are . . ." She shrugged helplessly.

"Works of the devil?" suggested Riker with an irreverence he hadn't meant to voice.

"We're not superstitious, Mr. Riker." Patrisha's annoyance was obvious, but fortunately she wasn't gravely offended. "As Farmers we try to avoid unnecessary technology, to lessen our dependence on machinery."

"But your credo allows stasis chambers," Riker pointed out. Of all the colonists, this woman seemed the least likely to take offense, but he should have brought Troi along to warn him if he pushed Patrisha too far.

"Only because our need is so great," she said. "We had no other choice. Despite that pressing urgency, many Farmers have opposed the use of such an unfamiliar method of transport for the animals. The stasis malfunction has strengthened the force of their arguments. So many arguments."

Riker sensed a lowering of Patrisha's reserve, as if she were too tired to maintain her distance. For the first time, she motioned him to sit down on the suite's couch. She perched on a smaller chair, tense but much less defensive.

"We are wanderers, Commander. Ziedorf, the oldest among us, was born on Titan nearly two hundred years ago. My mother and my aunt were born on

Yonada, and I was born during the voyage to Grzydc. Each world was deemed a perfect place, so we would adopt some smattering of the local customs, alter our names to fit the native language, but always the changes were superficial. First and foremost we were Oregon Farmers and eventually the differences forced a departure. With each move to a new planet our community and our possessions grew smaller."

"And New Oregon is to be another home."

"The final one, I hope." She smiled sadly. "Though my mother said the same of Grzydc." She shook herself and continued more briskly. "My daughter Krn is waiting for us on the terraformed land, making the final arrangements for our settlement. We named it after our original home, a place on Earth called Oregon. Nearly a thousand people left there some three centuries past. We're all that remains of that group. And the animal embryos are nearly all that's left of our possessions."

"I understand, Farmer Patrisha." Riker stood to take his leave. "The *Enterprise* will get you, and your livestock, safe to New Oregon." But he was relieved that she didn't ask him when.

"What time of year do you want?" asked Wesley. The computer blinked a steady query remark and patiently waited for new input.

Dnnys instantly whooped out, "Spring!" The Grzydc year was very long, and he had experienced that glorious growing season only four times in his life. He wasn't sure what a Terran spring was like, but he was sure it would be better than what Grzydc had offered, as was almost everything Dnnys had encountered since leaving that planet.

"And I'll put in a few fancy details," continued Wesley as he entered a series of numbers into the holodeck program. "Commander Riker says that if you can take the time to make a project good, then you might as well work hard enough to make it great."

"That sounds just like Dolora," sighed Dnnys. "But somehow I don't mind it so much coming from Mr. Riker. I like him."

"So do I." Wesley's fingers stopped their tap-dance on the keyboard. "Sometimes I wonder if . . ." But he didn't finish.

"Go on," urged Dnnys.

"Well, it's just that I was kind of young when my father died. I try to remember what he was like, but it's hard." It was equally hard to admit that to his mother. She would probably understand, but the knowledge that Wesley's memories of his father were fading would make her sad. "And so sometimes I wonder if he was anything like Mr. Riker."

"Not having a father must be like my not having an uncle," said the Farmer boy. "Except you miss a real person, whereas I just think about a make-believe one." He had never revealed that fantasy to anyone, but his friend would understand the desire that prompted it.

The simulation program was forgotten for the moment. "So it bothers you, too?"

"Not that often, really," said Dnnys, shrugging. Sometimes he didn't think about an uncle for weeks on end. Other times the sense of loss drove him to seek out Tomas, whom he didn't like much at all, but who was made of flesh and blood rather than air. "And I get along pretty well with my mother. Not like my sister Krn. They were always fighting. I think that's one of the reasons Krn volunteered to go to New Oregon ahead of the group."

Wesley tried to conjure up the image of a red-haired sister yelling angrily at his own mother, but the very idea set him laughing. "Don't they like each other?"

"Of course they do. Or at least they love each

other." He could see that more easily than the two women. "Tomas says they're two of a kind."

A deep male voice echoed this last phrase. "Two of a kind?" Riker had entered the room just as Dnnys finished speaking. "Are you building a farm or playing cards?"

The boys broke up laughing, then eagerly waved the first officer over to the computer to review their work. Thoughts of fathers and uncles gave way to the demands of the holodeck project.

Picard usually stayed on the command level of the bridge, but as the search for the Choraii dragged on he noted the unconscious frown Tasha Yar directed at her console. When the frown deepened, but she remained silent, the captain took a stroll onto the aft deck. His security chief was quick to speak her mind, too quick many times, but her dogged attempts to discipline her own temperament could go too far. Yar had good instincts which must not be lost beneath the weight of caution.

"Have you found something, Lieutenant?" he asked with assumed carelessness.

His question caught her off guard. "Yes, sir," she said, then amended that to, "I mean, maybe."

Picard looked down at the search grid. It appeared normal. "A hunch?"

She squirmed uncomfortably at the implied imprecision. "It's probably only edge distortion, Captain." With a pointing finger she drew his eyes to a tiny ripple on the outer perimeter of the scan field. "This coordinate isn't on Geordi's current trajectory."

"Mr. Data, what do you make of the lieutenant's reading?"

Data's interpretation of the disturbance was equally indecisive. "If it is the Choraii vessel, we are traveling far off course."

"What course?" asked Geordi. His visored eyes were fixed on the computer signal that traced a path on his navigation board. "These guys travel in loops, not straight lines. Their ship could end up anywhere."

Picard rapidly weighed the statements of his officers. The review was a rational process, but his final decision was based more on instinct than on logic. Unlike Yar, he had conquered his fear of playing hunches. "Mr. La Forge, set a direct course for the sensor disturbance."

"Aye, aye, Captain," said the pilot. The tumbling stars on the main viewer gave one final lazy swirl, then steadied into place.

"Computer navigation does have certain advantages," remarked Picard to Lieutenant Worf.

Worf nodded solemnly. An odd gurgling noise reminded Picard that the Klingon had scorned Dr. Crusher's offer of a horizone injection though everyone else had taken it willingly. Judging from the sounds emanating from the lieutenant's body, Klingon's were just as prone to nausea as humans, if far less willing to admit their discomfort.

Satisfied that the varied problems of the aft deck were now over, Picard returned to his command position. With a rapid series of taps to his chest insignia, he summoned Riker and Troi to the bridge; he would contact Ambassador Deelor after addressing the bridge crew. The captain had promised full cooperation on this venture, and Deelor would get it, but he would not get blind obedience. Picard wanted a close accounting of the ambassador's actions from this point on.

Andrew Deelor was a light sleeper. The call from the bridge brought him to an alert state immediately and there was no trace of drowsiness in his voice when he spoke with Picard.

The exchange was brief and Deelor slipped out of bed as soon as the contact was severed. Ever since the *Enterprise* had picked up the trail of the Choraii, he had gone to bed fully dressed, ready at any time for a summons to the bridge.

"Ruthe?" He switched on the cabin lights, blinking just once at the sudden glare, and searched for the translator's gray cloak. She would be huddled beneath it. The night before Ruthe had pulled all the pillows off his bed and slept on the deck, but tonight he found her curled up on a chair in a far corner of the suite.

Deelor shook her awake and whispered the news into her ear. Ruthe hated loud noises. She uncurled her body with a lazy stretch and was ready to leave the cabin. They had that much in common: they both traveled light.

The ship's corridors were quiet—the few people they encountered walked alone—but the bridge was a startling contrast, alive with voices and movement, and he felt Ruthe flinch as they stepped off the turbolift.

"The ship is skimming in and out of scanner range," explained Picard to Deelor and Ruthe as they joined him at the command center. "We can't get close enough for a solid reading."

"Don't even try," said Deelor. He waved First Officer Riker aside and took the seat at the captain's right. "The Choraii do not respond to direct pursuit."

"What do they respond to?" asked Picard with a touch of bad humor.

"This." Ruthe pulled her hands out from the folds of her cloak. She held three sections of an intricately carved wooden shaft. With practiced ease, the separate pieces were assembled into a single unit.

Dropping down next to Deelor's feet, Ruthe sat cross-legged on the deck. She lifted the musical instrument to her mouth, adopting the position of a flute player, but the sound that emerged was deeper in timbre, closer to that of an oboe or bassoon though without the reedy quality.

"Start transmission now," ordered Deelor. He noted Yar's resistance to his assumption of command. She waited until the captain nodded a confirmation before opening a broadcast channel. The time was fast approaching when Picard must cede his authority outright. Soon, but not quite yet.

The rise and fall of notes from the flute pulled Deelor's mind back to Ruthe. Her melody was simple, little more than a scale played over and over with subtle variations of tempo and rhythm, but haunting nevertheless. Each phrase led to the same note, lingered over it, then rushed away only to come back to it again.

"B flat," said Riker after listening for several minutes. "At octave intervals, but always B flat."

"That's as good a name for the Choraii ship as any other," responded Deelor.

Reaching the end of her greeting, Ruthe held the naming note until her breath died away. She dropped the instrument into her lap and waited.

The answering transmission was more intricate. Three separate flutes, or possibly voices, wove up and down crossing the B flat tone sustained by a fourth player. After listening for some time, Ruthe began to play again, melding her part among the others. The exchange lasted several minutes, then one by one the voices dropped out, leaving Ruthe solo again.

Eyes closed to the people around her, the translator was still playing when Yar announced that the Choraii ship had passed out of scan range. Deelor touched Ruthe lightly on the shoulder. She broke off abruptly, as if waking from a trance.

"They have a song to finish before they can meet with us, but they have agreed to another rendezvous."

"Even after the injury we caused their vessel?" asked Picard. "I would have expected that a greater amount of persuasion would be needed to arrange another contact."

"Oh, that." Ruthe shrugged off the previous encounter. "No one was hurt, the ship has healed."

"Where and when are we to meet with them?"

Ruthe hesitated, then returned to her flute. She replayed a short segment of the exchange, transposing the notes to human concepts. "In twenty of your hours. The choice of place was mine. I told them we would meet at coordinates eight five six mark twelve."

"We can reach the site in the allotted time by traveling at warp six," said Data after plotting the coordinates on his console. "But why there? The location has no obvious significance."

"I liked the sound of it."

Riker smiled at the android's consternation. "Sometimes presentation is more important than content, Data."

"I fail to comprehend . . ."

"Later, Mr. Data," said the captain firmly. "Now that the rendezvous has been established, the ship's saucer section can be detached and left behind. We'll meet the Choraii with the battle bridge."

"Under no circumstances," said Deelor. "The ship stays whole."

Picard stiffened at the countermand. "I can't deliberately involve passengers in the coming conflict."

"They are far safer staying with the heavy armaments section than they would be on their own. The Choraii are erratic in their navigation and could easily double back on course. The saucer section would be easy prey."

"I see your point," sighed Picard. "The population is at risk either way."

"Quite so." Deelor had no desire to continue debat-

98

ing the issue. He stood and beckoned Ruthe to leave the bridge with him. He called out one last order from inside the forward turbo compartment. "You may proceed to the rendezvous, Captain Picard."

"The ambassador needs better manners," muttered Picard after the turboelevator had carried Deelor off the bridge. He instructed the helm to lock in Ruthe's coordinates, though not without some misgivings. Picard was no musician; while Riker had been enthralled by the performance, the captain had listened with growing unease to the unintelligible transmission.

"We've only her word for what passed between them," he pointed out to Riker. "And while I have no reason to disbelieve what she says"—he threw up his hands in frustration—"I just don't trust her or Deelor."

The captain looked to Troi for an opinion, but the counselor had little to offer. "Ruthe thought solely of her music. And Deelor, as always, was very careful to shield his emotions. He knows I'm half-Betazoid, and his powers of concentration are very strong when I am nearby."

"I have a record of the entire transmission, Captain," said Data, next in line for the captain's attention. "Theoretically, the language computers can develop a translation, but the Choraii speech appears to be quite intricate, more emotive than literal. I will need additional information to speed the translation process and increase accuracy."

Picard turned to his first officer. "You're a musician, Number One. I've heard you play."

"I'm an amateur," protested Riker. "And I really know only jazz."

"Amateur or not, you're the only person with security clearance who has any affinity for the musical nature of the Choraii language." The captain considered the first officer's other off-duty interests and nodded at the appropriateness of his choice. "Yes, I'm sure you can persuade Translator Ruthe into discussing her work."

"But Captain . . ."

"She's not unlike Mistress Beata on Angel One. Your oratory moved her to grant clemency to the crew of the *Odin*." According to certain informal sources, Riker's persuasion had been based on more than just his debating skills. Picard gave greater credence to those reports when he noticed the tips of Riker's ears had turned pink.

"I'll give it a try, sir."

Despite the first officer's discomfort, Picard detected a certain amount of anticipation in his acceptance of the task. "Just make sure Deelor isn't around when you do. He strikes me as the jealous type."

A diversion was easily arranged. Dr. Crusher was none too pleased to have Deelor's medical exam used as a screen for Riker's activities, but when pressed she agreed to schedule an appointment with the ambassador. Drawing Ruthe out of her cabin was more difficult. Several minutes passed before she answered Riker's persistent touch to the door chime. His offer of a tour of the ship was met with a blank stare, but since she did not tell him to go away, he tried again with a more direct approach.

"I was fascinated by your flute-playing on the bridge. Would you play for me?"

"Here?" she asked, somewhat bewildered.

Riker insisted on treating her answer as an agreement to his request, but suggested a nearby recreation lounge as a more congenial location. With more prompting, Ruthe followed him to an open area filled with cushioned seats and brushy plants. The place was empty, which evidently pleased her because her resistance disappeared. She moved ahead of Riker and sat on a plush chair facing a large port window. The view must have pleased her as well. She smiled at the sight of deep space.

The informal surroundings were deceptive. Lieutenant Yar's security guards were posted at all the corridor crossways leading to the section. They had strict instructions to keep off-duty crew members away from the lounge. The effort to separate Ruthe from Andrew Deelor had been carefully worked out to take full advantage of the short time available.

Riker had framed his opening gambit after a quick review of the music files in the ship's library. "What little I heard of the Choraii message reminded me of Terran music during the Middle Ages. Western song forms displayed several voices, but they weren't tied together by either melody or rhythm—each part moved separately."

Ruthe was surprised by the comment. She pulled her gaze away from the stars to look at him. "Yes, the polyphonic development is similar, though the Choraii harmonic modes are closer to the scales developed in the twentieth century by Schönberg."

"So you're a professional musician?" he asked. The statement was the longest she had uttered in public, and he was eager for her to continue talking. The question had the opposite effect.

Ruthe looked back to the window. "I've studied music history," she said tersely, then lapsed into silence.

"The greeting you played"—Riker hummed a few bars of the melody he had heard on the bridge—"was it your own composition? Or do the Choraii have a standard form when they call another ship?"

"The notes are always the same," she answered, "but the rhythm is free." She drew out the pieces of her flute. "The song changes every time I sing it."

As Riker watched Ruthe assemble the instrument, he was struck again by her beauty. One part of his mind concentrated on the music she played, while another delighted in the clean line of her profile as she blew into the flute and her delicate fingers fluttered against its stops.

Ruthe did not break off playing when Data wandered into the lounge, though her melody slowed as she watched him take a seat. He was more interested in the printout report he brought with him than in her music, so she resumed her original tempo. Riker knew that the vocoder nestled in the palm of Data's hand recorded her every note.

Deanna Troi was the next person to enter. Riker feared the counselor's presence would disturb Ruthe, but the translator was too absorbed in her song to be troubled by an additional listener. Unfortunately, he couldn't restrain his own irritation at the growing audience.

Under cover of the music, Deanna whispered to him, "Perhaps you could concentrate better in more intimate surroundings."

A sustained B flat signaled the end of Ruthe's song.

"That was beautiful, even if I don't understand what it means," said Riker. "But then, I'm sure the Choraii find our speech just as mysterious."

Ruthe shook her head. "Not at all. The Choraii learned Federation Standard from the children. In fact, they speak it quite well, but it's such an ugly, clumsy way of communicating, they prefer not to use it."

That fact was certainly worth passing on to Picard, but it was the last useful bit of knowledge that Riker gathered from the translator.

"Will . . ." Troi's warning came when Ambassador Deelor was only a few yards away.

"I wondered where you were." Deelor spoke only to Ruthe.

"I got bored waiting in the cabin."

"That won't happen again," Deelor assured her. "My trips to sickbay are over." This last comment was directed at the first officer.

The ambassador beckoned Ruthe to his side. She rose from her seat and followed him out of the lounge.

Riker frowned as he watched the pair walk away. Ruthe had left without a parting word, without a backward glance. "I don't like the way Deelor orders her around."

"She doesn't seem to mind," said Troi. "Why should you?"

He turned to answer her but bit back the reply when he saw Data still sitting nearby. The android had abandoned his earlier pose of disinterest and watched them with undisguised curiosity.

"Data, it's time for you to go," said Riker.

Data frowned, searching his memory for some forgotten appointment. "I have no particular event scheduled for this hour." He studied Riker's expression more closely. "You wish for me to leave?"

"Yes, Data," said Troi quite firmly.

The android didn't move. "My understanding of human interaction would improve if I had more opportunities for direct observation. Your discussion promises many important insights."

"We'd like some privacy," Riker insisted.

"But it is that very privacy which obstructs my attempts at understanding the intricacies of interpersonal relationships."

"Good-bye, Data," said Riker. Data rose from his chair and left the room, but he walked slowly. The first officer wondered about the limits of the android's hearing and waited until Data was well out of sight before speaking. "Deanna, if I didn't know better, I'd think you were jealous."

"I have no *right* to jealousy. Our parting made that aspect of our relationship certain."

"And you have no reason for jealousy either."

"I know that, Will," she admitted with a sigh. "True, I can sense a passing interest in Ruthe, your admiration of her beauty, but no serious attraction. From her . . ."

Riker's vanity battled against a sudden concern for Ruthe's feelings. "You don't mean she's falling for me?"

"No. No, she's not," answered Troi with more certainty than he expected. "In fact, I sense no interest in you at all."

Troi smiled at the flicker of annoyance that crossed his features. Her next words soothed Riker's pride and explained her own troubled thoughts. "That's just it. She has no interest in anything except her music. She is empty, Will. Devoid of all feeling."

Chapter Eight

TEN MEN AND WOMEN were bunched in a tight knot in front of the holodeck gate. The portal was open. Just over the threshold, gently rolling hills led to a stand of shade trees. A breeze rustled their leafy branches. Wooden buildings painted a dusky red lined the far wall of the ship's hull, but the images of pastureland projected onto the flat surface created a vista of meadows stretching away to a distant horizon.

Farmer Leonard edged closer to the opening and sniffed at the air. It was fresh and carried the scent of honeysuckle. He inhaled deeply, savoring the familiar smell. "Early spring, just in time for planting."

Some of the more timid of the colonists watched him carefully, but he showed no ill effects. Others drifted to his side.

"I never saw so much green in all our years on Gryzdc," sighed Charla. "It looks just like Yonada."

105

Tomas snorted loudly and stepped back. "It's cheap theatrics. An illusion." He tugged peevishly at his beard.

"After all these months in space, I'll settle for an illusion," said Mry. "It can't be any worse than reality."

She was the first to step from the hard metal deck to ground that gave way beneath her feet, but Leonard followed immediately after her. The lure of open air and warm sunlight was too strong for the others to resist for long. By ones and twos they passed through the gate.

Tomas was left standing alone. "For shame," he called after them. "I said it before and I'll say it again: I'd as soon enter the maw of a dragon as step foot in a holodeck simulation." He raised his voice as they moved farther away. "You applauded my ethics then, but evidently your own principles can't stand up to temptation."

"Come, Tomas," responded Myra. The old woman still lagged near the entrance. "You can disapprove as easily from inside as elsewhere."

Tomas did not move. He hooked his thumbs over his belt to steady the trembling of his hands. "I can see quite well from here." His eyes narrowed as he watched his sister and Leonard laughing and tumbling in the meadow grass.

"Mry's an attractive woman," commented Myra with a dry chuckle. "And old enough to bear children."

"Perhaps so," he said. "But I'll have some say as to the sire." He gritted his teeth and stepped forward.

As soon as he walked through the portal, the metal doors meshed together with a soft hiss, then vanished. The illusion was complete. Tomas was standing in a field of rippling grass. A clear blue sky vaulted far above his head, and the warmth of the yellow sun prompted him to loosen the top buttons of his flannel shirt.

Young Stvn dropped down to his knees. He dug out a handful of soil, crumbling the black loam between his fingers. Old Steven plucked a stalk of grass and chewed on the root. "Not suitable for corn, but an acre of wheat would do pretty well."

"It's the animals that are being put here, not the seed," said Tomas, glaring at the two men.

"Still, it's a waste of good land not to plant something," said Young Stvn, exchanging approving nods with his uncle. "Decades of hard work will be needed to turn New Oregon into so pleasant a world as this."

Tomas glared next at Dnnys and Wesley as they raced out of the barn and across the meadow to greet the adults. "Another short circuit and our sheep will be grazing on a metal deck," he scolded Dnnys when the boys were within reach of his voice.

"I think they did a wonderful job," said Mry. Fluttering wings brushed against her cheek, then danced away. "Look at the orange butterfly! I've never seen a live one before. Who thought of such a lovely detail?"

"Uh, it was my idea," admitted Wesley.

"So you're an artist as well as an engineer." She plucked a stray wisp of straw from his hair.

"What's wrong with you?" Dnnys dug an elbow into his friend's side. "You're turning all red."

"The sun's too bright," Wesley said. Mry smiled at him and he blushed again. "I'd better recheck the construction code."

"I wish living on a farm were as much fun as writing the program for one," sighed Dnnys. "Then I wouldn't mind—"

His cousin lifted a hand to his mouth and touched his lips with her finger. "Hush, Dnnys. They'll hear you." She glanced nervously at the other Farmers.

Myra stumped up to them, frowning dangerously. "Don't lag about. I want to see the pens."

"There's no point in seeing any more," declared Tomas desperately.

Myra waved away his protest like a bad odor. "This is a farm and a farm means work. The youngsters have been idle for too long; they've forgotten the value of hard labor. I'll refresh their memories."

Under Myra's constant proddings, the entire group drifted toward the buildings. Tomas marched next to his sister, using his bulk to shield her from Leonard's attentions. Any objections to the use of the simulation were forgotten.

All preparations for the rendezvous with the *B Flat* had been made, but the time for Deelor to take control of the bridge had not yet come. Suspended between actions, he and Ruthe could do nothing now except wait.

Deelor sat still as a crouching cat, muscles coiled for a sudden spring. He hadn't moved from his chair for over an hour, but his mind flitted restlessly between the immutable past and an all too variable future.

Ruthe, on the other hand, was stretched out on the cabin bed listening to the mellow strains of an unaccompanied cello from the ship's music library. She was obviously content with the present.

"Riker likes you," said Deelor suddenly.

"Does he?" She looked up at him idly, lost in the music. Deelor wondered if the Choraii would think more highly of humans if they could hear this Bach suite or a Mozart concerto.

"How can you tell?" she asked.

"The way he looks at you."

"Do I have to do anything about it?"

"No. Not if you don't want to." The sarabande gave way to the gavotte, her favorite passage of the D major suite. He knew enough to keep silent until it was over. At the start of the gigue he continued. "He thinks we're lovers."

"Who does?" she asked.

"Riker."

"Oh, him." She frowned suddenly. "Is that why he asked me to play for him? Because he likes me?"

"In part. However, he was probably under orders to gather more information about the Choraii."

Ruthe curled into a ball, a sure sign that his words had disturbed her.

"What did you tell him?" Deelor was careful to project a casual curiosity. If she sensed any tension in the question, she would stop talking altogether.

"I don't remember."

She probably didn't. The past held as little interest for her as the future. Deelor rose from his chair. With a quick tap to the room controls, he cut off the music.

She sat up abruptly. He had her undivided attention.

"Ruthe, you know my position. If the captain and his crew see through your agreement with the Choraii, I won't be able to back you up. You're acting without official approval. For your own sake, be very careful around Riker and the others."

"I don't like him anyway."

"Neither do I," laughed Deelor. "But I like you." He sighed at her wary look. "And no, you don't have to do anything about it."

With a light tap at the ops panel, Data displayed a graphic representation of the Choraii energy net on the main viewer of the bridge. He tapped again, and the sprawling blue web glowed. "This is only a theory," the android cautioned the two officers seated at the command center.

"Yes, I understand," said Picard, squinting at the

STAR TREK: THE NEXT GENERATION

sudden brightness of the screen's image. He absently rubbed the bridge of his nose. "Please continue."

"The Choraii net is constructed of flexible strands of energy. I believe it is possible to capture one of those filaments and by bending it create a weak area that can be pierced by a specially constructed probe."

"For what purpose?" asked Riker, studying the schematic drawing of Data's design that appeared on the viewer. An animated sequence brought the probe in contact with the net.

"To draw on the net's energy source." As Data spoke, the blue lines lost their glow. "We can either bleed the energy out into space or use its power ourselves. In either event, the drained field will be ineffective against our shields."

"Sounds risky," said Riker frowning. "What if we can't control the flow?"

"There is a thirty-four percent probability of an explosive overload," agreed Data. "As I said, the model is theoretical and may require some adjustment during actual operation."

Picard considered the hazards of testing such a defense in the midst of combat. "Let's hope it doesn't come to that, Mr. Data."

"We're only four hours away from the rendezvous," said Riker. He was slumped in place, too weary to maintain his usual upright bearing. The bridge officers had worked several shifts without a break. "That doesn't leave us with many options."

"We shall have to rely on Andrew Deelor's diplomacy. Presumably, the ambassador possesses a store of tact that he doesn't waste on subordinates." The captain took a closer look at his first officer. "Our remaining time can best be spent in getting some rest. That includes you, Number One."

Riker sat up, quickly correcting the slouch that had betrayed him. "On one condition, Captain, that you

110

also leave the bridge." And he was prepared for resistance. "If asked, I'm sure your chief medical officer would insist."

A faint smile crossed Picard's face. Apparently, he had not hidden his own fatigue any better than Riker. "There's no need to disturb Dr. Crusher. I'll go to bed like a good little boy." Pushing himself up from his chair, the captain addressed the one officer on the bridge who did not need relief. "Commander Data, you have the conn."

However, once Picard had reached his cabin he simply could not fall asleep. He lay unmoving on his bed, eyes closed, thinking. Andrew Deelor would demand control of the *Enterprise* soon. Admiral Zagráth had made it very clear that the captain must give Deelor that control.

Don't waste your luck on us, Captain Picard. You'll need it more than we will.

D'Amelio's warning whispered in Picard's ear. He felt the weight of Phil Manin dying in his arms. The captain of the *Ferrel* had followed the ambassador's orders and lived long enough to regret it. At what point did obedience to authority become unquestioning stupidity?

Hours passed.

Picard had not yet answered those questions when Data called him back to the bridge. He rose from the bed feeling more tired than when he had first lain down.

Lieutenant Worf had stoically withstood the insult of Captain Picard's insistence that he rest, then marched dutifully to his cabin. As a Klingon, Worf followed orders to the letter. As a Klingon, he also felt free to violate the spirit of those orders if they did not suit him. He remained inside the room for some two minutes, then promptly returned to the bridge.

"Humans sleep too much," Worf told Data by way of explanation. "It dulls the reflexes."

Since Data did not require such periods of inactivity, he was unable to judge the validity of this statement. However, he had an observation of his own to add. "They seem to find sleep an enjoyable process."

"That's another reason to avoid it."

Worf set to work on the problem that had taunted him for days: the *B Flat*'s ability to overload a tractor lock. The Choraii spheres were slippery, they could still move inside the holding beam even if they could not escape it. By shifting into a long strand, they had put an increasing drain on the *Enterprise*'s power supply, and computer simulations indicated that a ring shape would have the same effect. Each configuration expanded the tractor beam beyond its assigned portion of ship's power.

"They never broke out of the tractor beam," said Worf when he showed Data the results. "They made us turn it off because the cost was too high."

"Perhaps the *Ferrel* tried to hold them for too long," theorized Data. "That could explain why the starship was so vulnerable to the energy matrix."

"According to the computers, we need more power."

"That is certainly the most direct solution," said Data. "Perhaps more power to the phasers would have stopped them as well."

Worf frowned at the unspoken portion of Data's argument. "But Commander Riker found a way to damage the *B Flat* with less power, by narrowing the phaser beam. In other words, ordinary solutions won't work with the Choraii."

He returned to the science station with a new perspective. Computers searched for answers based on established parameters, but if the parameters of the tractor beam were altered, new solutions might appear.

An hour later Worf found his answer.

"Theoretically, this could work," said Data as he viewed the new graphic simulation. Worf had split the tractor into four beams. Each locked onto a single sphere. Regardless of the arrangement the spheres assumed, the beams held fast to their individual target. Overall power expenditure was no higher than for a single beam.

"This time they won't get away," said Worf. The knowledge was quite refreshing, more so than sleep.

Dr. Crusher heard the sound of footsteps entering her office, but she didn't lift her eyes from the computer screen. "Go away. I'm busy."

The shadow across her desk did not disappear. "A nurse warned me you were in a snit."

Crusher's head snapped up at the sound of Deelor's mocking voice. "As the ship's chief medical officer, it's my responsibility to prepare for the arrival of the Hamlin survivors, but without any guidelines I can make only the most general preparations. Emotional disorientation is to be expected; vitamin deficiencies are also likely. Beyond that lie a host of maladies ranging from mild disorders to crippling disabilities." She tapped the screen that had absorbed her attention. "If the Choraii ships lack gravity, the captives could have no bones left, just soft cartilage that would bend under the weight of their bodies. And that's just the beginning . . ."

"Oh, stop worrying," he said lazily. "I have a cure for what ails the doctor." He flipped a cassette onto her desk. "These medical records will answer most of your questions about the captives."

"It's about time!"

"You're welcome." His flippant good humor only increased her irritation. "And, Dr. Crusher, about the records. I'm sure I needn't remind you that this is all highly classified material." The tone was light, but the words were serious enough.

"I'm well aware of that, Ambassador." She slipped the tape into the computer and began to read.

By the time Picard walked onto the bridge, his first officer had already assumed command and Data had returned to his position at the helm. Riker appeared unusually somber when he greeted the captain.

"Ambassador Deelor would like to see you."

Picard had expected as much. "Tell him to meet me in the Ready Room."

"Sir, he's already there."

When Picard entered the office, Deelor was standing by the star window staring out into space.

"Won't you have a seat?" asked Picard dryly. He indicated the captain's chair behind the desk.

Deelor moved away from the window. "The desk is yours, Captain, but the bridge is mine. I will assume full command of the ship from this point on."

"You have control of the mission, Ambassador," replied Picard. "Not the *Enterprise.*"

Deelor frowned, but showed no surprise. "Admiral Zagráth . . ."

"Is not here right now," said the captain evenly. "My primary responsibility is to my crew, and I will not place their fate in your hands."

"Even at the risk of a court-martial?"

"A court-martial would require open discussion of the Choraii and their Hamlin captives. And of the *USS Ferrel.*"

"Very astute," said Deelor. "Phil Manin didn't see through that bluff. But there are many ways to lose a

114

command, Captain Picard. Promotions to dead-end jobs on back water planets."

"Better that than lose this ship. You destroyed the *Ferrel;* you will not destroy the *Enterprise.*"

The ambassador's frown deepened. "Your concern is admirable, but misplaced. I've dealt with the Choraii before. I can make more informed decisions."

"Then tell me what you know."

"You're a stubborn man," sighed Deelor. "Don't let your dislike for me blind you. No matter what you may think, my actions are not capricious or inept." He tapped lightly on the glass of the wall aquarium, watching the fish inside nibble at the reflection of his fingers. When he turned back to Picard, he was smiling ruefully.

"Keep control of your ship, Captain. We can't afford to fight among ourselves; the Choraii would take quick advantage of any divisiveness. But if you value the *Enterprise,* listen to whatever advice I give you."

Picard felt the first stirrings of doubt. Deelor was clever and manipulative. He was also unexpectedly gracious in defeat.

The two men left the Ready Room together and walked back onto the bridge. Picard noted the scrutiny of his first officer but said nothing to assuage Riker's curiosity as to what had happened. Maintaining a poker face, the captain took his usual position at the command center; Deelor sat down at his left side. Then, and only then, did Picard look his first officer in the eye. "You may call the approach, Number One."

"Impulse power, Mr. La Forge," ordered Riker as the ship neared the rendezvous site.

"Leaving warp drive, now."

The first officer addressed the helm again. "Sensor readings, Mr. Data."

"Still no sign of the Choraii."

"Full stop to engines."

Ruthe's location had been reached. The *Enterprise* hung in empty space.

"Well, Ambassador?" asked Picard sharply. "We're here, at the appointed place and at the appointed time. Where are the Choraii?" He had put his career on the line for this encounter. If the *B Flat* failed to appear, the gesture would be somewhat anticlimatic.

"Patience, Captain. I'm certain they will come." Deelor looked over his shoulder and frowned. "As will Ruthe."

"Actually, we are somewhat ahead of schedule," Data pointed out. "We have arrived one minute and fifteen seconds early."

Picard was too tense to tolerate the overliteral statement. "Data, there are no ships within scan range, which means the Choraii will be late. If they come at all."

"Captain!" cried out Yar. "Long-range sensors are picking up an object now. Just entering . . . no, it's already well within range. Approaching fast, incredibly fast!"

Picard tensed in place. "Raise shields."

"Would you look at that!" said Geordi, pointing to the viewer.

Seconds before there had been no image on its surface. Now, a small dot appeared, then zoomed into prominence on the screen. The *B Flat* tumbled end over end, hurtling ever closer to the *Enterprise*.

"They're coming right at us," warned Yar as the cluster of reddish-orange bubbles filled the frame. A Yellow Alert klaxon screamed its protest at the approach.

Picard took a deep breath, then said, "Evasive maneuvers."

"No," countered Deelor. "They're not attacking."

"How can you be so sure?" But Picard held back his next order.

At the last moment before collision, the Choraii ship stopped, its spheres quivering and shaking from the sudden deceleration.

"Twenty-two seconds early," said Data. "Their punctuality is impressive."

"So is their speed," said Picard with an upraised brow. Now he understood why Starfleet had chosen an intelligence agent for a diplomatic mission.

Chapter Nine

Captain's Personal Log: For duty's sake I have often undertaken unpleasant tasks. Yet, I find this one especially distasteful. We are exchanging trade goods for human lives. We are paying for the return of those who should never have been taken in the first place. Is this the best that diplomacy can offer?

RUTHE GREETED the *B Flat* with an outburst of melody from her flute. The translator's appearance on the aft bridge had been as sudden as the approach of the Choraii ship on the front viewer. Playing as she walked, Ruthe strolled down from the elevated deck to the command center. Her gaze never strayed from the image on the screen.

"Can we get visual contact of the interior?" Picard asked Deelor as her extended song was broadcast to the other ship.

Deelor shook his head. "No, they seem to lack an equivalent to our visual technology, even though their audio system is highly developed."

Picard checked a second source of information. "Any comments, Counselor?"

Deanna Troi emptied her mind of her own thoughts, blocked the familiar impressions of the people around her, and studied what was left. "I can sense a strong presence that obscures the individual beings within the vessel. It's as if the ship itself is a living being, or perhaps an extension of its inhabitants."

Ruthe reached the end of her music. The Choraii crew answered as one in a return greeting. Four voices joined in lock-step progressions up and down the scale.

Ambassador Deelor waited patiently until the preliminary introductions were complete, then instructed Ruthe to confirm the conditions of the earlier exchange agreement. She translated his words into a new melodic form and paused for the response.

Picard heard the dissenting notes in the Choraii's answer even if he could not understand the cause. The look of concern on Riker's face indicated he had also caught the change in key. "What's gone wrong?"

"The Choraii want more lead," explained Ruthe. "Twelve pounds instead of the original ten," she looked to Deelor for his next directions.

"No. Tell them the terms have been settled. Ten pounds in all and remind them the first payment has already been made."

Ruthe proceeded to translate back and forth between the Choraii language and Deelor's Federation Standard. The captain wondered if the laborious process was a concession to the Choraii or an attempt to shield some portions of the negotiations from the crew. While his attitude toward Andrew Deelor had shifted over the last hour, and the captain was more inclined to trust him than before, there was still no way to confirm the accuracy of Ruthe's version of the transaction. Picard knew Data's language computers were making progress, but not enough to follow the complexities of this bargaining session.

The dissonance of the *B Flat*'s transmission increased. Ruthe shook her head at its conclusion. "The Choraii maintain this is a new vessel, so a new contract is in order."

"Agreed," said Deelor emphatically. "Three pounds for their captive since the *Enterprise* is a stronger ship and has defeated them in battle. Unless they wish to fight again and negotiate a new price when the combat is over."

Picard cleared his throat with a deep rumble, but he did not protest the ambassador's challenge. He had agreed to leave this part of the mission to Deelor. The captain's discomfort was noticed, however.

"The Choraii respect a hard bargain," explained Deelor in an aside to Picard. "Besides, the less metal they have, the sooner they'll be ready to trade more captives."

Ruthe must have conveyed Deelor's convictions to the aliens. "The original price is acceptable," she reported at the conclusion of another passage of song. "They are ready to discuss the exchange procedure."

"The captive must be brought over first."

Until now, the translator had repeated Deelor's statements without comment. This time she ventured an opinion. "They will expect a security."

"No security," he said firmly. "They forfeited that accommodation by their actions against the *Ferrel*. My terms or nothing."

She shrugged and lifted the flute to her lips. A staccato series of discordant notes emerged.

Deelor leaned back in his chair. "Relax," he advised the captain and Riker. "This one's going to take awhile."

"What happened with the *Ferrel?*" asked Picard in a low voice. He expected another evasion from the ambassador, but this time he received a straightforward reply.

"We beamed over a half-payment of the lead as proof of our trust." Deelor frowned at the result of his previous action. "And the *B Flat* took off like a bat out of hell."

"Then you tried to detain them with a tractor beam, depleting your power reserves in the process," suggested Data. "At least that is my theory, based on available data. Is it correct?"

Deelor remained silent for a moment, brooding over the helmsman's conjecture. Ruthe's music floated above their heads. "Yes," he said at last. "When they hit us with the energy matrix, we were too weak to break loose or even to fire our phasers."

The translator's song came to an end. She lowered her flute. "They are very upset by your restrictions."

"The Choraii have closed their frequency channel," Yar said, checking her console.

"But they're not moving away," observed Deelor thoughtfully. "So we wait."

"Damn!" said Beverly Crusher when she reached the end of the Hamlin file. "Double damn."

The doctor ejected the cassette, removing the security-restricted data from the medical computer system, and considered what she had just read. The developments should have been obvious to a doctor. She was annoyed at herself for not looking that far ahead and drawing the proper conclusions, but her concern had stopped short at the immediate medical condition of the Hamlin children. That misleading name again. Data had emphasized they weren't children anymore, but the image persisted nonetheless.

Still absorbing the implications of the new information, Crusher departed for the bridge. She had felt the shudder in the ship's deck as the *Enterprise* dropped out of warp speed. Negotiations for the *B Flat*'s captive should already be in progress.

She had expected music on the bridge, not a brittle silence. Her entrance drew the entire crew's attention. With unaccustomed self-consciousness, she walked the short distance from the front turbo to the command center. All the seats were taken, so she had to stand next to Ruthe, making Crusher feel even more conspicuous.

"Finished your homework, Doctor?" Deelor asked.

"Yes." She jammed her hands into the pockets of her med jacket and fought against the urge to whisper. "Very interesting reading." The captain's attention was fixed on the viewscreen; he was too distracted to pursue the meaning of her comment, and Crusher was not eager to elaborate in front of an audience. She joined the crew in their silent vigil.

"Incoming transmission from the Choraii," announced Yar at last, and put it on speakers. The dissonance in their music was muted, but so was the melody.

Ruthe listened intently to the Choraii singers, then spoke. "They agree, but the decision was not unanimous. I suggest we proceed quickly, before the discord can deepen." Another voice interrupted her with a jangling solo passage. "One of them warns that if the *Enterprise* tries to escape, there will be immediate reprisals."

"But of course," said Deelor. He gestured at her flute. "Tell them we would be dishonored if they failed to retaliate."

She translated his sentiment into a sprightly, almost impudent tune. All four Choraii echoed the comic lightness in their response. "You have amused and pleased them. Careful, or they will want to trade for you."

"They couldn't meet my price." Deelor jumped to his feet. "Mr. Riker, you can prepare the lead shipment while Ruthe beams over to the Choraii ship."

"Is direct contact really necessary?" asked Picard with alarm.

Data saved the ambassador the trouble of an explanation. "The dense organic nature of the *B Flat*'s structure makes exact life readings difficult to obtain. My sensors are unable to determine the transporter coordinates for the captive human."

"My away team is at your disposal, Ambassador," said Riker, rising to his feet. "We can beam over with—"

"Stay out of this," said Ruthe. "I don't want your help."

"Thank you for the offer, Mr. Riker," said Deelor quickly. "But I'm afraid that your landing party isn't trained to function on a Choraii ship." He addressed the rest of his explanation to the captain. "The interior is not dangerous, but you must breathe in the liquid matter of the ship's atmosphere; to wear environmental suits which hide your physical essence would be a gross insult to the hosts and a sign of deceit."

Picard still looked dubious, so Dr. Crusher joined in the discussion. "According to my medical records, the oxygen-rich fluid is quite breathable—you can't drown even when your lungs are filled—but the experience would be very unsettling to an air-breathing species."

"However," interjected Deelor. "I do want a back-up team available in case of trouble. Will you allow

Mr. Riker and Lieutenant Yar to accompany Ruthe to the transporter chamber?"

"Certainly," said Picard with an ironic smile. Only Crusher caught his softly uttered aside. "You don't usually bother to ask."

Then Deelor aimed a slight bow in her direction. "And, of course, Dr. Crusher. To provide the best of medical care."

"Come on," said Ruthe, and moved impatiently toward the turboelevator. "The Choraii are waiting."

Beverly Crusher reluctantly followed the translator. The doctor hadn't been given the opportunity to discuss the Hamlin medical files with Captain Picard. But then, not all of what she had read could be told.

Ruthe's preparation for boarding the Choraii ship was simple. She handed her flute to Lieutenant Yar, then shrugged off her gray cloak and dropped it onto the steps leading to the transporter. A communications emblem dangled from a chain around her neck. She wore nothing else.

Stepping up onto the circular platform, she waited unselfconsciously for her transfer. Riker, matching her aplomb with considerably more difficulty, established a signal code.

"One tap means an immediate return to the *Enterprise*. Two taps and our team will beam over to the *B Flat*."

"That won't be necessary," Ruthe said calmly. "No more delays, Mr. Riker."

The first officer moved away from the platform and nodded to Tasha Yar. As security chief, she supervised any procedures that affected the ship's defenses, and transporting required a momentary lowering of the *Enterprise*'s shields. Yar was adept at keeping the window of vulnerability to a minimum. As the lieutenant activated the transporter controls, a high whine filled the chamber. Ruthe disappeared in a flicker of light.

The first phase of the exchange had begun; Riker and Yar immediately prepared for the second. Dr. Crusher watched as the two officers pulled bars of lead from a small chest and stacked them neatly onto the platform near the area Ruthe had vacated.

"The payment is ready," said Riker when the last bar had been counted out.

"Yes," said Crusher with a worried frown. "But just whom are we buying?"

The leisurely pace of the Choraii greeting ritual had prepared the *Enterprise* crew for another prolonged interval during contact, but that knowledge did not lessen the tension of waiting. Conversation on the bridge faltered, then ended altogether. An hour passed without any signal from the translator. Then another.

Riker was the first to question the delay. *"I advise we go after her."* His voice echoed over the bridge intercom.

"Absolutely not," countered Deelor. "Ruthe has been on Choraii ships before—she knows what she's doing. We wait for her signal."

"She may be in trouble."

The ambassador dropped all pretense of courtesy. "I'm in command of this mission, Mr. Riker." He severed the contact with a savage flick at his chest emblem.

"His concern is only natural," said Picard in his first officer's defense.

"These matters take time," Deelor declared, glaring at the image of the *B Flat* on the viewscreen. "You can't rush the Choraii."

"Evidently not." Picard rubbed the back of his neck. Tempers had frayed as time passed, his own included. "Counselor Troi?"

Deanna shook her head in frustration. "I don't sense any distress, but my impressions from the ship are still very clouded. Even at close quarters I've never read any of Ruthe's feelings."

"Mr. Data, what can you determine from the translator's communications link?"

"She appears to be exploring the ship. I have tracked her path through most of the spheres in the cluster."

"And the Hamlin captive?"

"Also present," said Data, frowning. "However, the currents and eddies of the atmosphere are disordering my scan data. I am registering an echo in certain life-sign readings."

"Can you compensate?" asked Picard.

"The complexity of the problem presents a challenge. I will attempt a recalibration that will take the density and viscosity into account. If my controlling logarithm is increased by—"

"Thank you, Mr. Data. A detailed explanation is unnecessary."

"Yes, sir," sighed the android. He continued his work in silence.

At the end of the third hour, Lieutenant Yar recorded a single beep from Ruthe's com link.

"One or two people to beam over?" asked Riker.

"I can't tell," said Yar. "The site readings are too garbled." She entered the source coordinates into the system controls and specified a wide beam that would pull in Ruthe and any possible companion. As the flash from the transport energy filled the room, Dr. Crusher automatically reached for the medical kit hanging at her side.

Ruthe's body shimmered on the chamber platform, then solidified. Her bare skin glistened with moisture and liquid streamed out from her nose as she exhaled the Choraii atmosphere from her lungs.

She carried a young child in her arms.

Only one person was prepared for the sight. Dr. Crusher sprang forward and plucked the boy from the translator's careless grasp. The doctor placed a palm over the child's chest and pushed her hand gently but firmly beneath his rib cage. He coughed up fluid, then gasped in his first breath of air. Seconds later he began to cry.

"You'd better tell the captain," said Crusher to Riker. She wrapped the screaming child in a blanket and raced for sickbay.

"A child?" stormed Picard when Riker had completed his intercom report to the bridge. The captain turned on Deelor, who still sat beside him. "Were you aware of this situation, Ambassador?"

"Not in this instance," said Deelor, lowering his voice. "But we have recovered other descendants of the original Hamlin group."

"A fact you failed to mention during the briefing," Picard pointed out without any drop in his own volume. "And one that increases the complexity of the entire issue. The Hamlin Massacre is still a sensitive episode for the Federation, even after fifty years. That the humans held by the Choraii are growing in number can only inflame emotions."

"I am well aware of that, Captain, but this is neither the time nor the place to discuss the matter." Deelor nervously scanned the bridge. "This was one aspect of the Hamlin project which I had hoped to keep restricted to a smaller circle for precisely the reasons you just stated."

"I trust my crew's discretion," snapped Picard. "Which is more than I can say for—"

"Captain," said Troi. She had taken Riker's seat on the bridge and her call forced Picard to turn away from Deelor. "With your permission, I'd like to offer my assistance to Dr. Crusher. I haven't been of any use in our dealings with the Choraii, but I am certain I can help with the captive."

Picard granted the counselor's request with a curt nod. Troi rose from her chair and walked to the forward elevator. When the doors parted, she stepped aside to let Ruthe leave the compartment. "How is the child?" Troi asked anxiously.

The translator shrugged. "Well enough, I suppose," she said before Troi was whisked away. With an unhurried stride, Ruthe approached the command center. Her hair was still wet from her immersion in the Choraii ship's atmosphere, and small beads of fluid trickled down her neck, darkening the yoke of her robe. She was careful to hold the wooden shaft of her flute away from the damp cloth.

"Why didn't you tell us about the child?" demanded Picard.

"The exchange was for their captive. Age wasn't the issue." She lowered herself into the chair Troi had vacated. "Has the lead been transported yet? The Choraii will expect a parting song."

Picard shook his head. "Lieutenant Yar will beam the metal over as soon as the ambassador orders us to do so."

"We have waited patiently for the Choraii," said Deelor. Leaning back, he stretched his legs forward, out onto the deck, and crossed them at the ankles. "They can wait until we've checked the condition of the trade goods."

"And do we return the boy if he is damaged?" asked Picard bitterly.

"No, but I might insist on a reduced price."

"Your humor is offensive."

"I wasn't trying to be funny," said Deelor. "I'm looking at the situation from the perspective of the Choraii. You could do with a little more objectivity yourself, Captain."

Picard clenched his jaw. Several seconds passed before he tapped at his com link. "Picard to Crusher. Please report on the Hamlin child."

"Male, approximately two years of age. His lungs are handling the transition to an oxygen environment quite well." A wailing cry could be heard in the background. *"The results of my exam are still being compiled, but he appears to be in excellent physical condition. He's been very well cared for."*

"Of course he has been," said Ruthe at the conclusion of Crusher's evaluation. "Humans are highly valued by the Choraii."

"Valued for what?" asked Picard. "Their labor?"

Ruthe shook her head. "Humans are never put to work. They serve . . . a symbolic function. The gift of a child from one ship to another cements bonds of friendship within the cluster. In order for the tie to be honored, the child must be treated with kindness and consideration."

"Pampered pet or slave, the distinction is a fine one," observed Picard. His voice had regained its former edge. "And equally demeaning."

Deelor sighed heavily. "Let's leave the ethical debate until another time, shall we?" As he crossed his arms over his chest, one finger flicked his metal insignia. "Deelor to transporter room. Proceed with the exchange."

The three people seated at the command center stared at the image of the Choraii ship on the forward viewscreen, waiting silently for the trade to reach its conclusion. The soft chatter of Data's ops console filtered back to them. The android's hands moved back and forth over the panel, never still for more than an instant.

"Riker to Captain. The lead shipment has been delivered."

At a nod from the ambassador, Ruthe picked up her flute and began to play a loose, unstructured melody. The *B Flat* slowly drifted away to the strains of her farewell song.

Deelor watched the ship leave through half-closed eyes. When Picard stirred in place and opened his mouth to speak, the ambassador cut him off with an imperious wave of the hand. "Listen," he whispered.

The captain rose from his command chair and paced up to the helm, but he issued his orders quietly. "Mr. Data, set a heading for New Oregon."

Data used one hand to input course coordinates, but his other hand continued manipulating sensor input from the retreating Choraii ship.

"Mr. La Forge, prepare for engagement of warp drive."

"Captain, wait," said Data suddenly. He looked up from his console. "My life-sign readings were not in error after all. There is a faint but unmistakable profile of another human still on board the Choraii ship."

Chapter Ten

CAPTAIN PICARD PACED the deck of the observation lounge, circling the conference table and the three people seated there. He stopped opposite from Ruthe. "Data tracked your progress through every sphere in the *B Flat*. You knew there was another human on board."

"Yes," she admitted defensively. "But he doesn't count. He's too old to bring back."

"And who are you to make that judgment?" Picard switched his gaze to Deelor, who sat next to her. "Or was this your decision?"

"I knew nothing about it," said Deelor. "Federation policy is very clear on this issue. All Hamlin survivors are to be recovered."

"I spoke with Jason," said Ruthe. "I asked if he wanted to come with me and the child, but the thought of leaving the Choraii frightened him. He's been with them too long to want another life."

Picard paused in mid-stride, then took a seat at the table. "Of course, I should have realized—it's only natural for any captives to be confused by our appearance—but this man can be helped to readjust to his native environment. We can't abandon him simply because of his fear."

Ruthe shook her head. The captain's reassurance did not change her mind. "Tell them what happens," she asked of Deelor. "Make them understand."

Deelor did not answer her. He stared down at the tabletop as if searching for a reply on its glassy surface. He found none.

She grew anxious at his silence. "Please."

The ambassador flinched at the utterance of that simple word which she so rarely used. He raised his head, but looked only at Picard when he spoke. "Official Federation policy dictates that we must recover all Hamlin survivors."

"No!" said Ruthe. Her face, usually still and expressionless, was animated with resentment. "It's a waste. He'll die. They all do."

"Is that true?" asked Picard.

But Deelor fell silent again. Dr. Crusher answered the question instead. "Of the five Hamlin captives bought by the Ferengi, all three adults did eventually die. Only the two children lived."

"I see," Picard said, dragging the two words out ominously. He was disturbed both by the knowledge and by the doctor's possession of it. "Why wasn't I informed of this earlier?"

"I'm sorry, but I received the pertinent files only a few hours ago . . ."

Picard waved aside her apology; he knew who was to blame. Divide and conquer seemed to be one Deelor's favorite maxims. "Continue, Doctor."

"The exact cause of death was different in each

case, but emotional stress was recognized as a prominent contributing factor to their physical deterioration. One suffered a fatal heart attack; the second died of pneumonia." Crusher took a breath, then continued. "The third committed suicide."

"So, what is your medical recommendation?" asked Picard, wondering if the decision for future action would be his. Deelor had dropped all presumption to authority since Data's announcement on the bridge. "Will this man live if we bring him back?"

"I can't predict the outcome based on three people," protested Crusher. "It's too small a sample from which to draw any valid conclusions. In addition, there's no way to judge what effect the intervening stay with the Ferengi had on their final condition."

"Ferengi or human," said Ruthe. "Don't you see it's all the same? This place is too different from the Choraii ship. Leave him alone."

"We can't," said Deelor quietly. "The decision has already been made at higher levels. We have no choice but to bargain for the last captive."

"I won't translate," said Ruthe stubbornly.

"But the Choraii can speak Federation Standard." Picard's statement startled both Ruthe and Deelor. "Ruthe told my first officer they learned our language from the children."

"Yes, that is true," said Deelor with a reluctant nod. "However, our language form doesn't tend to facilitate communications. The harshness of the sound puts the Choraii on the defensive."

"We have no choice but to try," said Picard, and Deelor did not contradict him. The captain appealed to Ruthe next. "Surely you can see that?"

"No. And I won't help." With this last protest, Ruthe ran from the room.

* * *

Sound does not travel through the vacuum of space, but instincts forged by planet-bound evolution are not easily extinguished. So while the *Enterprise* shadowed the *B Flat,* the members of the bridge crew assumed the demeanor of a predator stalking its prey. They talked only when necessary and moved with soft, silent steps over the carpeted deck. Even the engines were subdued, reduced to impulse speed. The ship's pace was set by the leisurely progress of the Choraii vessel as it sang its private song of alien dreams. Data had established a correlation between the ship's spiraling path and the notes of its language, but the significance of the pattern was still beyond his comprehension. Perhaps Ruthe could have deciphered its meaning, but the translator had not returned to the bridge.

"Status report, Number One," demanded the captain as he crossed to the command center. His voice was automatically pitched low in deference to the hushed ambiance.

Riker answered with equal restraint. "The *B Flat* is moving slowly. We've been careful to keep it just within sensor range so our continued presence isn't detected."

"Ruthe refuses to help us lure them back," said Picard. He did not elaborate on her unwillingness. "We shall have to signal them ourselves."

"That calls for a bit of trickery—and I think Data may have just what we need." Riker looked to the android, who nodded in reply. "Ruthe played a version of the greeting for me in the crew lounge and Data managed to record it on the ambassador's vocoder. Since the Choraii have never heard this particular song before, they may think she's singing to them in person."

"Excellent," said Picard.

Data stepped away from the ops station to pass the vocoder on the Lieutenant Yar and instruct her in its operation. "The greeting is cued. Begin broadcasting as soon as we're in radio-contact range."

"You're a very persuasive man, Mr. Riker," observed Deelor as he took a seat next to the commander. "Do all young women fall for your oily charm? Or just the trusting ones, like Ruthe?"

Riker's jaw tightened, but he did not respond.

"Close in on the *B Flat*, Mr. La Forge," Picard instructed. "Maintain impulse power, but be prepared to go to warp speed on my order."

"Hailing distance reached. Ruthe's greeting is being transmitted now," announced Lieutenant Yar.

The *B Flat* responded to the strains of the flute by weaving an irregular path back toward the *Enterprise*. The bubble cluster grew larger on the main viewer. As before, the Choraii voices responded with their own melody, then fell silent waiting for Ruthe to explain the recall.

"Ambassador," said Picard. "Will you speak to the Choraii or shall I?"

Deelor roused himself from an unblinking stare at the screen. His former quicksilver manner had slowed. "I'll speak to them."

Animation returned to his features. The ambassador stood, took a deep breath, and answered the Choraii with the single sustained naming-note of the *B Flat*. His tenor voice was amazingly good, thought Picard.

"Who are you?" wavered a single Choraii voice, filtered through the liquid environment of the alien ship. Its words still rose and fell to the demands of a musical cadence and the effect on human ears was of a haunting siren call.

"I am Deelor," said the ambassador, though he kept

his voice soft, smoothing out the roughness of the spoken sound.

"Where's the other one? Why doesn't she sing for us?"

"She's tired and in need of rest. My speech isn't as pleasing as her songs, but will you listen to me?"

A second Choraii voice replaced the first. *"What do you want?"*

"The trade pleased us," explained Deelor. "We wish to trade again and provide you with more lead."

"But we can't pay for it."

"But you can . . ." Deelor faltered for an instant, then recovered. "You can pay us with the other human."

A clashing chord of notes echoed over the broadcast band. All four Choraii joined together in a jumble of sound until one of their number regained dominance. *"No trade."*

Picard recognized the voice of the fourth singer, who had opposed the arrangements for the first captive exchange. Deelor adopted the persuasive wheedle of a merchant trader. "We offer any metal of worth to you."

"Jason was a present. He isn't for sale."

"The boy had a price," persisted Deelor.

"Because he hasn't been named yet. Jason is different; we like him too much to give him up."

"If you are fond of Jason, you will return him to us. He should be with his own people."

"Go away, Wild Ones!" Deelor tried to respond but the Choraii drowned him out. *"Your notes are ugly. We will not sing with you anymore."*

"They've severed communications contact," said Lieutenant Yar.

"Moving away at warp one," added Data.

The ambassador looked to Picard for his reaction.

"If we try to stop them, your ship will be placed in danger."

The captain nodded gravely. "Yes, I know, but we have some new tricks of our own for dealing with the Choraii."

"Do what you can, then," said Deelor, leaving command of the ship to Picard, just as promised. "I won't interfere."

At Picard's command, the *Enterprise* sprang forward in pursuit of the retreating alien ship. The Choraii, unprepared for the acceleration of their enemy, called forth a burst of speed, but not soon enough to escape the rays that latched on to four bubbles in the cluster.

"Tractor beams locked on," said Lieutenant Worf.

The Choraii ship shuddered in place. A dimple formed in the center of the cluster, then deepened into a hole, creating a ring. The ring spread out, thinning its sides until the line of the circle was only one sphere thick. Four tractor rays swiveled in tandem with the moving spheres, firmly attached to their individual targets. The ring swiftly reformed its structure. Two spheres detached from each other and flew apart, forming the single-file line that had overloaded the previous tractor lock.

"As predicted, no increase in energy consumption." Worf's theoretical model was now fact.

Picard signaled Yar to open a hailing frequency to the alien ship. "This is Captain Jean-Luc Picard. We repeat our previous request. Let us bring Jason over to the *Enterprise.*"

The bubbles regrouped and parted, whipping through a series of geometric forms, but none of the variations shook the grip of Worf's energy lock. As a last resort, one of the trapped spheres was detached entirely. It floated loose, dragging the beam with it.

Within seconds Worf had switched the wandering beam back to the main cluster. The maneuver was not repeated.

The bubbles drew together into a clumped mass. Lieutenant Yar tried to initiate radio contact, but the *B Flat* was silent as well as still.

"They don't give up easily," said Riker. "They'll try something else, maybe the energy matrix."

Picard shook his head. "Our phaser fire discouraged the use of that particular tactic. Remember, they've lost four spheres now, a loss which reduces the size of their ship."

"And of their status," said Deelor. "Evidently each ship begins as a cluster of three or four bubbles, but as the crew matures, more bubbles are added. Grown, as far as we can determine. A larger ship commands respect by virtue of its age."

"So what's next?" asked Riker. "How do . . ."

The bridge deck rocked violently, shaking the crew from side to side. Yellow Alert sirens flashed into life, and Picard immediately picked up the escalating whine of the ship's engines. Overload indicators spread like fire across Worf's console.

"Report! All stations," shouted Picard, clutching at the arms of his chair to keep in place. "What is happening?"

Geordi La Forge was the first to pinpoint the cause. "The *B Flat* is trying to pull out of the tractor beam with their warp drive."

"Data, how long can we hold them?" asked Picard. The bridge had regained an even keel, but it was still trembling in place as the engines fought to maintain the starship's position. The scream of their effort deafened his ears.

"Unknown. The duration is dependent on their maximum speed, which has not been measured."

"Warp nine-point-nine," said Deelor, then smiled

wryly. "That's highly classified information, by the way."

Data tilted his head in contemplation of his completed equation. "In that case, our energy reserves will be depleted in approximately fourteen point six minutes."

Picard rose to his feet, bracing himself for the rolling movement of the deck. "Yar, prepare to fire on the Choraii."

"Phaser power at forty percent capacity, Captain," answered the lieutenant.

"If we divert power to phasers," said Data with a swift recalculation of his figures, "we will deplete our energy reserves in five point two minutes."

"Captain, look!" Riker pointed to the viewscreen. A violet globe had appeared among the orange bubbles of the Choraii ship.

"Damn," swore Picard. "They're going to hit us with everything they've got."

Riker turned to the captain expectantly, "Now what, sir?"

"Worf, maintain tractor beams." Even as he issued the command, Picard's mind sifted through the remaining alternatives. He could try Data's energy-field neutralizer, but the probe had never been tested. If the tactic failed, his ship could be destroyed.

Picard took a deep breath and broadcast a second order through his communicator. "All hands. Prepare for sudden acceleration. Engineering, cut power—"

Suddenly, there was a tremendous surge of forward motion as the Choraii ship shot away, pulling the unresisting starship in its wake. Inertia dampers absorbed part of the shock, but they couldn't prevent a severe jolt. Picard was thrown back into his chair with a force that knocked the breath out of him. On the viewer, stars were transformed to streaks of light.

"Warp two," said Data. His grip had kept him at the helm. And dented the edges of his ops panel with the imprint of his fingers. "Warp five."

Picard tried to speak again and managed a hoarse whisper. "Damage reports."

"Minor damage only," replied Riker as the information filtered through to the bridge. "All essential systems fully operative."

"Warp nine," called out Data.

Yar's report came next. "Captain, weapons power is back to full capacity."

"Sickbay to bridge." Dr. Crusher's voice stormed over the intercom. *"What the hell was that all about? A two-second warning isn't my idea of proper notice. I'm receiving injury reports from all decks."*

"Not now, Dr. Crusher." Picard's breath had finally returned. He snapped shut the connection with sickbay. Casualty reports would have to wait until later. "Lieutenant Yar, lock narrow phaser fire on the edges of the cluster, but steer clear of any spheres with life-sign readings."

"Warp nine-point-seven," warned Data.

Yar selected an uninhabited sphere at random. "Phasers locked and ready."

"Fire!" cried Picard.

Just as before, the target exploded at the beam's first touch and its interior atmosphere sprayed out from the shattered shell. Globules of liquid boiled away into the vacuum of space. Picard held his breath, waiting for the enemy's reaction.

At first there was no change. Then the deck lurched.

"The Choraii are reducing speed to Warp eight," said Data. "Warp six."

"They've given in," said Riker with an admiring grin. "I knew you could outsmart them."

The captain smiled back and tried to hide his own

relief at the outcome of the struggle. Data's count continued downward, keeping pace with the slowing of Picard's pulse.

"Wild Ones, enough!" came the message from the *B Flat* when it had coasted to a full stop. *"Take Jason, only stop your fire."*

"Agreed," answered the ambassador before Picard could speak. With the starship at rest, Deelor was back in control of the mission. He turned to the aft bridge. "Lieutenant Yar, prepare to board the Choraii ship."

"Alone?" asked Yar. Her eyes widened.

"I have no intention of going over myself, Lieutenant." Deelor glanced uneasily at the viewer. "The Choraii bear close watching during a trade, and I can best observe their actions from the bridge."

Riker was quick to jump to the defense of his away team member. "Request permission to accompany—"

"Denied, Commander," said Deelor flatly. "This isn't an invasion. And if Ruthe can handle these transactions by herself, I'm sure Lieutenant Yar can muddle through also."

The security chief reacted just as Picard knew she would. And as Deelor must have predicted as well. "I'll go over, sir. If there's any problem, I can signal for backup."

The captain protected Yar in the only manner open to him. "Mr. Riker, Mr. Data. Accompany the lieutenant to the transporter room."

As the turbolift compartment dropped downward, Data described the curious composition of the Choraii ship's environment in greater detail. Yar listened calmly to the detached clinical terms which were unconnected to the terror of submersion. Her composure was put to a greater test when they reached the transporter room; Dr. Crusher was waiting there and her advice went to the heart of Yar's fear.

"Don't fight against breathing in. Force as much air out of your lungs as you can, then inhale."

"I'll beam you in a few spheres away from Jason," said Data, taking over the transporter controls. "That will give you time to adjust to the environment."

"Let's go, then," said Yar, leaping onto the platform. She didn't want time to dwell on what was ahead.

Yar materialized in the calm sea of the Choraii atmosphere. Regardless of Crusher's instructions, she immediately held her breath. Her every instinct fought against exhaling the air in her lungs.

Treading in place with fine movements of her hands and feet, she concentrated on orienting herself in the alien surroundings. She was suspended in a sphere some ten meters in diameter. Music echoed faintly all around her, and a reddish glow radiated from the curving walls, filtering through the clear liquid to the very center of the orb. She could see no openings.

Yar knew she could hold her breath for several more minutes, possibly long enough to find her way through the next sphere and even to return the captive to the *Enterprise*. If all went well. If not, she would have to breathe in eventually. Better to do so now before her fear grew too strong to overcome. She quickly blew out a stream of air bubbles, then inhaled. Her mind was clouded by a momentary panic as her lungs filled with a thin, warm liquid, but against all expectation she did not suffocate. She took another deep breath. The fluid flowed in and out of her nose, more noticeable than air but just as breathable. The scent of cinnamon lingered behind.

A butterfly stroke carried her to the small flat circle that marked the intersection of two spheres. The opaque membrane was smooth and cool to the touch. Yar pushed the palm of her hand against it and felt the surface give slightly. She pushed harder but couldn't break through. Remembering Riker's narrow beam assault against the exterior of the spheres, she tried again with palms and fingers pressed together in a diver's pose, and this time her hands passed easily through the membrane. A swift kick sent her entire body gliding into the next compartment. It was empty, but the one after it was not.

A man was there, floating, eyes closed, listening to the lulling song of the Choraii that reverberated in the chamber. Yar's entrance stirred the fluid interior, and a current brushing against his bare skin alerted Jason to her presence. She expected him to flee at the sight of a stranger, but he swam toward her instead, curious and trusting. His age was difficult to determine. He was plump, with the smooth, unlined face of a child, but his brown hair was streaked with silver. When he reached her side, she signaled the *Enterprise*.

The embrace of warm liquid gave way to the sharp bite of air and the dragging weight of her body's return to gravity. She wasn't prepared for the shock of transition. A harsh flood of white light blinded her eyes.

Yar tried to breathe. She stumbled to her knees on the transporter platform, coughing convulsively as fluid and air mixed together in her lungs. Racking spasms choked her throat. Seconds later, she passed out.

Chapter Eleven

DR. CRUSHER'S CALL alerted the medical department to incoming casualties from the transporter room. Following her hurried instructions, a team of paramedics and nurses prepared for new patients.

Data was the first to arrive. He ran through the doors of sickbay with Tasha Yar's unconscious body. The lieutenant had pitched forward off the transporter platform into his arms and, rather than wait for a stretcher, he had carried her in himself.

"Over there," directed a waiting paramedic, pointing to an empty table.

Data swung the woman onto a scanner bed. Her uniform was sopping wet; her hair was plastered flat against her head.

"Swimming accident?" asked the nurse, but she was too busy checking the diagnostic output to notice that Data did not reply. "Readings approaching normal. Lungs clear of water."

"Tathwell, I want a chemical analysis of that liquid," gasped Crusher, coming up behind them. She could smell the lingering scent of cinnamon on Yar's skin and clothing. When Ruthe and the child had returned to the *Enterprise,* the Choraii atmosphere had been odorless.

Riker was the last to enter sickbay and hand over his burden to the medics. He had refused Data's offer to carry both Yar and Jason—however, the effort of keeping up with the android had left the first officer badly out of breath.

"If you're going to hyperventilate, do it somewhere else," said Crusher, pushing Riker aside so she could read Jason's scanner results. "I can't deal with more than one patient at a time."

Too winded to reply, Riker let Data ask about Yar and Jason's condition.

"Stable," she replied. Like the captive child, Jason had flailed about in confusion when he was beamed aboard, and Crusher's only recourse had been to sedate him. By the time the doctor could turn her attention to Yar, the lieutenant had already passed out.

"The captain will expect a prognosis for their recovery." Riker's chest was still heaving from the exertion of carrying Jason, but he could finally talk.

"Later," said Crusher brusquely. "After I've had a chance to examine them more closely." She was too preoccupied with monitoring her two patients to spare Riker any further attention, and dismissed him and Data from her mind as soon as they walked out of sickbay.

"Dr. Crusher!" Nurse Tathwell called out changing vital signs as Yar edged back toward consciousness. The lieutenant came awake with a strangled gasp as if she were fighting for air.

"Tasha," cried Crusher catching hold of the

woman's shoulders. "You're back on the *Enterprise*." The doctor didn't release her grip until Yar had stopped struggling and her eyes had focused, but Crusher noted that the pupils were still dilated.

"I must have been dreaming." Yar's voice quavered as she spoke. "I thought I was drowning."

"You're just not used to breathing a liquid atmosphere," said Crusher with a reassuring smile, brushing a damp curl of Yar's hair off her forehead. Yar was still breathing rapidly, but the colored lights of the diagnostic panel had stabilized. Her physical condition was good; her emotional recovery would take a while longer.

"What about him?" asked the lieutenant, nodding toward Jason, who lay prone on a nearby medical table. "Is he all right?"

"He'll be unconscious until the effects of the sedative wear off." Crusher signaled two nurses to carry Jason into another ward for continued observation, then turned back around at the sound of a metal latch coming undone. Yar had swung up the cover of the diagnostic scanner and was scrambling down off the table. "And where do you think you're going?"

"I'm fine now," said Yar even as she grabbed the edge of the platform to steady herself. "I should be at my post."

Crusher saw the woman's pallor give way to a flush of embarrassment at the thought of her collapse. Yar would have been further mortified to know that Data had carried her to sickbay. "You have been relieved of duty, Lieutenant. I want you under medical observation for a full twenty-four hours."

"But I was unconscious for only a few minutes."

The doctor knew Yar's stubborn temperament and didn't waste time on gentle persuasion. "Tasha, if you don't get back on that bed, I'll have you sedated."

The threat lacked finesse, but it achieved the desired effect. Dr. Crusher had no intention of letting the officer go until any ill effects from her exposure to the Choraii environment had been ruled out. And the spicy aroma had been explained.

"Lieutenant Yar passed out?"

"She seemed to be having difficulty breathing, sir." Data's intention may have been to reassure the captain that the rescue attempt had been successful, but his graphic description of the scene in the transporter room only heightened Picard's alarm.

Ambassador Deelor, however, appeared satisfied with the knowledge that the lieutenant and the captive were in sickbay. "Lieutenant Worf, open a channel to the *B Flat*," he ordered, then drummed his fingers impatiently as the Klingon looked to Picard for confirmation of the command.

"Thieves!" The Choraii were as one in their accusation. *"This wasn't a trade."*

"Well, let's see if I can salvage some shred of good accord," whispered Deelor to Picard. He raised his voice to answer the Choraii accusation. "The extra lead is still yours. We offer payment for what we have taken."

"Keep your metal, only let us go!"

Picard heard the disharmony in their voices and recognized the futility of the ambassador's attempt. "If we hold their ship any longer, the Choraii may resume fighting."

"Very well," said Deelor after a short pause. "Release them."

An impassive Lieutenant Worf cut power to the tractor beam. As soon as the four rays retracted, the *B Flat* shot away at full speed. The entire crew watched with fascination as the bubble cluster shrank to a pinpoint size on the viewer, then disappeared entirely.

"Moving out of long-range sensor range," announced Worf. "Gone."

As abruptly as it had begun, the confrontation with the Choraii was over. The *Enterprise* had won. Captain Picard reflected briefly on his ship's triumph, then moved on to the demands of the present. He looked over to the ambassador.

"I'm just a passenger now," Deelor said, divining the question in Picard's mind. "You can drop me off at Starbase Ten, along with Ruthe and the Hamlin survivors."

"That will have to wait until after we have taken the Farmers home," said Picard. "Our passengers have suffered enough inconvenience as it is." He expected a protest, but Deelor only shrugged. The man had an uncanny ability to know which issues the captain would give way on and which were not worth the effort of contesting. "Helm, set a course for New Oregon. Warp four."

Data had anticipated the order and the necessary coordinates were already prepared. "Course laid in, sir."

Picard settled back in his command chair. The passage of a few uneventful days would be quite welcome after the recent turmoil. "Engage."

Geordi started the ship on its journey, then double-checked a number on his control panel. "Data, this can't be right." The pilot turned around to address Captain Picard. "Estimated time of arrival at New Oregon is thirty-six days."

"What!" The captain jumped up from his seat. "Mr. Data, explain."

"More precisely, thirty-six days, five hours, and twelve minutes." Data puzzled over the agitation of his fellow crew members. "The Choraii ship towed us off course during the tractor lock."

"Yes, but over a month?" protested the captain.

"The original rendezvous site was only a day and a half away from New Oregon."

"The *B Flat* reached a peak speed of warp nine-point-nine for several seconds," said Data. "I can show you the exact distance/acceleration ratio of—"

"That won't be necessary, Mr. Data," said the captain. He sighed at the thought of prolonged contact with Ambassador Deelor's entourage and over a hundred contentious Farmers. "Mr. La Forge, increase speed to warp six."

Data obligingly recalculated their arrival time. "Twelve days, ten hours—"

"Understood," said Picard, cutting Data off. The captain's mood was not appreciably improved by the altered schedule, especially since the colonists would demand an explanation for the delay. Riker could provide it, decided Picard. One of the privileges of rank was the delegation of unpleasant tasks.

None of the Farmers had been hurt when the *Enterprise* was jerked into motion by the Choraii ship. Enticed by second-hand reports of beguiling farmland, the entire community had packed inside the holodeck for a first-hand look at the simulated wonder. Most of the colonists were still exploring the meadows when they were thrown down onto the springy grass by the sudden lurch of the ground beneath their feet.

A few of the more intrepid explorers had reached the cluster of wooden buildings, but the barn floors were lined with a thick layer of dry hay which padded their fall. Of them all, Tomas was the most unfortunate. He was rapped soundly on the back of his head by a swinging Dutch door and briefly lost consciousness.

"Tomas, my son, my poor boy," Dolora clucked, bending over the bulky form stretched out on the floor. She looked anxiously to the woman who was checking his pulse. A loose circle of Farmers were gathered around them, peering down at Tomas and waiting for Charla's pronouncement.

"I can't even find a bump," Charla laughed.

The man's eyes fluttered open and fixed on his mother's face. He groaned.

"Oh, don't move!" cried Dolora when he sat up. She pulled at his arm, trying to keep him from rising, but Tomas struggled to his feet. "You'll only make it worse, son."

"Please, Mother," he said through tightly pressed lips. He tried to avert his gaze from the other Farmers, but the audience was ringed all around him. "I'm not a child."

"No, fortunately. You're a grown man with a thick skull," said Patrisha.

Tomas ignored the jibe, but he brushed the straw off his clothes with great vigor and jammed a loose end of his shirt back under his belt. One by one the men and women drifted away. When Tomas looked up again, he caught sight of Dnnys and Wesley at once.

"Earthquakes, what a lovely detail," he cooed, mimicking his sister's earlier praise. "Who thought of that?"

"It's not in the program," protested Wesley, then lamely added, "but maybe there was a glitch somewhere." He suspected the true cause of the motion but shouldered the blame rather than draw attention to another of the starship's combat maneuvers. A programming error would be less likely to draw the wrath of the Farmers.

"And what other surprises do you have in store for us, Ensign Crusher?" Tomas was starting to draw the attention of the bewildered colonists. "Barn fires? Tornadoes? Perhaps a flood of biblical proportions?"

"Tomas!" cried his mother. "You go too far."

Her son flushed. "I'm very sorry, Mother. It must have been the blow to my head." He edged his way out of the barn as he apologized.

Taking advantage of the diversion, Wesley and Dnnys scampered up a tall ladder to the hayloft. From that dizzying height the concerns of the adults below seemed just as puzzling, but far less important.

"So what was that all about?" asked Wesley. "What was he apologizing for?"

Dnnys mumbled an unintelligible reply as they climbed over tightly corded bales of hay and waded through loose straw. Dust raised by their boots tickled their noses and set them to sneezing. They reached the hay doors and pushed them open, taking in great gulps of the clear air outside.

"So tell me," Wesley asked again, after they had taken a seat, dangling their legs over the edge of the loft. A late afternoon sun cast long shadows across the barnyard below.

"We don't talk about those things."

"What things?"

To Wesley's surprise, his friend turned bright red. Dnnys took a deep breath, then whispered the answer. "You know, religious things."

"Oh." Wesley was careful not to show any sign of amusement. His exposure to a wide variety of cultures had taught him to respect an equally wide variety of taboos, and this prohibition was certainly no stranger than others. He changed the conversation to spare his friend any further embarrassment. "When does the decanting start?"

Dnnys stuck a straw between his teeth and leaned back onto his elbows. "Tomorrow morning," he said glumly, as if uttering a death sentence.

Wesley understood. Once the animals were released into the holodeck, Dnnys would lose his excuse for working in the cargo deck. Which also meant losing his cover for roaming freely about the *Enterprise*. "Listen, if there's anything I can do . . ."

"There is," said Dnnys. "I have a favor to ask. A big favor."

Wesley waited for an explanation, but Dnnys seemed reluctant to continue. "What is it, Dnnys? You know I'll help."

"I have this plan." The Farmer boy wiped a bead of sweat from his forehead. "But it's got to be a secret."

Wesley listened carefully to his friend's explanation. And as he listened, he began to frown.

The medical isolation chamber had been cleverly designed for a wide variety of purposes. If a patient was contagious, the airflow seals locked the infectious agent within. For anyone with a depressed immune system, the same seals kept viruses and bacteria from entering. The low-intensity red lights were soothing to eyes weakened by fever and fatigue, while the soft cushions and lowered gravity were especially suited for burn patients in the last stages of healing.

It was also the closest approximation to the environment of a Choraii ship that Dr. Crusher could prepare on such short notice.

A diagnostic scanner monitored the patient lying inside, displaying a constant assessment of his physical condition and the effect of the last sedative injection, but the panel couldn't tell her what she really wanted to know. She studied the sleeping figure of the man known as Jason, searching for the answers to the disturbing questions raised by the deaths of the other adult captives. The skin over his knees and elbows was still raw. He had collapsed as soon as the transporter beam faded and his body lost the support of the buoyant liquid interior of the Choraii atmosphere.

Here, his face was slack in repose, but her own mind superimposed an image from the transporter chamber when she had looked into his eyes and seen only a wild terror.

Jason had plunged without warning into a vastly different world, and his cries had been strangled by the unexpected rush of thin air into his lungs. If he was one of the original Hamlin children, memories of that long-ago childhood had not eased the transition. Even Tasha, gone for only a few minutes, had been disoriented on her return to the ship.

Had the rescue come too late for this man? Would he die like the others?

Dr. Crusher laid a hand on the clear window. Her touch darkened the glass, granting Jason privacy in the confines of the chamber. He would remain unconscious for another few hours, but she stole out of the room as if afraid she might wake him.

In the room next door, a second isolation unit also held a sleeping form, but the child was deep in a natural slumber. His toffee-colored skin and curly black hair were a stark contrast to Jason's pale complexion.

"He's finally cried himself out," said Troi, who was keeping vigil over the boy. She followed Dr. Crusher's sharp glance at the blood-sugar-level indicator. "He was too upset to eat, but he'll be hungry when he wakes up. I'm certain I can tempt him with some food later."

Crusher nodded in automatic agreement, then shook her head. "It's not going to be that simple, Deanna." A brief review of the Hamlin medical records had made that much clear. "He's been raised in a liquid environment. A complete rehabilitation will be necessary to teach him how to function in our world."

"Which means he'll need constant supervision," said Troi. "So how will we explain him to your department?"

"Good question." Only a few people had seen Crusher whisk the child into the isolation chamber, and Troi had taken over primary responsibility for his care when the doctor had been called away, but his presence could not be shielded for much longer. The unannounced appearance of a two-year-old boy, one unknown to her medical staff, would give rise to a host of questions. "For that matter, how do we explain Jason?"

"Survivors of a shipwreck," suggested Troi. "It's unoriginal, but not too far from the truth."

"Good enough, I suppose," sighed the doctor. "Only we'd better make sure the rest of the bridge crew gives out the same story. Nothing will draw attention faster than conflicting accounts of how they got here." She moved toward the room's door. "I'll stop by later and we can discuss what to do when he wakes up."

"Beverly," called out Troi as the other woman reached the threshold. "We can't keep calling him 'the boy' and 'the child.' He needs a name."

"What about Moses?" suggested Crusher, and stepped out of the room to continue on her rounds.

Striding down the corridor, the chief medical officer shoved aside the distracting demands of the Hamlin captives and focused her attention on her next set of patients. Sickbay was at near capacity, and the heavy caseload meant she would be working through the night.

Captain Picard's warning announcement before the *Enterprise* was dragged off course by the Choraii ship had been brief, too brief to prepare every one of the thousand people on board for the sudden acceleration. A few people never heard the crew alert and were hurled through the air without warning. Others were simply a shade too slow in reacting. The extent of their injuries depended on what part of their body connected with the nearest solid object. Those with broken bones and lacerations reached sickbay quickly on float stretchers with paramedics in close attendance or were carried in by fellow crew members. Over the following hour, a gradually increasing stream of people had hobbled in to sickbay on their own, seeking relief for bruises and sprains.

"Duncan is doing very well," said the supervising nurse in critical care. He called up an encouraging pattern of regenerating nerves on a computer screen. Crusher was relieved to see that the astronomer's spinal cord had been bruised rather than cut by the telescope that had swung into his lower back.

"What about Butterfield?" The most badly injured of the crew had been a botanist who had crashed headfirst into a potted caudifera. Butterfield would be the first to laugh at the irony of being attacked by one of his own plants, if he ever regained consciousness. Dr. Crusher had mended the scientist's fractured skull, but only time could tell if his brain would function with its previous brilliance.

Doswell shrugged. "No change."

Recovery was out of her hands at this point. Dr. Crusher reacted to her impotence with a rage—and found a focus for that rage waiting in her office.

"Captain, I have a sickbay filled with casualties and because of Deelor's damn security restrictions, they don't even understand why they were hurt. This wasn't their fight, but they're the ones paying the biggest price."

Her harsh words echoed Picard's own thoughts, intensifying his guilt. He alone was responsible for the people lying in the medical wards.

"These are passengers. They should *never* have been

taken into a situation that you knew would be dangerous!" Crusher said bitterly. "You should have separated the ship."

In fact, his first instinct had been to order the detachment of the stardrive section from the main disk. He had been swayed by Deelor's arguments against that action. Or was it that he hadn't been willing to fight hard enough for his own command decision? What would have happened if the saucer section had been left behind—would the crew of the battle bridge have returned to find these people uninjured or to find all the passengers slaughtered by the wandering Choraii? "I chose not to," said Picard curtly.

"Tell that to my patients."

"I stand by my actions."

"At least you're still able to stand, unlike Butterfield and Duncan." She regretted that remark as soon as she said it—but Picard didn't give her time to retract the statement.

"It's your job to redress my errors in judgment," he said harshly. "Be thankful you can wash the blood from your hands."

"Jean-Luc, I'm sorry, I should never have said that. It was unfair of me."

"Never apologize for the truth, Dr. Crusher," said Picard, unwilling to accept absolution for his sins. He stalked out of the office before she could speak again.

One by one the senior officers had scattered to other parts of the ship until Geordi La Forge was left in charge of the bridge. Trading his position at the helm for the captain's chair, even during the prevailing tranquility, inevitably led to dreams of command. Having observed Picard in action against the Choraii, the lieutenant questioned how he would react to a similar emergency. Not that he would get the opportunity to find out any time soon.

"Geordi?"

Starting at his name, La Forge looked up to see who had called him. "Oh, hello, Wesley." He hadn't noticed the boy's entrance onto the bridge. Geordi was relieved that an ensign rather than an officer had caught him lost in thought. "You can use any of the empty duty stations . . ."

"I'm not here to work," said Wesley with a shake of his head. "I have a favor to ask."

"So ask," urged Geordi, sensing an unspoken urgency in the young ensign's somber expression.

"Well, it's not really ship business," apologized Wesley. "But a friend of mine needs some information."

"What kind of information?"

Wesley looked nervously over his shoulder, then bent down and whispered in Geordi's ear. Once Geordi heard the request, the identity of Wesley's friend was fairly obvious. "The best person to ask for that information is probably Logan."

"Oh."

Geordi grinned at the boy's unenthusiastic response. "Hey, I know our chief engineer isn't your biggest fan, but I bet he'll answer your questions. After all, it'll give him a chance to give *you* some answers for a change."

"Yeah, I guess so," said Wesley, turning away.

"And Wes, tell Dnnys . . . I mean, your friend, that I wish him luck."

"Thanks, Geordi," the ensign called out as he raced off the bridge ramp to the aft deck. "He's going to need all the luck he can get."

* * *

Riker had been on his way to his cabin when the haunting melody pulled him off course, sending him through a welter of corridors searching for the source of the music. He turned one corner and the sound strengthened, turned another and it faded to a faint whisper. Doubling back on his trail, he picked up the soft strains of the flute filtering down from an access chute in the ceiling. He stood listening for several moments, letting the sorrowful notes wash over him like falling tears.

Grabbing hold of a rung at the hole's entrance, he hoisted himself into the tunnel above. His shoulders brushed against the sides of the narrow, curving walls. He kept climbing, hand over hand up the ladder, until he reached a service chamber halfway between decks.

Ruthe was sitting cross-legged on the metal ledge that circled the opening like a catch basin. Her music trailed away when Riker climbed out of the chute, then stopped altogether when he sat down beside her. She dropped the flute onto her lap but didn't seem to resent the intrusion.

"You're hurt," he said, frowning at the line of dried blood that ran down her cheek. He brushed aside a lock of her hair and uncovered a purplish bruise on her forehead.

She shook off his touch. "Sharp edges and hard metal. That's what ships are made of."

"We've brought Jason on board. I thought you should know that." Picard had described his confrontation with the translator and her resistance to the rescue. "Dr. Crusher will do everything—"

"He lied," said Ruthe abruptly.

Riker almost asked her who she meant, but there was really only one person that she could be talking about. He let her continue.

"He knew what I was doing all the time."

The captain had suspected as much. "Then why did Deelor deny it?"

Ruthe didn't answer. She pulled her instrument into parts, then slipped the pieces into separate pockets in her cloak. Each section had its own place. "He knows other things. Dangerous things that he's not telling."

"Will *you* tell me?" asked Riker.

Her head jerked up. She studied Riker's face, as if seeing him for the first time. "I've told you things before. Now it's his turn."

Pushing Riker aside, she raced nimbly down the rungs of the access chute. He scrambled after her, but by the time he dropped back into the corridor below, Ruthe was gone.

Chapter Twelve

UNCOUNTED NUMBERS OF STARS glittered brightly outside the windows of the observation lounge, but their light cast no warmth on the three men inside.

"You knew there was an adult still aboard the *B Flat* and were prepared to let the Choraii leave with him. Why?" demanded Captain Picard.

"Ruthe acted of her own accord, Captain," said Deelor with a greater show of conviction than he had exhibited hours before in that same room. "I knew nothing . . ."

Picard made a deliberate show of losing his temper. He slammed his fist down on the tabletop and raised his voice to shout. "I'm tired of your self-serving games, Ambassador Deelor. Or Agent Deelor—or whoever you really are. No more evasions, no more crumbs of information. I want the whole truth of what you're doing out here."

The expression of innocence had frozen on Deelor's

face. He rubbed it away with one hand. Beneath that mask, his face was gaunt and weary. "Yes, I knew about Jason and I knew that Ruthe planned to leave him." He sagged deeper into his seat, as if in need of its support to continue. "I agreed not to interfere with her decision because I knew if we brought him here he would probably die. There have been other exchanges, ones that not even Ruthe knows about. In all, the Federation has recovered twelve of the original Hamlin captives."

"And they've all died?" asked Riker.

"Not all," said Deelor. "But those that aren't dead are withdrawn, catatonic. Only young children seem able to adjust to life outside of the Choraii ships."

Picard thought of the casualties in sickbay and his bitterness increased. "Why didn't you tell me this before we brought Jason aboard?"

His answer confirmed the captain's fear. "Because you might have let him remain with the Choraii," said Deelor. "And being a man of integrity, you would have recorded that decision in your Captain's Log. I have fewer scruples. I was willing to let Jason go, but only if no one knew. There are too many officials in high places that want the Hamlin captives brought back."

Picard might fault the man's ethics, but at least Deelor was finally being candid. "Why is his return so important?"

"Different reasons for different admirals. Some are under the belief, perhaps misguided, that the survivors can be salvaged or that a crippled life in our world is better than leaving them with the aliens who killed their parents. Others want the adult captives returned on the off chance that one of them will provide some useful information. You see, the children can't tell us how the Choraii stardrive works."

"No!" Picard brushed aside Deelor's explanation

161

with scorn. "I won't believe Zagráth would sacrifice lives for that knowledge."

"Don't judge her too harshly," said Deelor. He bit down on his lip, stifling the words that almost followed. Drumming his fingers on the table, the first nervous tic he had ever betrayed, he studied Picard, then Riker. The tapping stopped and Deelor's narrative resumed. "The Romulans are after that drive, or will be soon. At least one of their battlecruisers, *The Defender*, was destroyed in an encounter with the Choraii. There may have been other clashes, rumors indicate, but we don't know the outcomes." He had their undivided attention now. "My original mission was to discover how the Choraii defeated *The Defender*."

Riker caught the connection immediately. "By letting them destroy the *Ferrel*."

"If necessary."

"You're a cold-blooded bastard," observed the captain.

"Look beyond the nose on your face, Picard!" cried Deelor. "What do you think will happen if the Romulans unravel the workings of the Choraii drive? They could fly through the Neutral Zone to the very heart of the Federation and lay waste to entire worlds. I've walked through the carnage they leave behind. Imagine what would have happened at the border outpost if the Romulans had possessed a superior flight technology."

"The *Enterprise* was sent there to maintain a balance of force," reflected Picard, settling back into his chair. "And a very shaky balance it was."

"Yes, I know. I was there, too. Only I was walking on the other side—that's how I learned about the fate of *The Defender*. Fortunately, I made it back across the Neutral Zone before I bled to death."

Once again, Picard found his opinion of Deelor

shifting to accommodate a new facet of the man's character. He clearly possessed physical courage. The captain listened with growing respect to Deelor's impassioned speech.

"In the interests of Federation security. That's not a phrase to be used lightly. It means a few dozen captives, or the crew of a starship, may be sacrificed to save millions of lives. Captain Manin forgot that part of the equation when he tried to detonate the *Ferrel.* He wanted a clean death for his crew and he wanted revenge on the Choraii. I had to stop him."

Bit by bit the pieces of the puzzle were coming together in Picard's mind. "That's why you were shot."

"As you've pointed out on several occasions, people feel quite strongly about the Hamlin massacre—too strongly, perhaps. Violent hatreds demand swift military reactions, but the interests of the Federation are best served by the slower progress of diplomacy. Since the exchange of human captives between the Choraii ships serves as a bonding gift, we're hoping that our trade exchanges for the young children will lead to similar ties between the Choraii and the Federation and the eventual exchange of technological secrets."

"My actions certainly haven't improved those relations," said Picard with a weary sigh.

"Conflicting Federation policy set us up for a no-win situation. Some officials want the adult captives back, while others want to maintain cordial relations." Deelor shrugged philosophically. "The *B Flat* is just one ship in the local cluster, and not among the most important. I'll start again with another."

"You could have saved a lot of trouble by telling me all this in the first place."

"I shouldn't be telling you now," said Deelor. He revealed another part of himself to the two officers, one more chilling than the others. "And if what I've told you leaves this room, you'll both be dead men. I'll see to it personally."

When Deelor returned to his cabin suite he was surprised to find Ruthe comfortably curled on a low couch listening to a Vivaldi string concerto. She looked up when he entered, then returned to her contemplation of the music. Silence was no clue as to her mood since her greetings were always sporadic and perfunctory. As he had learned over the course of their association, Ruthe would remain remote and impersonal until she had need of him or he addressed her. Deelor had expected that the fight would change their tenuous relationship in some manner, but perhaps she had already relegated that scene to the past.

Or perhaps her betrayal of him had evened the score.

Settling down on a chair, Deelor let the rushing counterpoint of violins and violas sweep away the tensions born of his confrontation with the starship officers. If Ruthe held no grudge, neither would he.

Picard had stayed behind in the observation lounge after the other two men left. The view stretching outside the broad sweep of windows never bored him because the pattern of far-distant stars was always different, always changing. Those elusive beacons usually challenged and inspired him with their beauty, but just now the vista seemed bleak.

He heard the doors to the room slide open and thought for a second that Riker had returned, but the steps coming up behind him were too light to belong to his first officer. Then Picard caught Beverly Crusher's reflection moving across the glass window. She stopped a few feet away from him and followed his gaze out into space. They stood side by side in silence for several minutes before she spoke.

"If you look at the stars for too long, you can start to feel like a god. Or to think you should be able to act like one. Omniscient, omnipotent, infallible."

Picard did not respond.

"Captains and doctors are both prone to the syndrome. We expect to solve all problems and cure all ills, and then blame ourselves if we fail at impossible tasks. Or blame others."

Picard finally glanced over at her. "Am I being lectured, Dr. Crusher?"

"Something like that." Her eyes were still locked on the scene outside the ship. "I'm better at lectures than I am at apologies."

"I don't need either."

"You deserve both." Crusher took a deep breath and faced him squarely. "An apology for what I said to you in sickbay and a lecture for listening to me when I was in too foul a mood to make any sense."

The captain's stiff posture loosened. "I wasn't in a particularly good humor myself," said Picard wryly. "And you didn't say anything that I hadn't already told myself a hundred times over."

"Which proves we both need a vacation."

Picard smiled and the strain between them dissolved, only to be replaced by another, more familiar tension. Crusher took a step back and Picard looked out at the stars again. He wondered how he could have mistaken their brilliance for desolation.

"How is Lieutenant Yar doing?"

"Tearing apart my sickbay," sighed Crusher. "I'll release her soon, unless I strangle her first."

"And Jason?"

"Sedated," said Crusher tersely. "I've established his identity from the old Hamlin medical records. His DNA profile matches that of Jason Reardon. He was three years old at the time of his abduction, not much older than the child we recovered."

"Are they related?"

"No," she said. "However, I used genetic markers to trace the boy's ancestry. His father was one of the original kidnapped group but his mother was apparently born in captivity, the result of a union between two maturing children."

"A third-generation captive," said the captain. His brows lifted in alarm.

"Yes, and he's probably not the only one. Given their good health, the human population may be growing fairly quickly and spreading throughout the Choraii ships. How will we ever recover them all?"

"Is that even the right question?" asked the captain, recalling Andrew Deelor's revelation of the high fatalities among the rescued captives.

Crusher raised her hand to stop him. "I'm not ready to deal with that issue yet. Oh, Jean-Luc, if you could have seen Jason when he beamed aboard . . . those terror-stricken eyes . . ." She shook herself. "I've got to get back to sickbay. Jason's sedative is due to wear off soon."

They walked out of the lounge together but parted after crossing over the threshold. Picard was halfway down the opposite corridor when the doctor whirled around and called to him.

"By the way, Captain. Professor Butterfield requested a caudifera salad for his lunch."

Although Data had been assigned a cabin of his own like his human companions, he was more often found in Geordi's quarters or the ship's library. Both places fed the only hunger of which he was capable: curiosity. The android was free from the demands of a human body, but he delighted in the search for knowledge and acquired facts with the same relish some people experienced when they encountered a new culinary delicacy.

Since Geordi was still in command of the bridge, Data chose to spend the remaining hour of his off-duty shift pursuing his most recent line of research. He had mastered the texts explaining the physiological necessity for sleep among organic life forms, but certain psychological aspects still puzzled him. Upon entering the ship's library, however, Data was distracted by unusual activity in one corner of the room.

"Oh, hi, Data," sighed Wesley when the android approached the print terminal. He tried to gather up the hardcover books that covered the table, but Data had already picked up one of the volumes.

"Very interesting," said Data, inspecting the title on the spine. Personally, he found the printed format to be somewhat clumsy and time-consuming, yet its close association with humans lent the medium a certain charm. *"Basic Engineering Principles.* Is this for archival purposes? You have already mastered this material."

"I'm doing a favor for a friend." Wesley removed the final bound volume from the printer assembly. "And, Data, I'd appreciate it if you'd keep this to yourself."

Data frowned. The phrase was unfamiliar to him. "You wish me to have a copy as well?"

"No, I mean"—Wesley took a deep breath—"well, don't tell anyone about what I'm doing. You see, it's, uh . . ."

"A secret?" asked Data.

"Yes," said Wesley.

The android smiled and recited enthusiastically, "Secret: a clandestine operation, a sub rosa endeavor, a—"

Wesley interrupted his recital. "Sorry, sir, but I'm running late for class." With an apologetic smile the boy gathered up his printed materials and hastened toward the exit.

Data stood lost in thought, pondering the mystique of secrets.

Now that he had one, he wasn't entirely sure what to do with it.

Each time Riker met with Farmer Patrisha, the woman greeted him with greater civility. On this occasion, when he came to her suite, she offered the first officer some tea and he accepted. They sipped the bitter herbal brew in companionable silence before moving on to business.

Riker hoped Patrisha's cordiality would stand the test of his tidings. Setting aside his empty cup, he began. "I have good news. We're back on course to New Oregon."

"Will we arrive in time for the decanting?" asked Patrisha.

"No, I'm afraid not." Riker was frank about that aspect, then launched into his deception. "Our warp engines are undergoing some routine maintenance work that will slow our progress." Fortunately, Logan wasn't likely to come in contact with the Farmers. The chief engineer wouldn't appreciate having his department maligned.

"How long will we be delayed?"

Smiling, he tried to downplay the answer. "Only two weeks." His bravado was unnecessary; Patrisha accepted the news without comment. Riker wondered if her composure was influenced by Dolora's decision to live full-time on the holodeck farm. That thought brought a second issue to mind. "About the decanting. The easiest way to move the stasis machinery to the holodeck is to use the transporter."

"My people will never agree to that," said Patrisha immediately. Her brows flew upward at the heretical proposal. "Transporters are definitely against Farmer creed."

"I was afraid that would be the case." The entire community and their belongings had come aboard the *Enterprise* by shuttlecraft, a process that should have taken only one hour but lasted for five instead. Shuttles had flitted back and forth between the starbase dock and the hangar deck with colonists riding both ways in a noisy muddle of lost baggage and separated families. The first officer wanted to avoid a replay of that episode. "The alternative is to dismantle the machine so that the stasis cells can be carried by hand."

"Which means the entire project would end in disaster for the animals," concluded Patrisha without any prompting. Evidently, she remembered the disorganized boarding just as clearly as Riker.

"It's not my place to say so," demurred Riker, uncertain as to how far he could push her.

"And not mine either." Patrisha set her mug down onto the table. "These matters are decided by a community consensus."

And they both knew what the community would decide. At least he had tried, thought Riker as he stood to take his leave. Perhaps the Farmers could be persuaded to allow members of the starship crew to assist in the delivery process. He wondered how many of his own people would be needed to counteract the inefficiency of the colonists.

"Of course, if you don't ask, they can't refuse," said Patrisha, also rising from her chair.

"I beg your pardon?"

She couldn't meet his eyes, but she made her position clear as they walked to the door. "If the stasis equipment is in place tomorrow morning, it will be too late for anyone to object. And possibly no one will even wonder how it got there."

"Thank you for the tea, Farmer Patrisha," said Riker, smiling broadly. "And for the advice."

"Please don't mention it," said Patrisha firmly. "To anyone."

"I can't stand another minute of bedrest," cried Tasha Yar, storming into the doctor's office. "I could be on the bridge doing something useful. We're in the middle of a highly classified mission, and my confinement is interfering with essential security duties." She planted her fists on Crusher's desk. "Besides, I feel fine."

"I'm glad to hear that, Tasha," sighed Beverly Crusher. She leaned back to put a little more distance between herself and the lieutenant. "But I've been holding you here until I got this back." She held up a tape cassette. The lab analysis report had been on her desk when the doctor returned to sickbay. She'd initiated the tests as a routine precaution—but the results had been an unpleasant surprise. "What do you remember about the Choraii ship's atmosphere?"

"It was just like drowning," Yar shuddered. "The first few moments were the worst. After that, breathing in wasn't as bad as I expected. The liquid was actually rather pleasant. It had this smell, almost a taste, of cinnamon."

That had been the telltale clue. "I had a sample of the scented liquid tested. It's laced with a drug, a narcotic."

"Does this mean I have to stay in sickbay?" Yar's concern was single-minded.

"Yes!" said Crusher emphatically. Persistence was admirable in security chiefs but not in patients. She headed out of the office and the lieutenant trailed after her down the corridor. "I can't release you until I'm sure your system has metabolized all traces of the drug. Even then, we won't know what long-term effects you may suffer."

"But I feel fine!" exclaimed Yar.

"Tasha, you say that even after a game of Parrises Squares with Worf. I've watched your body turn black and blue and you won't admit to a single ache."

"But that's not a fair comparison."

"Enough!" Crusher stopped abruptly and turned to face Tasha. "One more word and I'll call your own security team to take you back to the ward."

An anguished cry from the room ahead brought the argument to an abrupt conclusion. Both women raced down the passage and burst into the isolation area. Dr. Crusher took in the scene at once. "Tasha, take care of Troi." She moved directly to the chamber.

Jason was awake. His whimpering cries mixed with Troi's sobbing. The doctor retracted the protective cover of the isolation chamber in order to reach him directly. He was crouched in a corner of the unit, rocking back and forth in his agitation. Though his eyes were open, they stared blankly and didn't seem to register Crusher's approach.

"Jason." She reached in and touched him.

The man screamed at the contact. His body curled into a fetal ball with his head buried against his knees. His arms and legs trembled uncontrollably.

"No," cried Troi. "Don't get any closer." Despite Tasha's comforting embrace, the counselor was also shaking. Her face was contorted in a mirror image of Jason's emotional distress. "Your presence only frightens him more."

"What can I do to reassure him?"

"I don't know," sobbed Troi. "Nothing. Leave him."

Jason had retreated into an even tighter huddle, and his cries had taken on a disturbing rhythmic chant.

"Damn." Crusher pulled a hypo from her medical kit. Jason flinched at the touch of the cold metal against his skin but otherwise took no notice of the contact. Seconds later, as the sedative took effect, he fell silent and slumped in place. Crusher lowered the man onto his side and gently untangled his limbs into a comfortable sleeping position. He would remain that way for at least another six hours.

The doctor activated the chamber-control panel and the shield slid back over the unconscious form, hiding it from view. The diagnostic panel indicated that Jason's body was healthy even if his mind was not, but his intense emotional reactions would have a depressive effect eventually. Changing a setting on the hypo, Crusher turned her attention to the counselor.

"No," protested Troi, but she was too late to stop the hissing dose of medication from entering her system. "Really, I'm fine now."

"That's what they all say," murmured Beverly Crusher. "This should calm you down until you reach your cabin."

"But I can't leave Moses." The Counselor was as determined to stay in sickbay as Yar had been to leave. "He's just starting to recognize me."

"I'll keep you company," volunteered Lieutenant Yar.

Crusher looked up with disbelief. "I thought you wanted to get out of sickbay."

Yar shrugged sheepishly. "I hate to see Troi cry."

Troi laughed even as she wiped away the last of her tears. "Thank you for the offer, but what do you know about babies?"

"Not much," admitted the lieutenant. "But the exposure might be good for me." She paused. "As long as there aren't too many messy biological functions involved."

"Oh, do what you want," said Crusher, exasperated with them both. Troi was quickly recovering her emotional equilibrium, but the doctor's own reaction to Jason's awakening was only now taking its toll.

In the privacy of her office, Dr. Crusher was unable

172

to ignore her growing despair. She sat at her desk, calling up a succession of case files on the computer without absorbing the material on the screen. Her mind kept returning to the Hamlin captive, searching for ways to help Jason adjust, but the situation was far removed from any she had ever dealt with before. She needed help. Raising a hand to her chest, Crusher tapped at her insignia.

"I was expecting your call," Andrew Deelor replied. *"And I have a pretty good idea of what you want."*

"Will you ask her?"

"Yes, I'll ask," he said reluctantly. *"But I can't guarantee she'll help."* He broke contact.

And I can't guarantee Jason's life, Crusher admitted for the first time.

Chapter Thirteen

PATRISHA STOOD APART from the other Farmers. The
men and women of the community were ranged in a
semicircle around the front face of the barn, talking
among themselves in whispered voices, stamping
their feet to keep warm in the chill morning air. She
held back, observing them as they watched the barn.
An early dawn light washed over the wooden structure. The stage was set for the drama to come.

A hush fell over the group as Dnnys and Wesley
pushed their way through the crowd and marched up
to the barn, conscious that their every movement was
being watched. Exchanging nervous grins, the boys
unbarred the great doors and swung them open. The
Farmers edged forward, necks craning to catch sight
of the cryogenic equipment stored inside. Beyond a
few murmurs of contempt at the intricacy of the
machine, there were no other comments.

Patrisha was almost ashamed of the unquestioning

174

acceptance of the stasis equipment on the holodeck. No one, not even Tomas, was bothered by the absence of tracks on the packed hay floor. But then, good Farmers didn't know enough about transporter technology to look for the signs of its use. Patrisha was thankful that Mr. Riker had worked his magic during the night and was not present this morning. An outsider was sure to laugh at people who were so easily fooled, yet Patrisha had invited that ridicule with her advice to the starship officer.

Dnnys initiated the first step of the actual decanting process by detaching a single cell from the honeycomb structure. Wesley emerged from the back of the machine unwinding the coiled loops of a thin, flexible hose. He handed the socket end to the Farmer boy. Moving with an assurance born of much practice, Dnnys deftly attached the threaded fitting to the cell's drainage port. He flicked a switch and a suction pump kicked into operation with a series of gurgles and burps.

"Dnnys was never this swift with his farm chores," said Tomas, sidling up beside Patrisha.

"He's older now than when we left Grzydc." And when had his skinny child's frame filled out with solid muscle? "Besides, you should be glad someone can do this job." Patrisha had defended her son's decision to assume maintainance of the antiquated equipment during the long voyage to New Oregon since the community would have been hard pressed to afford a qualified technician. Now she saw firsthand the boy's easy familiarity with the stasis equipment and wished his actions were not so visible to the other Farmers.

She and Tomas watched as Wesley repeated the same motions with other cells, frequently looking to Dnnys for instructions. Clearly the Farmer boy was the main operator of this equipment, not the starship ensign.

Another observer joined them. "He's your son, all right." Patrisha did not mistake Dolora's comment for a compliment.

A high-pitched buzzer signaled that the first cell was emptied of its preserving fluid and the gathering of men and women stirred and whispered as they waited to learn the condition of the contents. Dnnys flipped open the cover and reached inside the container. He pulled out a pink newborn rabbit, then another. "They're alive," he announced with pride when the small, fleshy bundles squirmed and squeaked.

"Damnedest birth I've ever seen," declared Old Steven, and spat onto the ground for added emphasis.

Patrisha saw Dolora's mouth tighten, a sure sign her aunt had heard the cursing. Old Steven was the only Farmer who dared curse in Dolora's presence. The two of them no longer kept company, but he had fathered her children and that sentimental connection apparently bestowed a certain immunity on the man's actions.

"Hey, look at this!" cried Wesley with great excitement. He had unlocked a cell with a litter of puppies. Their eyes were closed, and when he picked up one with black and white markings, it nuzzled against the palm of his hand in search of milk.

Myra snatched the puppy away from him. "Get to work before the boy kills them all," she snapped, passing the animal on to Charla.

Patrisha moved forward to take the next one. Galvanized into action by the woman's sharp tongue, Farmers carried away animals as quickly as the stasis workers could deliver them. The puppies were followed by a litter of piglets and clutches of chicken and duck eggs ready to hatch. All the newborns, bereft of their mothers, would have to be hand fed and tended around the clock. After ten months of enforced leisure the colonists were called back to duty.

The hard labor would continue for the rest of their lives.

"And day after tomorrow we start decanting the horses!" said Wesley. His mother was looking straight at him as he talked, but she didn't react at all. "Mom, you're not listening."

"Aren't I?" said Dr. Crusher, then sighed. "No, I guess I'm not." She laid aside her medical padd and sighed.

"And you haven't been to see the Oregon farm either." He shifted a bulky package from one arm to another. "I'm heading there after my last class. Want to go with me?"

"I'm sorry, Wesley. I know you worked hard on the holodeck project and I really want to see it, but . . ."

"But you've been working hard, too," Wesley said without resentment. "In fact, you look kind of tired." Just a few months ago he wouldn't have noticed.

"I haven't had much sleep lately." In fact, Wesley couldn't even remember the last time his mother had been to their cabin. "But as soon as things calm down here, I'll come see the farm."

"The captives, they're not doing too well, are they?"

She didn't answer the question. "You'd better hurry or you'll be late for your physics class."

"Astronomy," Wesley corrected her as he backed out of the office. He paused at the doorway. "Mom, if a friend asked you for a favor, one that maybe meant getting him into trouble with his family . . ."

"What was that, Wesley?"

"Nothing," he said. "'Bye, Mom."

Dr. Crusher waved an absentminded good-bye to her son, then picked up her padd again. It seemed heavier every time she lifted it. She checked the next item on her agenda—a listing of those in the patient ward. Most of the beds had been cleared that morning.

She was especially looking forward to releasing the next patient.

"Get back to the bridge," she ordered. "Your last exam shows you're fine."

"That's what I've been telling you all along," said Lieutenant Yar, jumping off the bed. "I never felt any effects from the drug."

"Beyond fainting," pointed out Crusher. Fortunately, Yar's exposure to the narcotic had lasted just a few minutes. If only Jason could have recovered so easily, but he had spent the last fifty years aboard that ship and short of returning him to the Choraii . . . The glimmer of a solution began to form. "Did the drug affect your memories of the ship?"

"Oh, no. I'm not likely to forget that experience very soon." Crusher was pleased by the lieutenant's answer, but Yar was too elated over her medical release to ask why. "About Troi . . ."

"I know she's tired. I've already chosen someone to help her out with the boy," said Crusher. Too many details kept interrupting her thoughts, but Yar's departure would reduce the interference considerably. "And, Tasha, stay out of trouble. I don't want to see you in sickbay again for a long time."

"Don't worry," said Yar, speeding toward the door. "I'm not coming back."

Dr. Crusher stood in place, developing her sketchy idea into a more solid concept. Her next step was to sound out Data. He answered her com link call and listened patiently as the doctor outlined her requirements.

"*Yes, technically the project is feasible,*" said Data after due consideration. "*I have access to most of the pertinent information."* He explained what else he would need to know.

"Tasha may be able to provide some of that," said Crusher thoughtfully. "But Ruthe definitely can." If the woman would agree to help.

"Do you wish to begin now?"

"Not yet, Data," said Crusher. "I'll let you know when." She was still waiting to hear from Deelor about her first proposal. If Ruthe refused that one, she would never agree to the second.

Lisa Iovino tracked down Counselor Troi by listening for the howling of her young charge. The woman and child were in the dietician's cubicle, which its resident nurse had evidently fled in search of more peaceful surroundings. Troi was too absorbed in what she was doing to notice Iovino's approach. The doctor had the opportunity to observe for a few minutes.

The counselor was seated at the food synthesizer table with the squirming child on her lap. A wide assortment of dishes had piled up in front of them, most of them barely touched. The missing portions were spread over Troi's face and chest.

"Here, try this one," she coaxed, holding a spoon heaped with mashed potatoes. The boy opened his mouth to scream. With perfect timing she popped the spoon inside.

After a moment's silence he spit the food back at her, adding a new ingredient to the soiled uniform. Then he began to cry again. Troi looked close to tears as well.

"I'm the relief crew," announced Lisa, moving into the room. "Dr. Crusher said you needed a break." Her own opinion, after seeing the counselor, was that the break was long overdue. The boy's piercing screams had echoed throughout the medical section for hours.

"But he's not used to strangers," said Troi wearily. Children were very direct in broadcasting their emotions, and shielding herself from this boy's unhappiness had taken a great deal of energy. "I'm afraid he'll be frightened if I leave."

"Well, he certainly can't get any louder no matter who is with him." Iovino reached out and gathered up the crying child from Troi's arms.

The transfer startled Moses into temporary silence. He stopped crying long enough to survey his new keeper, then broke into a suspicious whimper. He clutched tightly at the soft green blanket in which he was wrapped. It was liberally smeared with a sticky goo, as was his tear-stained face.

"Not very hungry, are you?" Iovino asked the boy.

"On the contrary, he's very hungry."

The boy turned his face back to Troi at the sound of the counselor's voice. Despite his steady sobbing, Moses was listening intently to the conversation between the two women, but Troi wondered if he could understand their words. The sound of human voices spoken in a liquid atmosphere was probably quite different from what he was hearing now.

"He's just not used to our food," Troi continued, wishing the Choraii trade had included some of their common dietary staples. She could sense the child's frustration at the unfamiliar taste and texture of what she had offered him. "I've tried soups, pudding, ice cream, pureed fruits, and vegetables."

"He'll eat eventually," said Iovino. "Children don't starve to death if there's anything edible in arm's reach."

Iovino's soft brown hair and peaches and cream complexion projected an appearance of innocence and sweetness, but Troi could tell that the intern's matter-of-fact answer was a more reliable indicator of her personality. "This is a special child." The counselor hesitated, unsure of how much more she could tell without breaching security restrictions. "He's had an unusual upbringing."

"Yes, I know," said Iovino. She had read an obviously edited medical file on the mysterious ship-wrecked survivors. The child's case history was not very detailed and certainly not up to Dr. Crusher's usual exacting standards, which meant unanswered questions were probably meant to remain unanswered. "Just leave him to me."

Despite her mental and physical exhaustion, Troi was somewhat reluctant to deliver Moses into someone else's care until she realized that the child had stopped crying. She lowered her empathic shield and read his puzzlement. Just what about the newcomer had roused his curiosity, she couldn't tell. "You're very good with children."

"Yes, I'm afraid so," sighed Iovino. Moses fixed Iovino with an unblinking stare and hiccuped. The young intern patted him absently on the back to ease the spasms. "I come from a large family, a very large family." She shook her head at the memory of her homeworld. The sprawling continents of LonGiland had been populated in just a few hundred years by its prolific colonists. "Early marriage is a deeply entrenched tradition, so I've been taking care of younger brothers and sisters, not to mention nephews and nieces, all my life."

"But you joined Starfleet instead of following in that tradition," said Troi thoughtfully. "I know how difficult that decision can be. I broke with the customs of my own people also."

"I haven't entirely escaped," laughed Iovino. Moses had fallen asleep in her arms. "Everyone in sickbay keeps harping on my rapport with children. If I'm not careful, I'll end up in pediatrics."

* * *

The argument had begun in the outer area of sick-bay, but Dr. Crusher saw the hastily averted glances of her nursing staff and realized her temper was getting out of control. Either the ambassador was being unusually exasperating or her lack of sleep was affecting her emotional control; Crusher preferred to assign the blame to him. She guided Deelor into the privacy of her own office.

"I can't keep him fully sedated until we reach Starbase Ten," Crusher continued. "He's already been under far longer than I would like."

"Try lighter doses," suggested Deelor.

"Dammit, I don't need your medical advice—" But that was exactly what she had been asking for. She took a deep breath and spoke more calmly. "I tried reduced dosages but being in a partially drugged state just increases Jason's confusion. He's slipping away from me."

"It happens."

"Not to my patients!"

Deelor shrugged. "I can't help you."

"But Ruthe can."

"I asked, but she refused."

Crusher abandoned any attempts to contain her anger. "Then ask again!"

"No!" Deelor matched her heat with his reply. "Surely you realize what that request entails?"

"I'm trying to save Jason's life."

Their shouting covered the sound of approaching footsteps. Captain Picard walked into the room and paused, waiting for some explanation of their behavior. When it was not forthcoming, he broached his own concerns for coming to sickbay. "I've received your medical report concerning the Choraii atmosphere. What is the nature of this drug?"

"Chemical analysis indicates that it's a mild narcotic," answered Crusher distractedly. "It may have contributed to Lieutenant Yar's collapse after her return from the *B Flat,* but she doesn't show any prolonged ill effects and I've released her from sickbay." The doctor's frown was directed at Deelor. "However, I'm still trying to determine whether Jason or the child are undergoing withdrawal. My tests on a possible chemical dependence have been inconclusive."

"And you believe Ruthe may have more information?" So Picard had overheard enough of their conversation to guess the issue under contention.

Crusher nodded assent. "Only she won't give me the opportunity to ask questions."

"Ambassador, you're the only one who has any influence over her," challenged Picard.

"Me?" Deelor scoffed. "I've known her a long time, but don't mistake that for influence. Ruthe follows her own will." By his tone, Crusher suspected he admired that trait in her.

The captain persisted. "I realize that Ruthe opposed the transfer, but surely she won't let Jason suffer for our actions."

"Ruthe wants nothing to do with the captives."

"Why?" asked Picard.

"I can't answer that," Deelor said.

"Never mind," said Picard angrily. "I'll ask her myself." He moved toward the office door, but Deelor blocked his way. "Are you ordering me not to try, Ambassador?"

"No," said Deelor at last, and stepped aside.

He and Crusher settled into an uncomfortable silence as they waited for the captain's return.

Picard's request for entry was granted, but Ruthe was not in the front room of the cabin and he was forced to go in search of her. He walked through a suite empty of personal effects. The captain knew

Deelor and Ruthe had lost all their belongings when the *USS Ferrel* was destroyed, but evidently they had not made use of ship's stores to replace any of those items. Deelor, at least, had procured a new suit of clothes, but the translator was always wrapped in the same worn gray cloak.

Picard found Ruthe in the back bedroom. "Dr. Crusher has some questions regarding Jason's condition."

"It's nothing to do with me now." She sat on the room's single bed, hugging her knees to her chin. "I told you not to bring him on board."

Her pose was not seductive, but Picard would have preferred conducting their conversation in the day area of the cabin. The informality of their surroundings implied an uncomfortable degree of intimacy. "And Jason's death would prove your point. Is your pride worth a man's life?"

"My job is to translate, nothing more. The Hamlin captives are not my concern."

"You can't simply deny responsibility because it is inconvenient or even distasteful," argued Picard— but he could see that he was not getting through to her. Ruthe plucked fitfully at the disheveled covers of the bed as her initial defensiveness gave way to restlessness. "You said the Choraii value their humans, but they've harmed Jason."

This accusation drew Ruthe's immediate attention. "Why do you say that?"

"Dr. Crusher has found traces of an unknown chemical substance, a drug, in the Choraii atmosphere, which has affected him. It may have also affected the child. Under the circumstances, I can't regret my decision to bring them both aboard and I will strongly recommended to Starfleet that we make every effort to recover as many other adult captives as possible."

Ruthe uncoiled her body, standing straight up on the bed, glaring down on the captain. For a moment, Picard thought she was going to attack him. Instead, the woman leapt down to the deck.

"Show me this drug." She drew the billowing folds of her cape back around her body and followed Picard out of the cabin.

When they arrived at sickbay, Beverly Crusher assumed the neutral manner of a medical professional, but not before Picard caught the look of relief in her eyes. He also saw Deelor's surprise . . . and a hint of displeasure at the captain's success.

Ruthe repeated her demand to see the drug, and Crusher handed the translator a small glass vial holding a few milliliters of amber liquid.

"I noticed the scent when Lieutenant Yar returned from the Choraii ship."

Ruthe unstopped the end and took a tentative whiff of the contents. "Cinnamon," she whispered.

She remained frozen in place, cupping the vial in her hand, until Deelor called to her. "Ruthe?"

"I'd forgotten." Her eyes were still focused on some inner vision. Then Deelor's touch on her arm pulled her back to the room in which she stood. She slipped the top back onto the vial, sealing in the aroma.

"You've encountered this drug before?" asked the captain.

"Years ago," Ruthe said. "When I was a child."

Picard did not understand. "But how is that possible?"

She slipped the vial into the folds of her cloak. "I was born on a Choraii ship."

Chapter Fourteen

"She doesn't usually tell anyone," said Deelor as he and the captain walked into the Ready Room. With a pointed look at the doorway of her office, Dr. Crusher had made it clear she wanted to speak to Ruthe without the distractions of an audience. "And it wasn't my secret to reveal."

"Yes, I can understand that," Picard said, nodding. "The surprises on this mission never seem to end," he added.

The captain took his place behind the office desk, leaning back in his chair and swiveling to the side in order to talk to Deelor, who was admiring the lionfish. "When was she rescued?"

"In the first exchange, fifteen years ago." Now that her origins were known, Deelor decided there was little point in keeping back the details. "She was one of the five captives traded to the Ferengi." By settling down onto a chair, he exchanged his view of the aquarium for that of the star window behind Picard.

"And all three of the adults died," recalled Picard. "No wonder Ruthe refused to help bring Jason back to the *Enterprise*. What of the other child?"

"Alive and well. She was younger than Ruthe and adjusted to living with humans rather quickly." According to their case histories, Ruthe's transition had been more difficult, but that was none of Picard's business.

"Well, I certainly admire her courage," said the captain. "This mission must be a painful reminder of her own captivity."

"She volunteered for the work. With her help, the Federation has recovered five Hamlin offspring over the last few years." Though Deelor suspected that several captives had slipped away before he learned of her aversion to trading for adults.

"I suppose the opportunity to help rescue other Hamlin survivors makes the distress worthwhile," said Picard.

"Yes, it must." At least Deelor had thought so at first. Yet once the exchanges were complete, Ruthe never asked about the children. That thought brought another to mind. "How did you persuade her to come to sickbay?"

"Reverse psychology." Picard outlined the strategy he had used. "So the only way she could fight my decision to rescue more adults was to come to sickbay and prove they aren't being mistreated by the Choraii."

"Yes, of course. Quite clever, Captain." Deelor had spent his career manipulating people in just that manner, and often his life, as well as his mission, depended on that skill. Such a simple ploy should have been obvious to him. Why hadn't he thought of it?

Once the question had been posed, he touched on an answer and immediately shied away from it. Deelor always traveled alone. He didn't need complications.

Dr. Crusher had never spoken to Ruthe alone before. At close quarters, without the distraction of Andrew Deelor's strong personality, the woman's reserved manner was even more accentuated. The lack of expression would go unremarked in a Vulcan, but in a human such behavior was oddly disturbing. For the first time Crusher saw Ruthe as more than just a passenger. She was also a patient.

"The drug is harmless," said Ruthe as she handed the vial of cinnamon-scented liquid back to Crusher. "The Choraii were probably trying to help with the transfer. Without its influence Jason would have been much warier of Lieutenant Yar's approach."

The doctor was not mollified by the translator's interpretation of the drug's purpose. "That may be the case, but it increased his agitation when he was beamed over."

"They always react violently at first, even the young ones." Ruthe cocked her head. The faint cries of a child could be heard through the walls of sickbay. "Is that the other one?"

"Yes," sighed Crusher. Iovino's magical touch was no substitute for food, and the boy still wasn't eating.

"The cinnamon would calm him down."

"He needs food, not drugs." The doctor fought to keep anger out of her voice. She couldn't afford to alienate the translator now. Instead, Crusher used the subject to lead into a discussion of Ruthe's past. "What did you first eat when you left the Choraii ship?"

Ruthe shrugged indifferently. "I don't remember."

Crusher had expected continued resistance. Even

without the psych profiles in her medical file, the doctor would have guessed that Ruthe's emotional distance served as a shield, protecting her from a painful past. Yet Jason's best hope for survival lay in getting Ruthe to remember what she would rather forget.

"I have a plan for treating Jason, but I need your help."

"I've already answered your questions about the cinnamon," said Ruthe. "That's all I agreed to do." She turned her back on the doctor.

"I want to recreate the Choraii interior on a holodeck," said Crusher calmly. "If Jason can return to a familiar environment, he might be lured out of his emotional withdrawal." She watched for the slightest sign of a reaction from Ruthe, but the woman was difficult enough to read face-to-face. Trying not to exert any obvious pressure, Crusher continued the explanation. "Data has enough sensor-scan information to determine the broad characteristics of the bubble structure and the composition of the atmosphere. Lieutenant Yar can provide some idea of the interior, but not many details. You're the only person who can confirm the authenticity of the final effect."

"That child is very noisy," said Ruthe. "Don't you get tired of all that crying?"

"Yes, I do." Don't force, Crusher reminded herself. Let her choose to help on her own.

"Try grapes." Ruthe turned back around to face the doctor. "Or anything round with a soft center. The Choraii food always came in bubbles." Having delivered that one piece of advice, she left sickbay.

Dr. Crusher tapped her com link. "Data, I'm ready to begin the holodeck project." Ruthe hadn't said no, and that was promising enough to start work.

* * *

At first glance the construction of the room was simple, its boxlike dimensions established by plain, undecorated walls and an uncarpeted flooring. Appearances were deceiving. The holodeck was one of the most highly sophisticated technological features of the *Enterprise*.

This particular holodeck was smaller than the one that held the Oregon farm, and the illusion it created was confined to the center of the room. A single transparent bubble quivered in place, its curving lines flattened at the contact point with the deck. The slick surface glistened in the sourceless ambient light used to illuminate the early design stage of the project.

Inside the sphere, Tasha Yar hung suspended, treading water with lazy strokes, her blond hair drifting like a halo around her head. She waved one hand and the simulation faded, dropping her down to the deck with a thump.

"Data!" she cried in protest. Rising from the crouch that absorbed the shock of her fall, she swept aside a lock of hair trailing down over her eyes.

The android looked up from the control panel at the entrance to the room, his brows contracting in puzzlement. He caught the irritation in Yar's voice, but it took him a moment to construct the reason for the emotion and infer that an apology was necessary. "Sorry. The gravity field is tied to the other program parameters. An entry portal will be necessary eventually, but I have concentrated on the interior of the Choraii vessel. However, I can take the time to . . ."

"Don't worry about it." Yar brushed absently at her uniform, then stopped when she realized the material was dry. When Data had suspended the program, all the liquid had been removed along with the exterior shell. "The feel of the program is getting better, though."

"Could you be more specific?" he asked.

"The temperature feels right and so does the density of the liquid. I think." She concentrated on recapturing the physical sensations of her brief visit to the Choraii ship. The memories, which she had thought were indelible, blurred a little more with every exposure to the holodeck projection. "But something's not the same."

Data opened his mouth to speak, but Yar held up a hand to stop him. "I know, please be more specific," she said. The android nodded and she tried again. "The buoyancy is still wrong."

"In what way?" asked Data. Dr. Crusher had provided samples of the interior atmosphere, a few milliliters wrung from Yar's clothing, but the properties of the substance were difficult to determine from such minute quantities. As the mass of the liquid increased, its qualities changed. This mutability was fascinating from a theoretical point of view, but frustrating for his attempts to duplicate its effects.

"I can't tell. It just feels off." Yar hurried on with more items before he could try to pin her down. "And the walls are still too stiff."

"Ah. That particular logarithm is also very interesting," said Data as he adjusted the program parameter for the bubble construction. "The Choraii exhibit an amazing ability to control surface tension."

"And can we try it with the color added?" asked Yar. "Maybe that will help make it seem more real."

Data nodded and entered another series of numbers into the control sequence. The broad structures of the Choraii ship were set, but these subliminal details played an equally important role in establishing a proper credibility. Unfortunately, human imprecision was further lengthening the time-consuming process. If Data had beamed over to the *B Flat* instead of the lieutenant, the project would be completed by now. He initiated the program run once again.

"Hey!" Yar was pulled up into the air without warning as the low-gravity field reactivated. A translucent orange sphere popped into existence around her.

When Wesley Crusher entered the Farmer holodeck, the sunlit meadows were still wet from morning rain and a faint rainbow stretched across the sky. The idyllic vista was completed by the sight of white lambs bounding over the rich carpet of moist green grass and a leggy colt racing around a grazing herd of calves. Walking through scattered patches of wildflower, Wesley wondered how soon the mushrooms would come up and whether anyone would notice them.

"Fine weather we're having," said Old Steven when Wesley passed by the orchard. The man was sitting on a fallen log, carefully peeling an apple with his pocketknife.

"It certainly is," answered the boy. He couldn't tell whether Old Steven meant the comment as a compliment or a simple observation. In either case, it would be rude to admit credit. He walked on.

Wesley was a frequent visitor to the farm, and despite his starship dress, the ensign managed to blend remarkably well into the Farmer community. He cultivated the same purposeful stride that Dnnys used on his way to chores, and kept his opinions to himself like a well-behaved Farmer boy. Eventually even the most hostile of the colonists had grown accustomed to his presence. Most were content to ignore him; others, like Old Steven and Mry, were openly friendly in their greetings.

"Dnnys is up in the loft," said Mry when Wesley entered the barn. She was in charge of feeding the rabbits and was busily preparing bottled milk for their next meal.

Scooping up one of the young animals, Wesley

stroked the long ears and marveled at the soft texture of their fur. "You get wool from the sheep and milk from the cows, but what do you do with the rabbits?"

"We eat them," said Mry.

He looked down at the soft brown bundle. "Eat them?"

"Of course. Why so surprised?" She reached her hands out for the animal he held.

"I don't know." He gave over the rabbit, but not without a pang of remorse. "I guess I just assumed you were vegetarians."

"They are cute at this age," agreed the Farmer as the rabbit licked at the bottle. "But they also taste good. And the fur is warm."

"Watch out!" cried a voice from above, but not soon enough for Wesley to sidestep the load from a pitchfork. Dnnys peered down over the edge of the loft and grinned at the sight of his friend coughing his way out of the loose hay. "Come on up where it's safe."

Wesley scrambled quickly up the ladder. At close quarters he could see the strain behind the Farmer boy's smile.

"How did I do?" whispered Dnnys. He stabbed the pitchfork into a cut bale, rustling the dried grass to cover the sound of their voices.

"I checked the test answers this morning. Passing grade, but just barely."

Dnnys frowned for a moment, then sighed in resignation. "If I had more time to study, I think I could do better."

"I *know* you could," said Wesley. "You've picked up the math concepts really quickly and you've got a lot of practical experience from your journey. Now all you need is more practice." He took the pitchfork from Dnnys's hands and tossed a load of hay over the edge. "So get to work. I can't cover your chores for more than an hour."

Dnnys scrambled to the back of the barn and pulled a book out from under a loose board. The pages fell open to the middle of the volume. Squinting in the dim light of the loft, the boy began to read.

Iovino plucked the last green grape from a denuded stem. Several other bare branches were scattered about the table. "Grape?" she asked, enunciating clearly.

Moses nodded vigorously and reached out for the piece of fruit. Snatching the food from her hand, Moses placed the grape against tightly pursed lips, then sucked. It entered his mouth with a faint pop. He held out his hand for more.

"That's enough grapes for now," said Iovino. The boy had eaten nothing else that day, but it was a good beginning on solid food. He even recognized the sound of the word. Another more serious difficulty remained, however. He refused to swallow liquids. Perhaps the food on his homeships had provided sufficient water, but on board the *Enterprise* he was chronically dehydrated.

Iovino had a plan for changing that.

Making a deliberate show of her actions, exaggerating all her body movements to capture the boy's attention, she reached for a glass of water on the table. A brightly colored straw stuck up from the rim. Iovino slowly lifted the glass up to her mouth and sucked noisily on the straw until her cheeks were puffed out with the water she held in her mouth.

Pushing her face up to his, Iovino squirted the liquid right at Moses. Water dribbled down from his forehead over his face and cheeks and down his chin. He laughed with delight at the trick.

"You like that one?" she asked. "Want me to do it

again?" He didn't react to the words, but when she lifted the glass again he crowed.

She repeated the sequence several times, then presented the boy with the drinking straw. He didn't need any coaching on its use, which added an interesting note to his sparse file, and filled his mouth with water just as she had. His technique was better than hers. A jet of liquid splattered against Iovino's nose.

"Very good," laughed the intern. "Now it's my turn again." The game continued back and forth until they were both drenched. She refilled the glass and offered Moses the straw, but this time slipped her hands up to his mouth before he could spew out the water. Her thumbs sealed his lips and an index finger pressing in on each cheek forced the water down the boy's throat.

He didn't laugh, but before he could cry Iovino offered him a chance to play the same trick on her. She swallowed a mouthful of liquid when his clumsy fingers poked at her face. "Wasn't that fun?"

Moses evidently agreed, because he sucked from the straw and puffed out his cheeks but didn't spit out the contents. Instead, he waited for the doctor to play her part in this new game.

Dr. Crusher read parts of Iovino's report aloud to the captain, but out of deference to the intern's dignity she refrained from showing him the visual record. The sight of the boy gleefully squirting water into Lisa's face had provided the chief medical officer with some much needed comic relief, but the scene would remain private.

"A resourceful approach," agreed Picard. He smiled at the doctor's description of the water fight, but he was disturbed by the drawn quality of Beverly Crusher's face. Fatigue accentuated her high cheekbones and washed the color from her fair skin.

"She's one of my best doctors," said Crusher proudly, unaware of Picard's scrutiny. "The boy is making good progress under her care. He may be walking by the time we reach Starbase Ten. Of course, it helps that he's so young. Children have an amazing ability to adapt to new environments."

Fifteen years ago the translator had gone through the same rehabilitation. Picard tried to calculate the time difference, but her present age was difficult to determine. "How old was Ruthe when she was rescued?"

"The results of her initial medical exam indicated she was about ten, but that estimate could be off by several years. There's practically no information on the effects of the Choraii environment on early physical development."

"Ten years old," said Picard thoughtfully. "Imagine learning to breathe air, to walk and talk, to drink water, all for the first time at that age."

"Worse yet," said Crusher, "imagine that effort at over fifty years of age." Her expectations for Jason's rehabilitation were more modest: to keep him alive. The holodeck project had seemed promising at first, however Yar's recall was limited and Data was increasingly guarded about the chances of designing a convincing simulation.

"Beverly, you're limping," said Picard sharply as he watched the doctor cross the room to her desk.

"I hadn't noticed." Now that he brought it to her attention, Crusher felt a dull throb in her right leg. The realization didn't trouble her. She had experienced intermittent pain since injuring the leg two weeks before.

"I thought the wound had healed." The laceration had been deep and the resultant loss of blood very nearly proved fatal. In fact Picard had never really admitted to himself how close Beverly Crusher had come to dying on the planet Minos.

"It has healed. I've just been on my feet for too long."

"Aren't you the one who warned me about feeling invincible?"

Crusher laughed wanly. "I feel more like a squashed bug."

"Then get some sleep, like the rest of us." He refrained from telling her how tired she looked.

Dr. Crusher was too preoccupied to listen to the advice. She turned to him and for a moment her professional composure dropped away, as if she were lowering a piece of armor that had grown too heavy to hold in place. "Jean-Luc, if we don't succeed in creating the Choraii ship holo, I don't know what else I can do for Jason."

Her voice betrayed a quality of fear Picard had never heard before, not even when her own life had been in danger in the caverns of Minos. Then, as now, he had no answers.

The simulation released Yar from its hold. She had learned to anticipate the fall now and landed upright on two feet without losing her balance. Her legs ached from the repeated impact and the deck was marred by scuff marks from her boots, but she was too proud to ask Data to add the entry portal ahead of schedule. Especially since her performance was hindering their progress.

The android looked at her expectantly, waiting for a comment.

"I can't tell anymore," cried Yar, throwing up her hands in despair. "Warmer, colder, more pressure, less pressure. Data, we've tried it so many different ways that I'm all mixed up now." At one time her mind had retained a crisp, clear image of the Choraii ship, but that picture could no longer be trusted. Whenever she reached out to touch it, the image shifted away like a desert mirage.

"Perhaps we should work on the viscosity index next," suggested Data. "You said that was near completion."

"When did I say that?" groaned Yar. "Data, it doesn't make any sense to go on." She turned her burning face away from the android.

Data possessed an infinite store of patience, and he would have continued for as long as necessary, but he felt the futility of their efforts as well. "Dr. Crusher will be disappointed." Human emotions often puzzled him, but he had detected Dr. Crusher's reliance on this project. And her urgency.

He called up the projection image again and studied its appearance critically. Regardless of the interior programming, the exterior of the Choraii bubble matched his visual records. "Perhaps this will be sufficient for the treatment."

"Maybe," sighed Yar. She tried one last time to summon a memory that had not been overwritten with the trial and error of their design experiments, only to sense a further retreat of that reality; her brief experience had been too fragile to withstand hard use.

Data resigned himself to the fact that the project had reached its end. He prepared to lock in his most recent model when the startled look on Yar's face alerted him to the presence of a third person.

Neither of them had heard Ruthe's approach. The translator appeared as if from thin air at the holodeck entrance. She stood silent and unmoving, mesmerized by the translucent orange sphere inside. Then, as if pulled over the threshold against her will, she took one step closer, then another, gliding across the floor until she was within an arm's reach of the image.

Ruthe stretched out a hand to touch the bubble's surface. When her fingers met resistance, she pulled back as if burned by the contact. She turned to face Yar. "How can I get inside?"

Chapter Fifteen

RUTHE FLOATED FREELY in the warm ocean at the very center of the Choraii cluster. The innermost sphere was large, several times her length, bounded on all sides by the flat ovals marking its joining with the spheres around it. With lazy strokes she swam up to the faceted surface and kicked her feet against the smooth shell, stretching the flexible fabric. The spring of the wall's return pushed her across the interior to the far side. Her steepled fingers pierced an entry membrane to another sphere. She glided through to the other side and heard the pop of the closing gate. Stamping the flat of her foot against the nearest surface, she gained another burst of speed. She sped onward in that manner through a succession of spheres.

Her race through the cluster of bubbles had begun for the sheer joy of it. She moved in time to a lilting music which rippled through the surrounding liquid and shivered across her skin. She tumbled and bounced with careless ease until a darker, deeper thrumming sound began to drown out the dance. Fear chased after her. The game became a hunt and she was the prey.

As Ruthe swam onward, the spheres of the cluster grew smaller. She shot through them faster and faster, but the chase continued. Kick, glide, kick glide. When she saw the defracted light of stars sparkling and glittering through the curved hull, she knew she was trapped in the outside layer of the Choraii ship. The sound of snapping gates grew louder as her pursuer drew closer. A current washed over her, carrying an unfamiliar smell, one that reeked of danger.

Terror overcame all reason. Ruthe dove through the last wall, screaming as she hit the icy cold vacuum of space beyond and the liquid was sucked from out of her lungs . . .

Deelor scrambled through the dark of the cabin, led by the sounds of Ruthe's screams to the corner where she had been sleeping. He wrapped himself around her thrashing body and called her name over and over again until her cries gave way to sobbing and she stopped struggling against his embrace. Gradually, as he stroked her hair and continued a constant whisper of reassurances, the tension in her muscles eased. Toward morning, when she fell back into a restless sleep, Deelor left her side.

"Don't look down," said Yar as she led the others into the holodeck.

Beverly Crusher automatically checked her feet. She was standing over a black pit, light-years away from the stars shining below. Fighting against a wave of vertigo, the doctor raised her eyes and concentrated on the orange sphere suspended in front of her. Data had suggested placing the Choraii bubble in a cosmic setting and Crusher had agreed that it would add to the reality of the experience. The result was stunning. And disorienting.

"You were warned," said Troi with a sympathetic smile.

"Now, remember, don't fight against breathing in." Yar didn't bother to disguise her obvious enjoyment at the opportunity to quote the doctor's advice back to her. "Just inhale the liquid. Nothing to it."

"Thank you, Tasha," said Crusher dryly. She reminded herself that this was only a holodeck simulation, not an actual Choraii ship, but that knowledge was of little help once she had slipped through the entry portal into the alien environment. Bobbing gently in the liquid interior, her body refused to accept her mind's order to breathe.

With expert breast strokes, the doctor swam to Jason's side. Yar had transported him directly from sickbay to the center of the projection. He was still floating in a ball, but one less tightly curled than before. Crusher reached for the scanner strapped to her side and began her medical inspection. A wide pass over his body showed that his system had fully metabolized the last trace of sedatives; brain activity indicated that he was aware of her presence. That was a definite improvement in his condition.

Crusher swam back to the portal, but just before leaving the bubble she forced herself to take a quick breath of the atmosphere, filling her lungs with the unaccustomed weight and pressure of liquid. Crusher's respect for Yar increased severalfold. The security chief had guts.

"It's working," said Crusher upon her exit. She gathered up her hair and wrung out the remains of the watery interior. Rivulets of liquid coursed down over her uniform, pooling on the surface of the invisible deck. "He's coming out of it."

"Yes," agreed Troi with less enthusiasm. The emotions she sensed from Jason's awakening were far from reassuring.

Patrisha was still holding the textbook in her hands when Dnnys entered the room.

"That's mine," he said tightly.

"I'm sorry, Dnnys. I didn't mean to pry." She laid the book down on the cabin dresser, next to the clothes she had pulled out from the drawers. "I was packing your things for our arrival on New Oregon. You've been so busy lately . . ." Her finger trailed over the title of the book. "I can see why now."

He dropped his gaze to the floor. "I'm not sorry. Whatever the punishment, I won't say I'm sorry."

"No, I wouldn't expect you to," sighed Patrisha. "If Tomas hasn't beat any sense into you by now, there's no hope left."

Her son's head jerked back up, his eyes flashing with anger. "You don't believe in their silly rules. Why should I?"

Patrisha felt her throat tighten with fear. "Is it that obvious?" she asked.

"Maybe not to the others, but I could tell."

"And this book. What will you gain from reading it?"

"A mechanics license," said Dnnys. "And passage off New Oregon on the first freighter that needs an extra hand."

Jason could be seen from the outside of the Choraii bubble, but only as a pale, ghostly shape drifting from one place to another. His eyes were closed and he did

203

not react to the three people who watched him and talked about him in low voices. Although his arms and legs had unfolded from around his body, their movements were listless and limited.

"What if Data repeats the bubble pattern and creates a cluster?" suggested Beverly Crusher. Her brows had pulled together, marking her forehead with worry. "The structure would be even closer to the original . . ."

"That won't help," said Troi. "The construction of the sphere is not the issue. He is reaching out for something we cannot provide." Once again, though with some trepidation, the counselor thinned her emotional shields and felt what Jason felt. She searched for words to describe his yearning, the sense of abandonment, but her voice choked with tears.

"He's listening for the Choraii," said Ruthe quietly. She stood apart from the other two women. "Even though he knows they've gone."

"Will you play for him?" Crusher asked. "Maybe your music can reach him."

The translator stood still for a moment before speaking. "When I was little and my mother and I still swam through the waters of our homeship, she would tell me the story of Hamlin. How a child heard the song of the Choraii and laughed and clapped with joy at the glorious sound of their music, even though everything around her was turning to dust and fire. And the Choraii saved the child, and all the other children, so they could listen to the melodies for the rest of their lives."

"How horrible," cried Troi.

"Do you think so?" wondered Ruthe softly.

"Ruthe," Crusher asked through the tightness in her throat. "Please help us save Jason."

The woman shook her head. "You missed the point. The weak breath of my flute can't compare with the

music of the singers. Besides, all I feel are sad songs."
She turned and walked out of the holodeck.

"Damn her," said the doctor angrily.

Troi reached out and grabbed hold of Crusher's arm. "Beverly, this is affecting her, too. When Ruthe first came on board, she had insulated herself from all feelings. Now she is being forced to relive her past through Jason and through the child. I can sense so many emotions coming to life in her. We must be very careful in what we ask her to do."

"Well, it doesn't make any sense to me," said Riker as he and Data strolled through the corridors on their way to the bridge. "How can you even have a religion if you can't talk about it?"

"Some cultures forbid discussion about sex and yet they manage to reproduce." Data hadn't meant to provide amusement, but the first officer laughed at the remark.

Data shook his head. "You never evince the same response at my jokes."

"That's because they're never funny," Riker said, and laughed even harder.

"The subject requires much study," admitted Data.

"I'm not sure you can develop a sense of humor by studying," said Riker. He caught sight of a familiar form and sought to overtake the woman walking ahead of them. "It comes naturally."

"Like sleep?" Data absently matched the first officer's lengthening stride. "That is also a difficult concept. So far I have failed to comprehend the appeal of unconsciousness."

Riker was no longer listening. "Deanna."

Troi didn't turn until he had called her name twice over. "What's wrong?" Riker asked sharply when he saw her face.

"I'm just tired," said the counselor. Her hand lifted

up and touched the dampness on her cheek. "Oh, I've been crying."

"Deanna . . ."

"I'm fine, Will. I've just spent too many hours with the Hamlin captive. He's so lonely, so filled with despair."

Acutely conscious of the side glances of passing crew members, and of Data's undisguised curiosity, Riker was still unwilling to abandon Troi. "I'll walk you to your cabin."

"Thank you, Will," said Troi, then quickly added, "but I'd rather be by myself just now. These are only borrowed emotions, but until I untangle their influence . . . I'm vulnerable." Quickening her pace, Troi followed two passengers into a turboelevator.

"Deanna!"

The doors snapped shut between them.

"I also have a number of questions concerning the production of tears," said Data. "Perhaps this would be a good—"

"Not now, Data," snapped Riker, and broke into a fast walk.

"Then again, perhaps not," said Data to himself. He added another query to his running list of perplexing human behaviors.

Dr. Iovino wiped the water off the front of her uniform. "I guess you've had enough," she said, pulling the glass away from Moses. She hadn't yet convinced him what fun it would be to stop playing the drinking game with his meals.

"No!" shouted the boy emphatically.

"I thought you might say that." She talked to him constantly and his understanding seemed to be growing rapidly, almost as if he were already familiar with the language, yet he had been slow to talk. At the moment he possessed a vocabulary of one word. "In case you're interested, your behavioral development is right on schedule."

"No!"

"Exactly my point. That's why it's called the 'terrible twos.' Right?" Then she answered her own questions so that together they cried out the inevitable, "No!" Moses giggled with delight at the chorus of their voices.

A shadow fell across the floor and Iovino looked up to see who had entered the room. She recognized the woman as one of the survivors of the *USS Ferrel* and suspected that Ruthe was somehow connected to the child's unexplained appearance in sickbay. She seemed something like a shy child herself. Lisa ignored Ruthe's presence and continued talking to the boy.

"Look what I've got." Iovino held up a piece of chocolate. Moses had made the leap forward to solid food and this was one of his favorite items. "Do you want some?"

"No!" he declared happily.

She whisked it behind her back and waited for his reaction. When he started to whimper, she spoke very clearly. "But you said you didn't want it."

Despite his sulking, he listened carefully to what she said.

"Do you want some?" Iovino proferred the treat again. "Yes?"

His lower lip stopped quivering. "Yesss," he said with an exaggerated sibilance. He grabbed the treat from her hand and was all smiles again.

"He looks happy," said Ruthe with a hint of surprise in her voice.

"He's got a good disposition. Moses will do fine wherever he ends up." The doctor frowned at her own comment. She had been so busy with his present welfare that she hadn't really thought about his future. Suddenly, she was curious as to what would happen to this strange child.

"I wonder if they're all like him."

"All of who?" asked Iovino. Now the surprise was hers.

"The other children. I've tried not to think about them, but maybe they're happy, too."

The woman left as abruptly as she had appeared, leaving Iovino alone to ponder that tantalizing scrap of information. Thoughtfully, the doctor watched Moses eat the last crumbs of candy. He nibbled with dainty bites that left his face remarkably clean for such a young child, but then, the boy hated to get dirty. Wet was all right, however. "Just think, Moses. More kids like you."

"Yesss," he said with great conviction.

Jason slipped out of life quickly and quietly.

He floated in peace for a full minute before the medic team reached the holodeck and shattered the illusion of the Choraii sphere. A knot of people, with Beverly Crusher at the center, gathered over the man laid out on the hard surface of the unadorned compartment. Harsh mechanical chatters and raised voices echoed between the flat walls as the emergency revival equipment was activated over and over again.

Ruthe watched the doctors fight over the pale, still body, but she knew their frantic efforts were in vain. Jason had escaped.

Dr. Crusher was slumped over the desk, her head cradled in her arms, but Picard saw there was too much tension in her spine for her to be asleep. He took another step forward into the office.

"Beverly?" She straightened in place but didn't speak to him. "You've lost patients before," he said softly.

"Injured ones, yes," she answered at last. "With wounds too severe for me to heal or diseases that can't be cured. Those deaths are unavoidable. But Jason was well and I couldn't keep him alive."

"It was my decision to bring him on board."

"I'm not blaming you. I'm not even blaming myself. At the time, it seemed the right thing to do, but Ruthe knew better. We should have left him where he was."

"In captivity?" His abhorrence of the Hamlin children's circumstances was not easily dismissed.

"To him, *this* was captivity," she said, waving at the enclosure of the ship's hull. "Jean-Luc, Jason committed suicide. Not outright, not by damaging his body, but simply by deciding to die."

Picard listened to the tremor in her voice with deepening concern and was struck anew by her pallor. "You're much too tired for this discussion."

"I can't sleep," she said brusquely, rising from behind the desk. "I've got work to do."

"You won't bring Jason back to life by running around sickbay."

"I've got other patients to care for."

"Don't you trust your own staff, Dr. Crusher?"

"Well, of course I—"

"Then what's the problem?"

"Actually, I think I'm too tired to sleep."

Picard knew the feeling. After a certain point, exhaustion fed on itself and the mind raced on without regard to the body's need for rest. "A sedative would change that."

"Don't practice medicine without a license," she advised, heading toward the office doorway. "And I won't give orders on the bridge."

He let her brush past him and stalk out into the anteroom, then followed in her wake. She didn't go far before another doctor waylaid her.

"What is it, Iovino?" Crusher asked impatiently.

"I have a question about Moses."

Picard waited until the young intern was standing by Crusher's side, then he called out, "Beverly . . ."

She looked back toward him. With admirable slight of hand, Iovino whipped out a hypo spray and placed it against the chief medical officer's arm. Crusher jerked away at the sound of the hiss, but not before the contents had been injected into her system.

"What the hell are you doing, Iovino?"

"Following my orders," said Picard, walking up to them. He had hoped to avoid this surprise tactic, but given Crusher's obstinacy, there seemed little alternative. Fortunately, Dr. Iovino had readily agreed to the maneuver.

"Dammit, nobody orders my medical staff around but me," Crusher stormed at Picard. He was unmoved by her fury. She turned on Iovino. "Retranine?"

"Ten cc."

"I should put you on report for this."

"Just don't spit at me," said the intern without any remorse. "I'm tired of being spit at."

Crusher swayed in place. The sedative was already taking effect. With a sigh of exasperation, she said, "Five cc would have been more appropriate."

Iovino shrugged. "I knew I had to inject through your jacket."

"Oh, right," said Crusher. Her head was suddenly very heavy.

"Come on." Picard took her firmly by the elbow. "I'll walk you to your cabin."

* * *

The night-shift crew on the bridge was small. Data supervised the helm while Lieutenant Worf controlled the aft deck. Other support personnel were close at hand, but the Klingon did not call for assistance. He ran another check on the communications board, his third so far, and reported the results with an impassive expression. "No response."

"Damn." Riker leaned forward in the captain's chair. "Data?"

"We are within contact range, sir," said Data, turning from his position at the ops control. "The lack of radio transmissions indicates something is amiss."

The first officer ticked off the possible reasons for New Oregon's silence. "Equipment malfunction, ion storm interference . . ."

"That possibility had already occurred to me," interceded Data. "I ran the requisite sensor scan and found normal ion levels."

Riker continued with, "Frequency confusion . . ."

"Checking all communications bands," declared Worf as his heavy hands touched lightly on the console surface. "No transmissions from that sector on any frequency."

Riker sighed heavily. "Which leaves us with equipment malfunction on the planet surface or . . ." He let the unfinished phrase dangle in air.

"Further conjecture would be highly speculative," Data pointed out.

"I know, Data, but we'll have to assume the worst until we know otherwise; standard procedure demands that interpretation. What's our estimated arrival time?"

"Fifteen hours, twenty-three minutes—" Data paused, then continued hurriedly, "And five seconds."

Riker was too busy thinking to cut Data off. A lot

could happen in fifteen hours. "Increase speed to warp seven."

"Warp seven," confirmed Data, and the ship responded with an almost imperceptible shudder.

The captain would feel it though. This time Riker hit the com link before Picard could demand an explanation. "Captain, request your presence on the bridge."

Chapter Sixteen

DR. CRUSHER WAS the last member of the crew to receive a summons. She rubbed at sleep-weary eyes and tried to make sense of the tableau on the bridge. A full crew complement was assembled. Worf and Yar were hunched over the tactical console, too caught up in their observations to acknowledge the doctor's entrance. They worked with the concentration typical of an alert status. With growing unease, Crusher walked down to the command center, where the captain stood huddled in discussion with Riker and Andrew Deelor. Both Geordi and Data were at the forward stations.

Picard looked up at her approach and broke off his conversation with the other men. He had waited until the last minute before calling the doctor, allowing her to get as much rest as possible, but it was time for her to learn what had happened. She was the only medical officer with the proper security clearance for the work ahead.

Crusher studied the image on the main viewer—a beige planet streaked with pale green bands. "New Oregon? We're ahead of schedule."

"Yes," said Picard. "There's been a problem."

"Problem? What kind of problem?"

"We believe the colony was attacked."

The flat tone of Picard's voice should have alerted Crusher to what was coming, but her mind rejected the implications. "Why have I been called to the bridge? I should be down on the planet with my medical team."

Riker opened his mouth to reply, but the captain silenced him with an uplifted hand. Picard preferred to break the news himself. "It's too late for any medical assistance, Dr. Crusher."

"No survivors?" Stunned, she sank down onto a chair. An exhaustion of spirit as well as body swept over her. Sickbay had already been prepared for the upcoming medical check of the colony's Federation workers, over twenty terraform engineers, mechanics, and technicians. "All of them dead?"

Picard forestalled any false hope. "There are no life signs left on the planet surface. Even the vegetation is dying." By the time Geordi La Forge had brought the *Enterprise* into orbit around New Oregon, sensor scans had proven that the need for urgency had passed. The radio bands would continue to be silent.

"How? Why?" Crusher asked, then found the answer for herself in Andrew Deelor's presence. "The Choraii."

"Possibly," said Picard. "Data detected a faint trace of organic particles on the outskirts of the solar system. The evidence is still circumstantial, but highly suggestive. We won't know for certain until the away team has checked the surface."

Data turned from his ops console. "I have established transporter coordinates for both the terraform-

214

ing station and the Farmer outpost. What is left of them. I sorted through considerable scattered rubble for a clear spot that would accommodate a landing party." He pointed to an ominous red patch on his sensor screen. "And weather conditions will be quite harsh. The atmosphere-control fields have failed."

"Two teams," ordered Picard briskly. "One to each location." One of the hardest lessons of command had been to accept the away team as a substitute for his own presence, to use it as his eyes and ears and hands. Riker would quote safety as the reason for keeping the captain on the bridge, but Picard had come to realize that he usually could do his job better at a distance, calling alternately on the resources of his ship or the mission crew.

Riker quickly assembled the first group. "Data, Yar, check out the Farmers' settlement."

The designated officers abandoned their stations, leaving La Forge and Worf alone at opposite ends of the bridge. The first officer pointed to Deelor and Crusher next. "We'll cover the control station. The greatest devastation will be there."

Crusher pushed herself up from the chair, drawing on a reserve of energy that was nearly depleted. "I'm supposed to save lives," she said to no one in particular. "But lately I've done nothing but record death."

Riker's landing party materialized on a broad, featureless plain. Cold, driving rain lashed down over them, and clouds of deep purple hid the overhead sun from view, turning mid-afternoon into late evening. Beneath their feet, a thick carpet of plants lay rotting in the water-logged soil. The first officer scanned the horizon for signs of habitation.

"Over there," said Deelor, pointing to a spot several dozen meters away.

Riker lowered his gaze. Terraforming stations were built for utility rather than for beauty, but the structure on New Oregon now lacked both qualities. The squat tubes and bulbous domes of the operations center had been torn apart and smashed flat.

Leading the approach to the attack site, Riker picked his way through the standing water which covered the ground. Despite his caution, he stumbled over a piece of debris hidden in the mud. Reaching down, he pulled out a chunk of contorted metal. Its original function was impossible to determine, but the falling rain washed away the covering grime and revealed charred patches on its surface. Riker handed the fragment over to Deelor, who inspected it with great interest.

"The outer layer is completely carbonized," he observed. His thumbnail scratched a thin bright line across the surface.

"I'll look for the bodies," said Crusher, and walked on slowly. Her eyes swept over the burned construction materials. When her tricorder beeped suddenly, she took a closer look at a blackened lump in her path. "I've found something, Commander."

"That's a body?" asked Riker when he had answered her call. His face paled and he swallowed convulsively.

The doctor nodded and held up her tricorder. "Elevated calcium levels indicate the presence of bone inside." She waved the instrument over the outer perimeter of the collapsed station. "I register several more corpses over there, buried beneath ashes and rubble. Also burned."

"The fire must have been very intense to cause this much damage," said Riker.

"Not fire." Deelor kicked aside a loose metal plate lying next to the body. "The signs of a pressure impact are unmistakable. A hammer blow from a force field crushed the area. That was followed by an acid bath."

"How can you be so sure?" asked Riker.

"I've seen records of a similar pattern of destruction on another planet. It's Hamlin all over again."

Data monitored the open channel of Riker's communicator, comparing Deelor's description of the terraforming station to the blackened ruins of the farming settlement. Spars of timber lay rotting in jumbled piles. The hard rain had turned tilled fields into seas of mud.

"The Choraii have been here as well," Data reported to Picard. "There is very little remaining of the wooden structures. Even less remains of the people who lived in them."

"I joined Starfleet in order to stop things like this from happening," said Yar, surveying the destruction. Her mouth settled into a hard line. "This time we arrived too late."

Once again the conference room was filled to capacity. Captain Picard contrasted this briefing session with the one that had occurred some two weeks ago and noted the differences. Wesley Crusher, who usually made a point of sitting away from his mother, had headed straight for her side in search of comfort. Counselor Troi, also shaken by the news of the colony's destruction, was less obvious in her need, yet she was seated next to Riker. Their close proximity would mean little to most of the room's occupants, but the captain recognized its significance.

One person was conspicuously absent. Picard turned to the ambassador. "Where is Ruthe?"

"I didn't have time to tell her about the attack," said Deelor, and quickly added, "she wouldn't have any useful information to offer anyway."

Picard dismissed the rationalization and touched closer to the truth. "You can't keep this from her. She'll have to hear of it sooner or later."

"Then let it be later," the ambassador murmured uneasily. "Let's get this over with, shall we?"

The first few minutes of the meeting were spent reviewing the observations of the landing teams. Data summarized the common pattern of structural damage at both sites with his characteristic precision. Picard wondered what feelings, if any, lay hidden behind the objective account. He did not doubt that the android was capable of emotion, but the captain also considered that Data, like a young child, might be unable to connect the planet-side disaster with his own life. Perhaps that association process could not begin until Data had lived through a personal tragedy. Dr. Crusher was equally professional in her presentation of the autopsy results, but with one free hand she gripped her son's arm.

At the conclusion of Crusher's evidence on acid burns, Deelor further clarified the Choraii attack based on his knowledge of the Hamlin Massacre. "It had to have been a large ship, much bigger than the *B Flat*. Only the oldest of the Choraii ships can survive entry into a planetary atmosphere. We're not sure of the exact dynamics involved, but evidently the spheres compress under atmospheric pressure until the nonorganic components of the hull become concentrated, forming a rigid metal exterior."

"Whereas a young ship, with smaller bubbles, would compress to the point of crushing its crew," deduced Data. "Or lack sufficient metallic components to complete the hull."

"But why the attack?" demanded Riker bitterly. "Hamlin was a mining colony, but New Oregon is . . . was strictly agricultural. What metals could the Choraii have expected to find?"

"We may never know." Deelor's dark brows pulled together. "If they were running low on supplies, they could have acted out of sheer desperation. Or maybe just curiosity. Their last pass through this solar system would have occurred before the terraforming process. The changes on the planet's surface may have attracted their attention."

"And the wanton killing?" asked Picard. "What excuse for that?"

Deelor stiffened. "I'm not defending them, Captain."

"But will the Federation continue to develop diplomatic relations with the Choraii?"

A chorus of protests broke out from the crew as they assimilated the far-reaching implications of the raid on New Oregon.

"Impossible," declared Lieutenant Yar, overriding the others. "First Hamlin, now New Oregon. I saw what they did to the Farmers' settlement. The Choraii are butchers!"

Picard continued, his voice still deceptively soft. "What price for diplomacy, Ambassador Deelor?" And for the secret of the aliens' stardrive.

"That's not up to us to decide," said Deelor steadily. "It's the job of Starfleet admirals to weigh ethical considerations against the demands of defense. Until they change existing policy, I will follow standing orders. Which means that for now, the New Oregon incident is to be treated like any other Choraii encounter. All information is under strict security restrictions."

"You can't keep this a secret!" cried Riker. "Terraform Control will need to know their team was killed. And there were Farmers down there as well. We can't hide those deaths from our passengers any longer."

Deelor frowned. "Yes, entirely too many people on

board the starship are aware of the results of the landing parties' probe. We have no choice but to tell the Farmers of the attack, but for now the identity of the attackers is unknown."

Picard resented Deelor's easy dismissal of that most difficult of duties to be discharged: announcing death. As captain, this responsibility was traditionally Picard's, and he loathed it above all others associated with his rank.

He stared across the table at Beverly Crusher, focusing on her profile, thinking of her face as it had appeared years before when she first learned of her husband's death. Picard had delivered the news in person. His unannounced arrival, without Jack by his side, had been enough to warn Beverly of what was coming. Shock had clouded her eyes even before Picard began to speak. She probably never even registered the actual words, but he remembered them all too well. . . .

The captain pulled away from that morbid train of thought, but his concentration had been shattered. Deelor's closing comments were only so much noise to be endured.

Troi was the first to approach the captain at the conclusion of the briefing. "Captain, I would like to accompany you on your visit to the Farmers."

Picard nodded curtly. So the counselor had sensed his turmoil. Troi was an invaluable resource in judging the emotional health of his crew, but he was uncomfortable when that same empathic talent was used on him. She probably sensed that reaction as well.

"Captain Picard?"

"Yes, Mr. Crusher?" said Picard, turning to the young ensign. Another reminder of Jack's death. "What is it?"

"I thought you should know that one of the settlers on New Oregon was Farmer Patrisha's daughter."

"Thank you, Ensign," said the captain. The boy was right; the information was important. It also made Picard's duty that much harder.

At least he always knew where to find Ruthe, thought Deelor as he crossed the threshold of their cabin. She hadn't left the room once since Jason's death.

Looking up from the floor where she had curled for a nap, Ruthe said, "You've been gone a long time."

"I'm sorry," Deelor replied, not sure whether she had uttered the words as an accusation or merely as an observation. Usually she viewed his movements with indifference. "I beamed down to New Oregon." Then he told her why.

"When did it happen?" she asked after he had finished a brief description of the raid.

"Nearly a week ago. At least, that's Dr. Crusher's best guess from her study of the condition of the bodies. Data's estimate is a little more conservative. He claims the attack occurred at least four days ago, but won't commit himself to any greater length of time."

Ruthe stretched lazily; bare feet peeked out from under the folds of her robe. "Then they could still be in the area. Will we try to contact them?"

"Not with the *Enterprise*. Captain Picard wouldn't welcome the suggestion. Perhaps we can get another starship when we reach Starbase Ten."

"The Choraii will be gone by then," said Ruthe scornfully. "They may follow a circuitous path, but they follow it with great speed."

She didn't ask any more questions, but then, Deelor's talks with Ruthe never lasted long. She lost interest so quickly. Nearly an hour of silence passed between them before Ruthe uttered her final comment on New Oregon.

"The ship must have been very large."

When he heard her say that, Deelor feared Ruthe shared his own suspicion.

"She's alone," Troi told the captain as they stood in the corridor in front of Farmer Patrisha's cabin.

Picard hesitated, one hand raised halfway to the door chime. "Perhaps some of the other colonists should be with her when I break the news."

The counselor considered what she knew of the woman inside. Their few encounters had been brief, nevertheless Troi felt secure in her understanding of that strong personality. "No. Actually, I think she would prefer to be alone at this time. She is not always comfortable with the members of her community. In fact, Patrisha's sense of isolation from the other Farmers has been growing stronger over the journey."

"Very well, Counselor. I'm sure you know what's best." Picard was out of his depth in this situation, and depended heavily on Troi's judgment. For his own sake, Picard was just as glad there would be no further delay. If he waited any longer, he would start to worry whether he lacked the proper somber mien or whether he had overcompensated and looked too severe. Taking a deep breath, he activated the door chime.

When they had leave to enter, Picard and Troi walked into a cabin that had been stripped of personal belongings. Luggage containers were stacked neatly in the center of the cabin day area.

"Why haven't we been allowed to land?" asked Patrisha. "What's gone wrong?"

"The colony on New Oregon has been destroyed."

222

The blow could not be softened with any preamble, but Picard spared Patrisha the harsh details of the Choraii attack. He told her that her daughter was dead, but not that her last seconds of life had been filled with searing pain. Not that there was nothing recognizable left of the body.

"Our landing party has confirmed there are no survivors," Troi explained gently.

"We're very sorry," added Picard when there was nothing else left to say. From that point on, matters went much as they always did on these occasions. His words were met with initial disbelief, then accepted with growing anguish. Some people immediately dissolved into tears, but Patrisha was one of the quiet ones. The wrenching grief would come later, after the starship officers had left. Troi was right; this woman would not have welcomed any additional company.

After an awkward silence, Patrisha finally spoke. "Captain, what would have happened without the schedule delays?"

Over the years, Picard had trained himself to avoid such profitless speculation, but he understood the concern that prompted her question and he answered the query with respect. "Your entire community would have been wiped out. One hundred unarmed colonists, even twice that number, could not have changed the outcome in any way." Small comfort perhaps, but all that he could offer.

"I haven't seen Krn in nearly two years," said Patrisha. Her face was blank and expressionless. "Two years since she and her lover volunteered for the scouting trip. Krn and I were fighting so often that I was actually relieved to see them go."

Picard exchanged glances with Troi. There seemed no graceful way to leave, and the counselor silently indicated they should simply listen for the moment.

Picard did not want to hear any more, but he would
endure it. His discomfort was nothing compared to
Patrisha's pain.

"Yet Dvd always tried to patch things up between
us. He wasn't a typical Farmer. He was a silversmith,
an artist . . ."

Silver. That one word jumped out at Picard, over-
shadowing all that followed. He could trace the chain
of Troi's startled reactions as the counselor sensed the
surge of alarm in his mind and then made the
connection herself. Refined metal, in small quantities,
but sufficiently pure to serve the needs of the Choraii.
The captain was so distracted by the discovery of the
motive for the alien attack that he almost missed the
significance of what came next.

"He was a gentle man and so devoted to their
daughter that she called him uncle."

"There was a child?" asked Picard sharply.

"Yes, my granddaughter, Emily. She would have
turned four soon after our arrival." The intensity of
the captain's question penetrated Patrisha's shock.
"Why is that so important?"

Picard couldn't answer her. Not yet. Perhaps not
ever.

Ruthe paced back and forth in front of the windows
of the observation deck while the assembled group
settled into place. Out of habit, Ambassador Deelor
and Captain Picard both walked toward the seat at the
head of the conference table, but the diplomat gave
ground with an ironic smile and moved to another
chair next to Dr. Crusher. Riker and Data, just
returned from a second trip to the storm-tossed
surface of New Oregon, were the last to sit down.
Ruthe stopped pacing but remained standing.

"We have no proof the girl is still alive," said

Picard, opening the discussion with his greatest concern.

Riker was more optimistic than his captain. "We haven't found her body."

"Which doesn't mean she wasn't killed," warned Beverly Crusher with a frown. "She was only four years old. Her body could have been completely destroyed by acid, or so badly damaged that we simply couldn't identify the organic remains as human."

"They wouldn't kill a child." Ruthe uttered this belief with conviction.

"I wish I could believe you," said Picard. "But the Choraii slaughtered the entire community on New Oregon just as they slaughtered the miners of Hamlin. They're proven killers; why should they scruple over one child?"

"You don't understand," said the translator. "The Choraii consider human adults to be untractable and dangerous. Like wild animals. And if animals are in possession of something of value, well, then it is necessary to remove them. Killing is easiest. But human children are worth saving because they can be gentled."

Picard grimaced at the explanation. "A reprehensible attitude, but one that will work to our advantage this time. We must assume the Farmer girl has been taken aboard the Choraii ship." He locked eyes with Andrew Deelor. "What does existing policy dictate in this situation?"

"We've moved beyond the realm of policy," admitted Deelor with a shrug. "The imagination of Starfleet admirals had not extended to the possibility of another abduction, so the decision for action is ours."

"I say we go after them," said Riker at once. "Now, while Data can still detect the organic particles of their trail."

Data was more cautious. "But once found, what course of action do we take? The ship that attacked New Oregon is even larger than the *B Flat*. How do we force them to give up the child?"

"Not force," said Ruthe, stepping up to the table. "Persuasion." She turned to Picard. Her voice was tight with urgency, and her hands dug deeply into the upholstered chair between them. "When we find the Choraii, I can convince them to give up the girl."

Data continued the role of devil's advocate. "If you do not succeed, the *Enterprise* could end up in a battle it cannot win. All for the sake of a child who may be lying dead in the ruins of New Oregon."

"But what if she's alive, Data?" asked Crusher. "I'd be haunted by the uncertainty of Emily's fate until the issue is settled one way or the other. We have to make certain."

"The Choraii have her!" cried Ruthe vehemently. "And she's been with them for nearly a week now, carried off to an alien world that isn't her home. We must go after their ship and get her back."

"Agreed," said Riker, hitting the tabletop with a clenched fist. "Besides, we stand a good chance of winning any fight they start. Data and Worf are still refining their countermeasures against Choraii technology."

Picard suspected first-hand exposure to the destruction on New Oregon colored Riker's desire for a pursuit of the attackers. That and the natural exuberance of a young officer. Both motivations had merit if they were kept in perspective. "What are your views, Ambassador?" asked Picard, curious as to why the man had not expressed an opinion yet.

Deelor had stared at Ruthe, absorbed by the intensity of her pleading, but at the captain's prodding he shook himself out of his reverie. "I have complete confidence in Ruthe's ability to negotiate with the Choraii. The encounter can be peaceful."

Picard held up a hand to forestall Data's rebuttal. "Nevertheless, the potential for violence still remains." He lowered the hand with a gesture of finality. He had followed the debate intently, listening for any comments that would influence the decision he had reached hours before in Farmer Patrisha's cabin. His mind remained unchanged. "Number One, instruct the bridge crew to prepare for battle configuration. The stardrive section will pursue the Choraii ship."

"Yes, sir," responded Riker with enthusiasm, ready to spring into action as soon as the captain declared the meeting over.

Picard observed Ruthe's exultation at the resolution. Her smile was stiff and unpracticed, lasting only a few seconds, but her eyes shone bright and impassioned.

Chapter Seventeen

"PREPARE TO INITIATE separation sequence."

Picard's warning echoed through every corner of the *Enterprise*.

"Begin."

With that simple word, the massive latches joining the disk-shaped command module to the engineering hull were uncoupled, sundering the structural unity of the starship. The two sections slowly eased apart while metal links retracted into their housing. Then, powered by its twin engine nacelles, the stardrive section sheared away from the saucer in a wide swinging arc and broke free from the orbit around New Oregon.

Riker followed the accelerating flight of the departing engineering section on the viewer of the main bridge. With a sigh he settled back into the captain's chair.

"I wish I could have gone with them, too," said Troi softly from her position next to him.

The first officer shrugged away his disappointment. "Someone had to stay with the ship . . . and the Farmers. The Choraii could always double back and endanger the saucer section."

"But you're more worried about the captain and the others. You want to share their danger."

"Yes," admitted Riker. "But if Ruthe does her job properly, they won't be in any danger."

Captain Picard surveyed the battle bridge from the command dais. This captain's chair was a broad, solid throne, and he sat with back erect; a thin furrow on his brow marked his unconscious effort to adjust to altered surroundings.

The stardrive bridge echoed the layout but not the graceful design of the saucer's command center. Utility demanded a room of reduced dimensions, with less distance between the compact duty stations. The main viewer was smaller; the ramp to the aft deck was replaced by a high step. Instrument readings were displayed across the back wall, but all other walls were smooth and featureless.

The bridge officers had moved to their accustomed positions, but few provisions had been made for passengers. Andrew Deelor no longer had a chair next to the captain; he stepped to one side and leaned against a span of bridge railing instead. Ruthe chose to sit cross-legged on the deck by his feet. Beverly Crusher had claimed a vacant seat at an auxiliary station.

"Sensors detect definite indications of the Choraii's passage," announced Data from the helm. "Navigation coordinates established."

"Proceed at best warp speed, Mr. La Forge," ordered the captain.

"Aye, sir," answered the pilot, and set the *Enterprise* on a matching path to the alien ship. However, in less than an hour he was forced to slow the starship to impulse speed.

"Sensors are losing the trail," reported Yar from the tactical console.

Picard acknowledged the woman's statement with a curt nod. "Thank you, Lieutenant," he added deliberately, shaking off the influence of the sterile confines of the battle bridge. "Mr. Data?"

The android alone appeared unaffected by the oppressive interior. He replied with his customary enthusiasm for commentary. "The Choraii ships shed a continual stream of decayed organic particles, much as human beings shed dead cells from their outer layer of skin. However, over time, the concentration of residue disperses as the inertia of the drifting particles carries them in different directions, so . . ."

"So we've arrived too late to track this ship's departure from New Oregon," said Picard, jumping ahead to the conclusion of Data's exposition.

"We can't turn back now," cried Yar. "There must be a way to keep after the Choraii."

"We shall find them," said Picard, announcing his agreement with a studied calmness that subdued Yar's hotheaded manner without open rebuke. "Mr. La Forge, can you sense any pattern in the progress of their ship?"

"Definitely," said Geordi. His visored eyes tracked the curving path marked on the conn navigation panel; the end of the line was already fading away. "But the movements are very complex. I doubt I could get very far without a sensor feed."

Ruthe sprang up from the deck and approached the helm. Peering down over the pilot's shoulder at the console panel, she studied the visual display for a moment, then shook her head. "If only I could hear where they've been."

"Ah," said Data with a self-satisfied nod. "That can be easily arranged. I have established rough musical equivalents for the travel coordinates." He tapped his ops panel to call forth a record from the language computers. "Unfortunately, the reconstructed rhythm is arbitrary and lacks the free-flowing variation of Choraii song."

"If there is a melody, I will find it." Eyes closed, breath stilled, Ruthe listened twice to the sound of the starship's journey from New Oregon to their present location. "It's a traveling song," she declared at last. Her eyes fluttered open.

"You've heard it before?" asked Deelor.

"It's a popular melody sung by many of the ships in the local cluster," said Ruthe. "We don't have to follow the trail any longer. I can play the rest of the song and show you where it will end."

The translator pulled the sections of her flute from out of her robe and strung the instrument into its full length. Pursing her lips over the embouchure, she blew lightly and called forth the same notes the computer had played, but the stiff mechanical quality of the rendition was transformed into a fluid musical line. Ruthe continued the song past the point where the computer had stopped, carrying the melody on to its conclusion. As the last note died away, she lowered her flute. "That's where they're going."

"Reversing the translation process now," Data said, then checked the output of the language computer. "Final destination coordinates computed."

"Set a direct course for that location," ordered Picard. "Warp eight."

With a satisfied smile Ruthe sank back down on the deck. She held the flute in her lap, but her fingers continued to slide over the silent stops as if she sang to herself. Except for the flutter of her hands, she sat motionless.

Wesley Crusher crashed down onto the hard dirt of the open barnyard but absorbed the shock of his fall with an outstretched arm, just as Tasha had taught him. Then he automatically raised the other arm to guard his chest from the blows that followed the tackle. Dnnys was a clumsy fighter, easily blocked, and Wesley could have thrown him off with ease. Instead, the ensign concentrated on self-defense.

"Tell me!" shouted Dnnys. He was too blind with fury to notice his fists never connected with their target. "Why was the captain asking about Emily?"

Wesley blocked another blow. "Stop hitting and I'll explain!"

Dnnys pulled back from his attack. "I'm sorry," he stammered as his anger subsided. "But she's my niece. You know what that means to me, to any Farmer uncle."

"That's why I think you should know," said Wesley, sitting up. He brushed at the bits of dirt and straw clinging to his tunic, stalling for time as he phrased his answer to fall within the limits of his security oath. "There's a chance that Emily's still alive. She may have been taken off the planet."

"You mean the raiders have her?" asked Dnnys. His flushed face drained of color.

"Yes," Wesley said, skirting dangerously close to a security breach. "She's being well cared for, but getting her back is going to be difficult." He gingerly touched a stinging patch of skin on his cheek and wondered if the scrape would be healed before his mother returned. The thought of his mother on the battle bridge was more painful than the bruises. Wesley never gave much thought to danger when the two of them were together on the ship, but waiting for her return filled him with worry. Was this how his mother had felt while Jack Crusher was on board the *Stargazer?*

Dnnys shook his friend by the shoulder. "When will we find out?"

"I can't tell you, because I don't know," said Wesley, throwing off the hold and scrambling to his feet. "Come on, I have to finish your chores before sunset." He wanted to think about something other than the outcome of his father's last voyage.

The *Enterprise* had reached a patch of space no different from any other within a distance of several light-years. No different at that moment, reflected Andrew Deelor. If the Choraii followed their usual habits, the situation was subject to change without any prior notice.

"This is the place," announced Geordi. "I've double-checked the navigation settings."

"Sensors do not detect any traces of organic particles," reported Data. "Either our coordinates are incorrect or the Choraii have not yet arrived."

"We are at the right place and they will come," said Ruthe without rising from the deck. "The song is a long one."

"Not that long," Lieutenant Yar exclaimed. "I'm picking up a faint radio transmission. Boosting reception to the maximum." She released a thrumming sound into the air.

The bridge crew stopped in mid-motion, entranced by what they heard. The throaty chorus was far deeper than that of the *B Flat* singers; it possessed the broad resonance of a cathedral organ and a wide range of voices which rose and fell in complex harmony. Deelor waited for Ruthe's reaction; she displayed none that he could observe. Either she was indifferent to the character of the sound or she already knew what to expect.

"Not a single note," said Picard with surprise as he listened to the undulating music. "More like a chord."

"A D major chord, to be precise," noted Deelor. He stepped up to the captain's chair. "We're in trouble."

The quiet statement snapped Picard's attention away from the Choraii song. "Explain."

"Pitch is an indication of a ship's age. In addition, listen to the number of voices," Deelor instructed. "Only five different tones are present, but I suspect many of the parts are doubled or even tripled. A conservative estimate indicates eleven singers, which means the ship is very old and therefore very powerful. More than a match for the *Enterprise.*"

Ruthe's answering song caught him by surprise. She had mounted the aft bridge and played as if from a stage. The tripping notes from her flute hovered several registers above the drone of the Choraii D major chorus as she wove an intricate counterpoint to their melodic line.

"Captain, shall I broadcast her response?" asked Yar, lowering the growing volume of the Choraii transmission.

Picard hesitated. "Is something wrong, Ambassador?"

"What?" Then Deelor realized he had been frowning as he listened. "No, nothing's wrong."

The captain waved an assent to Lieutenant Yar. Ruthe played on and the tempo of the intertwined sounds quickened.

"They've heard her." Deelor's own heart began to beat more rapidly, as if striving to match the pulse of the music.

"And here they come," announced Geordi from the helm. His energy-sensitive visor had picked out the first glimmer of the approaching vessel on the battlebridge viewer, but by the time his warning drew the crew's attention to the screen, the image of the Choraii ship had tripled in size.

Deelor caught his breath at the sight. Even without any reference point in space, he could sense how massive the ship must be. Whereas the *B Flat* had been composed of some two dozen neatly packed bubbles, the *D Major* was a jumbled conglomeration of over a hundred spheres. An elongated stream of large bubbles formed the central mass, with smaller ones tucked into crevices and dotted here and there over the outer edges. Deelor had never faced a ship of this complexity before.

"Reduce magnification," ordered Picard as the *D Major* filled the frame, then spilled beyond its borders. His brow furrowed. "So these are the destroyers of New Oregon."

The approaching cluster tumbled in space. As a new side rolled into view, Deelor spotted several purple spheres nestled in the exterior layer. "Captain . . ."

"Yes, I see them," said Picard tersely. "Data, prepare your neutralizing probe for launch. Just in case we end up inside another energy net."

"Neutralization efforts would be ineffective," said Data. He further reduced the screen magnification as the Choraii ship threatened to outgrow the frame once again. "The net draws power from the mother ship and the *D Major* can release a far greater energy surge than can be siphoned off by the probe."

"Which means their net would crush us faster as well."

"Captain, we would still have time to drill through the spheres with our phasers," said Worf.

"Yes," agreed Data. "But my calculations indicate a seventy-eight point five percent chance that such a scenario would end in mutual destruction."

"That's enough talk of battle," said Deelor impatiently. "This is going to remain a peaceful encounter."

"So far, the peaceful intentions have remained ours and ours alone," said Picard bitterly. "The Choraii loot and destroy and then we pay them for their ill-gotten gains."

The flight of the *D Major* came to an abrupt halt. The glowing orange spheres quivered with the strong currents of their liquid interior.

"Ambassador . . ."

Deelor hushed the captain with a wave of his hand. "Listen." The journey song had ended, but Ruthe continued playing with the Choraii, modulating without a break into a new melody. "They're singing the greeting."

Shifting his weight in the captain's chair, Picard leaned closer to Deelor and spoke more softly. "The exchange sounds friendly."

"Yes, it is." So even the captain could detect the joy of the meeting. "Once Ruthe establishes our good intentions, we can—" Deelor broke off.

"What's happened?"

"Ruthe has begun a third melody," explained Deelor. She hadn't looked to him once for a sign of what to do, yet apparently she was moving beyond the ritual preliminaries. In what direction? Deelor tried to make sense of her exchange with the Choraii, to untangle the mix of high flute and booming organ voices, but the scales they used were unfamiliar and his understanding of the exchange faltered.

Dr. Crusher edged up behind him. "Do they have the child?"

"Yes, I think so," answered Deelor, less certain than he sounded. He had lost track of the melodic line and could grasp only scattered phrases of meaning.

"So how do we get her back?" Picard's voice rang

out over the bridge. All singing had stopped abruptly, replaced by an unvarying bass hum emanating from the *D Major*.

Snapping off a section of her flute, Ruthe answered the captain. "Arrangements have already been made for the girl's return." The translator rapidly disassembled the remainder of her instrument and tucked the pieces inside her cloak. "Emily was found when they plundered New Oregon for silver. She isn't a bonding gift, so they are willing to let her go for the proper price."

The palms of Deelor's hands grew moist. He rubbed them dry against his uniform. "What price is that?"

"Three pounds of gold, some few ounces of zinc and platinum." Ruthe stepped down from the aft deck. "I'll beam over while the metal is gathered."

Deelor was too shaken to reply. He had trusted Ruthe with his life over and over again; he would do so now. Yet he knew her well enough to sense a lie in what she told him. A lie to what purpose?

Picard stepped down from his chair to confront Ruthe. "I don't like the appearance of this transaction. They've agreed too easily."

"Would you rather fight the Choraii?" asked Ruthe, arching one brow. "I'm not so certain you would win."

A full beat passed before the captain spoke again. "Lieutenant Yar, Dr. Crusher, please accompany Ruthe to the transporter chamber." Picard fell back and the translator swept past him.

Deelor stared after her until the doors of the turbo cut her off from his sight. "I trust Ruthe's judgment." Then he wondered if he had jumped too quickly to her defense and betrayed his growing unease to the captain. "She knows what she's doing."

Picard settled back into place, his feet braced firmly

on the dais, his hands gripping the armrests. He focused his attention on the viewer. "You may trust Ruthe, but I don't trust the Choraii."

Tasha Yar felt uneasy about opening a window in the ship's shield for the critical seconds when Ruthe would transport over to the Choraii ship. Her tension eased very little even after the deflectors snapped back into place; she couldn't relax while the massive vessel loomed so near to the *Enterprise.*

"I hate this part," admitted Yar leaning against the console. "Last time we waited for nearly three hours before Ruthe's contact signal."

Crusher sighed heavily. "If the ritual swim through the *B Flat* took hours, how long will she take to go through the *D Major?"*

"Days, weeks . . ." A high-pitched tone jerked the security chief back to the controls. "The beam signal," Yar announced, swiftly reversing the procedure that had sent Ruthe out of the ship only minutes before.

"It's too early! Something must have gone wrong." Crusher rushed to the dais as white light flooded the chamber once again. When the blinding beam died away, the doctor found a young girl standing on the platform. And only the girl. Around her neck she wore the chain with Ruthe's com insignia.

"Get her out of the way," cried Yar as she hastened to broaden the reception beam around the coordinates. Each second she spent adjusting the controls increased the ship's risk.

Crusher swept the child off the platform, drawing the small body to her chest with a fierce hug, rejoicing in the recovery of at least one life from the devastation on New Oregon. The face that had peered out from behind water-soaked brown tresses bore a strong resemblance to Dnnys. "Emily!"

"I was having fun," answered the girl happily when the doctor loosened her embrace. Emily had made the transition to breathing air without assistance. "Can I go back to play soon?"

"No, honey. You're going home," said Crusher, trying to smile back. Had the Hamlin children been this untouched by their parents' deaths?

"Is that nice lady coming, too?"

Ruthe. The doctor looked across the room. Yar's hands were on the transporter controls, but they weren't in motion any longer. "Tasha, where is she?"

"I couldn't lock on to her," said the security chief. Her face was wooden, her eyes downcast. "Shields are raised."

"The entire ship registers as a life form," boomed Worf across the smaller bridge. "Sensor readings are garbled. I can't pinpoint her exact position in the interior." He checked another section of the tactical console. "Still no answer on hailing frequencies."

"What can have happened over there?" Picard had doubted the Choraii's intentions from the start, but he mustn't let his suspicions override judgment. A misreading of the alien motives could embroil both ships in unnecessary combat. "Would the Choraii send over the child without receiving payment first?"

"It's possible, I suppose. Perhaps as a statement of extreme arrogance."

Another thought increased Picard's concern. "Or would she have snatched the child away without the Choraii's knowledge?"

"No," said Deelor firmly. "She's not that foolish."

"We're blind to what's happening over there, but unless they make a hostile—"

"Captain," broke in Data. "The *D Major* is moving away."

239

"Helm, full speed pursuit!" ordered Picard. He followed quickly with a shipwide announcement. "All hands to battlestations."

The *Enterprise* surged forward after the Choraii bubbles. The wide gap between the two vessels began to narrow, but very slowly.

"Ambassador, we can't force Ruthe's return," said Picard. "Not without placing her in grave danger."

Deelor nodded. His face was pale but composed. "Just get their attention and buy me some time, Captain."

"Understood." Picard took a deep breath and issued his next order. "Worf, lock tractor beams as soon as the Choraii are in range."

Worf's clawed hand hovered above the tactical console like a raptor, then swooped downward. Contact. Deck tremors racked the starship as a half-dozen tractor beams latched onto the spheres of the *D Major*. White bridge lights guttered out; bloodred emergency lights flickered to life. On the viewer, the Choraii ship shuddered to a slow halt.

"Humans, release us!" Deep, slurring voices thundered like an angry Greek chorus.

"You still carry one of our people within your ship," shouted Deelor, but his solo tenor was weak in comparison. "Return her to us."

"You mean the lost one? We were forced to give her up many years ago, but now she's come back."

"Damn her," cursed Deelor under his breath.

Picard signaled Worf to cut off communications. Silence blanketed the bridge. "Ambassador, what do they mean by 'the lost one'?"

"I suspected this earlier. There are only a few ships in the local cluster that are large enough to land on a planet, but I thought sure Ruthe would tell me . . ." He trailed off distractedly.

"Tell you what?" demanded Picard.

"The *D Major* is Ruthe's homeship. She was born and raised there." Deelor raked his fingers through his hair, leaving a wake of angry spikes on the top of his head. "She must have known as soon as she heard their song, but she didn't tell me."

"Why not?"

"Because I would never have let her beam over." Deelor waved urgently to Worf and raised his voice to resume his exchange with the Choraii. "We'll give you any metal you want. Just let Ruthe return here."

"No, Wild One. This is her home. She agreed to stay if we gave you the young one in her place."

Rising from the captain's chair, Picard brought his deeper voice to the ambassador's service. "We will not accept her sacrifice."

"But it's not a sacrifice, Captain." Ruthe's words quavered and echoed, distorted by the liquid that filled her lungs. *"I'm here of my own free will."*

"No, I don't believe you!" cried out Deelor. "You've struck a bargain for the girl and this is the price."

"A small price." Her laugh rippled through the waters.

"An unacceptable price," countered Picard angrily. "The Choraii have brought death to so many people without thought, without remorse. How can we abandon you to live with them?"

"But I can stop the killings. I will sing them your songs! Songs of Mozart, and Beethoven, and all the others! I will show the Choraii that even beasts can make music. Once they recognize your worth, they will learn to ask for what they need."

"This action is too drastic, too final. There are other ways to—"

"You still don't understand. I have always wanted to return here, to my real home. I've betrayed many of my kind in the search for this ship, but only the children,

241

because they are young, and can forget. I was too old to forget and too young to die for the memories."

"Is she telling the truth?" demanded Picard of the man standing frozen beside him. "Can this be what she really wants?"

"Yes," whispered Deelor hoarsely. "Damn her, yes."

Ruthe's voice sang out again, more insistent than before. *"Let us go, Wild Ones. We have many songs to sing."*

"Lieutenant Worf," said Picard in a low voice. "Let them go."

The Klingon quickly obeyed, releasing the *D Major* from the tractor beam hold. The bright lights and chattering sounds of the battle bridge, muted by a lack of power, sprang back to full intensity.

"They're not leaving," observed La Forge of the alien craft. He lowered his hands closer to the helm controls.

A deep humming sound reverberated from the communications link with the *D Major*. Resonant Choraii voices swelled into a dirgelike song, flooding the bridge with their music. One high soprano echoed the somber melody.

The oppressive sound raised a prickle of apprehension in the captain. "What's happening?"

Deelor didn't answer. Instead, Data turned from the helm. "I believe that is their way of saying good-bye."

Chapter Eighteen

New Oregon's soil was still sodden from the long rains, but the standing water had finally drained away from higher ground. The smell of rotting vegetation remained, masking the sweeter scent of new growth. Scattered patches of bright green promised a return of grasses and shrubs; they would grow faster than before, feeding on the decay of the first generation. The violent winds that had racked the surface were now reduced to gentle breezes, and overhead a mid-summer sun shone through clear skies of azure blue.

While starship technicians had labored to restore the planet's weather controls, the Farmers had put their steel shovels to work, but not for planting seeds of grain. A dozen graves scarred their new land.

On the morning of her seventh day on this world, Patrisha carried a sprig of greenery to Krn's gravesite;

when the flowers bloomed, she would bring a bouquet. The ritual was an old one, stretching back to the beginnings of their community, and a familiar one to the woman who had spent her own childhood visiting her mother's grave. Perhaps, as grass spread over this pile of fresh brown dirt, her sharp pain would fade and she would come here out of habit rather than aching need.

Patrisha looked up at the sound of heavy footsteps. Her cousin's boots were caked with mud, his hands red and swollen from unaccustomed labor, yet Tomas had recovered a measure of his dignity in the last week. Although he was still an aggravating man, he was also a Farmer. He belonged here.

"I was looking for Dnnys, but I hear he's gone up there." Tomas pointed an accusing finger straight up into the sky. "By transporter!"

"Blame me if you must blame someone. I gave him permission to go." The leaves of the twig on Krn's grave were already wilting in the heat. "He's saying good-bye to his friend."

"The boy was too long aboard that ship," pronounced Tomas, although with more resignation than spleen. "Take my word for it, he won't abide by our creed anymore. Soon he'll dream of leaving the community."

"I won't ask him to stay," Patrisha replied quietly. She had lost her own faith many years ago, but not soon enough to forge a life elsewhere. Her place was here on New Oregon, with Krn's daughter, because there was nowhere else to go.

The last meeting between Wesley and Dnnys was uncomfortable for many reasons.

Dnnys had never experienced a molecular transport before, and though he had always scoffed at Farmer stories of bodies mangled by equipment malfunctions, he was overcome by a last-minute terror when the beaming lock took hold of him. The boy materialized on the transporter platform with a pale face and trembling legs, certain that both Wesley and the console operator could see his cowardice.

For his own part, Wesley felt an unreasoning guilt for the good fortune of living aboard a starship. He had tried to share this advantage, but when he observed the sour expression on his friend's face, the ensign wondered if the Farmer wouldn't have been happier knowing less about the life he was missing.

After an awkward silence, Dnnys stepped down from the dais. He carried several books in his arms. "I won't be needing these anymore," he said gruffly, and thrust the engineering texts into Wesley's hands. He scowled to cover the welling of tears in his eyes, then made an effort to explain his actions. "All my life, I've been without an uncle. I can't leave Emily without one, too."

"I figured you'd decide to stay," said Wesley, untroubled by the return of his gift. He stepped over to a table by the operating console and exchanged the Farmer's books for another set which he had prepared. "So I brought along these."

Dnnys accepted the new books. "What are they?" he asked, though without real interest. There seemed little point in reading anything Wesley could provide; a Farmer's life would leave him little time for dreaming.

"The technical specs on the terraforming station." Wesley was pleased to see his friend look down with sudden astonishment at the books he held. "A replacement crew is already on the way to rebuild the control center, but terraform engineers are in short supply, so the station will probably be under-staffed."

"And anyone who can help . . ." started Dnnys with the beginnings of a smile.

". . . will be very welcome," finished Wesley with an answering grin.

No more time remained for them to talk. "We're about to break orbit," announced the transporter operator. "You'll have to go now."

Dnnys stepped back onto the dais, books clutched tightly to his chest. As the whine of the transporter rose in pitch, he thought of one last pressing question. "How long does the finishing stage of terraforming last?"

"A lifetime," called out Wesley. And his friend was gone.

Ships of the sea sailed out of harbor with the tides, but the *Enterprise* was free to leave New Oregon at a time of the captain's choosing. Picard chose to leave when the lights of the ship's interior were dimmed to the level of a setting sun.

"Engage," he ordered, leaning back against the cushioned contours of his command chair. Given the lateness of the hour, some captains might have delegated this duty to their first officer, but no departure was routine for Picard, and he was always present when his starship left planetary orbit. He would remain on the bridge for a few more minutes, savoring the promise of adventure which lay hidden in each new beginning.

The captain listened without comment as Counselor Troi engaged in mild banter with Will Riker. The barbs flew back and forth from either side of the command center.

"A conference is not a recreational event," said

Troi. "The gathering serves an important professional purpose."

"Right, like finding out how many psychologists can fit in a transporter booth?" shot back Riker.

His derisive comment raised a muffled laugh from Tasha, listening from her perch on the aft deck. "Deanna, I watched you pack for the trip and some of the clothes you chose . . ."

"Tasha, hush," said Troi sharply.

Picard exchanged smiles with his first officer, but was careful to keep his back to the counselor. Unfortunately, she could probably sense his amusement.

"If you will excuse me, Captain," Troi said with studied politeness. "I have some more preparations to make for my journey."

Riker's grin faded slightly when the counselor rose to leave. "Deanna, I was only joking."

She turned back, and Picard wondered what impending mischief was hidden in her innocent smile.

"If I remember correctly, you have first-hand experience in determining how many first officers can fit in a shuttlecraft." Troi sailed off the bridge now that the crew's attention was riveted on Riker.

Picard could not resist an attack of his own. He raised an inquiring eyebrow and watched his first officer squirm.

"It was an experiment in emergency evacuation procedures," said Riker. He managed to keep a straight face during this explanation, but his ears were turning bright red. "And the answer is twelve."

Data swiveled his ops console to face the commander. "If the object of the exercise was to determine maximum passenger density, then even the smallest shuttlecraft model can accommodate more than twelve people."

"Yes, but at the time we could find only twelve first

officers who had shoreleave on Mardi Gras. So we had to make up the difference with some of the locals."

"You were on Mardi Gras?" Picard reflected on his own shore-leave experiences on that particular planet. "Are you sure Data is old enough to hear the rest of this tale?"

"Sir?" The android looked somewhat confused by the captain's comment. Geordi's laughter only added to his puzzlement.

Riker grinned broadly. "Well, he has expressed curiosity about human interpersonal relationships, Captain. How else is he going to learn?"

"Then by all means continue, Number One," said Picard. "And that's an order."

As chief medical officer, Crusher was responsible for the staffing of her sickbay. She prided herself on having assembled an ensemble of first-rate medical personnel for the *Enterprise*. Assignment to the new starship was already considered a prize, one much sought after by Starfleet doctors and nurses, so turnover in her department was exceptionally low. Nevertheless, the nervous intern who stood before Dr. Crusher's desk was requesting a transfer.

"How did you learn about the other children?" demanded Crusher. Her voice was sharp with disappointment; Lisa Iovino's departure would be a genuine loss to sickbay. "Never mind, it doesn't really matter."

"Can I join them?" persisted Iovino, not at all sure where she was asking to be sent. All that mattered was that the children were there.

"Yes," sighed Crusher. She admitted to herself that the Hamlin children had a greater need of the intern's talents than did the starship crew. "I'm sure I can arrange your transfer to the proper facility." Ambassador Deelor owed her that much. "And the authorities at Starbase Ten will fill you in on your eventual destination."

"Thank you, Dr. Crusher," said Iovino, looking a little dazed at the speed with which her life was changing from its prescribed course. "I never planned on working with children professionally, but these kids—"

"Lisa!" The howl from the medical ward was quickly followed by an ominous crash. "Lisa?"

"He's supposed to be asleep," said the intern, racing for the door. "I bribed him into walking, but now he's starting to climb."

Still smiling over the destructive antics of the rambunctious Moses, Dr. Crusher left sickbay for a long-overdue field trip. Her own child, no longer a boy so much as a young man, met her at the entrance to the holodeck. Beyond the gates, she glimpsed a sunset sky streaked with magenta and blue. Enough light remained for a stroll over the rolling hills.

"It was even better when the animals were here," said Wesley as he and his mother approached the first run of fences. The farm seemed eerily quiet, as if a sorcerer had cast a sleep spell over the land.

Beverly drew in a deep breath of the honeyed air. Old memories, overlaid by her life with Jack and a career in Starfleet, stirred to life. "Oh, I can imagine what it was like. After all, I was born on an agricultural colony."

Her son unlatched a wooden gate and they passed through. He took the time to close it, even though no lambs would get loose now. Standing in the empty main yard, Wesley pointed out the pens for pigs and the hutches that had held the rabbits. The dripping of a leaky water pump echoed loudly when he stopped talking. Absently rubbing a callus on his hand grown from drawing water for the horses, Wesley tried to make sense of his labors. "I still don't see why they've chosen to live this way. The whole point of technology is to save people from so much hard work, to give them time to do other things."

"Yes, I suppose," said Crusher. "But I can understand the Farmers' reluctance to use complicated machinery. The people of my homeworld would have suffered far less if they hadn't been so dependent on technology." The devastation on Arvedda III had occurred before her own birth, but Crusher's grandmother had passed on the memory of those harsh years. "When essential equipment broke down, they were helpless. The survivors were forced to relearn the old ways on their own, without teachers."

"I hadn't thought about that," said Wesley.

They rambled on in companionable silence until their circuit of the room brought them back to the gates. With one last look at the darkened fields, Wesley shut off the program.

Picard crossed the threshold of the observation lounge, then stopped short when he saw a shadowed figure standing by the windows. He traced the outlines of the silhouette. "You're up late, Dr. Crusher. Another call from T'sala's firstborn?"

"No, I'm just brooding," the woman replied, but she smiled at Picard when he walked up beside her. "Careful, my mood may be contagious."

"I'll take my chances."

"I was thinking about Ruthe," said Crusher. "She's lived with humans for the last fifteen years. Jean-Luc, what if she's changed too much for a return to life with the Choraii?"

Picard felt the muscles of his neck and shoulders

tighten under the heavy weight of her question. "Then she will have no place left to go." The sadness of that knowledge overwhelmed him for a moment before he shook his head. "No, that's not true. She will have to learn to live in both worlds."

The doctor carried the thought even further than he had intended. "That's what we've done here aboard the *Enterprise.* We've left our homes and chosen to become wanderers, just like the Choraii."

"We're a trifle less bloodthirsty," said Picard dryly. "But I grant the similarity." And the comparison helped to still the last of his doubts at having left Ruthe behind. "Have you finished brooding, Beverly?"

"Yes, I have."

"Good," Picard said. "Then you'll appreciate hearing about one of our first officer's adventures." The story would make its way through the entire population of the starship by the end of the next day, and the captain wanted the chance to tell it at least once.

Andrew Deelor hadn't slept, but he waited until the arrival of morning before throwing off the cover from his body and rising from the bed. He wasn't hungry but he would go in search of food rather than remain here any longer. Gathering up the crumpled cloak that had served as his blanket, he headed toward the cabin door.

As he walked the length of the passenger suite, Deelor realized Ruthe had made no imprint on the interior. Her only possessions had been the cloak and her flute, and she had dropped both to the floor of the transporter chamber. He had given the flute to the young Farmer girl. Children taken from Choraii ships developed into exceptional musicians; perhaps her brief time with them would have an effect. Now all that was left of Ruthe was the worn garment he held in his hands. A faint trace of cinnamon still clung to the fibers.

Deelor stuffed the gray cloth into a disposal chute and left the cabin empty-handed. He traveled light and the weight of her cloak was more than he could bear.

THE

STAR TREK

PHENOMENON

___ ABODE OF LIFE
70596/$4.99

___ BATTLESTATIONS!
70183/$4.50

___ BLACK FIRE
70548/$4.50

___ BLOODTHIRST
70876/$4.50

___ CORONA
70798/$4.50

___ CHAIN OF ATTACK
66658/$4.95

___ THE COVENANT OF
THE CROWN
70078/$4.50

___ CRISIS ON CENTAURUS
70799/$4.50

___ CRY OF THE ONLIES
740789/$4.95

___ DEEP DOMAIN
70549/$4.50

___ DEMONS
70877/$4.50

___ DOCTOR'S ORDERS
66189/$4.50

___ DOUBLE, DOUBLE
66130/$3.95

___ DREADNOUGHT
72567/$4.50

___ DREAMS OF THE RAVEN
70281/$4.50

___ DWELLERS IN THE
CRUCIBLE
74147/$4.95

___ ENEMY UNSEEN
68403/$4.99

___ ENTERPRISE
73032/$4.95

___ ENTROPY EFFECT
72416/$4.50

___ FINAL FRONTIER
69655/$4.95

___ THE FINAL NEXUS
74148/$4.95

___ THE FINAL REFLECTION
70764/$4.50

___ A FLAG FULL OF STARS
64398/$4.95

___ GHOST-WALKER
64398/$4.95

___ HOME IS THE HUNTER
66662/$4.50

___ HOW MUCH FOR JUST
THE PLANET?
72214/$4.50

___ IDIC EPIDEMIC
70768/$4.50

___ ISHMAEL
73587/$4.50

___ KILLING TIME
70597/$4.50

___ KLINGON GAMBIT
70767/$4.50

___ THE KOBAYASHI MARU
65817/$4.50

___ LEGACY
74468/$4.95

___ LOST YEARS
70795/$4.95

___ MEMORY PRIME
70550/$4.50

___ MINDSHADOW
70420/$4.50

___ MUTINY ON
THE ENTERPRISE
70800/$4.50

___ MY ENEMY, MY ALLY
70421/$4.50

___ THE PANDORA PRINCIPLE
65815/$4.99

___ PAWNS AND SYMBOLS
66497/$3.95

___ PROMETHEUS DESIGN
72366/$4.50

___ RENEGADE
65814/$4.95

___ ROMULAN WAY
70169/$4.50

more on next page...

THE

STAR TREK

PHENOMENON

___	RULES OF ENGAGEMENT	66129/$4.50
___	SHADOW LORD	73746/$4.95
___	SPOCK'S WORLD	66773/$4.95
___	STRANGERS FROM THE SKY	65913/$4.50
___	THE TEARS OF THE SINGERS	69654/$4.50
___	THE THREE MINUTE UNIVERSE	65816/$3.95
___	TIME FOR YESTERDAY	70094/$4.50
___	TIMETRAP	64870/$4.95
___	THE TRELLISANE CONFRONTATION	70095/$4.50
___	TRIANGLE	66251/$3.95
___	UHURA'S SONG	65227/$4.95
___	VULCAN ACADEMY MURDERS	72367/$4.50
___	VULCAN'S GLORY	74291/$4.95
___	WEB OF THE ROMULANS	70093/$4.50
___	WOUNDED SKY	66735/$3.95
___	YESTERDAY'S SON	72449/$4.50

• •

___	STAR TREK–THE MOTION PICTURE	72300/$4.50
___	STAR TREK II–THE WRATH OF KHAN	74149/$4.95
___	STAR TREK III–THE SEARCH FOR SPOCK	73133/$4.50
___	STAR TREK IV–THE VOYAGE HOME	70283/$4.50
___	STAR TREK V–THE FINAL FRONTIER	68008/$4.50
___	STAR TREK COMPENDIUM REVISED	68440/$10.95
___	MR. SCOTT'S GUIDE TO THE ENTERPRISE	70498/$12.95
___	THE STAR TREK INTERVIEW BOOK 61794/$7.95	
___	THE WORLDS OF THE FEDERATION 66989/$11.95	

Simon & Schuster Mail Order Dept. STP
200 Old Tappan Rd., Old Tappan, N.J. 07675

POCKET
BOOKS

Please send me the books I have checked above. I am enclosing $_____ (please add 75¢ to cover postage and handling for each order. Please add appropriate local sales tax). Send check or money order-no cash or C.O.D.'s please. Allow up to six weeks for delivery. For purchases over $10.00 you may use VISA: card number, expiration date and customer signature must be included.

Name _____

Address _____

City _____ State/Zip _____

VISA Card No. _____ Exp. Date _____

Signature _____ 118-40

The First Star Trek: The Next Generation
Hardcover Novel!

REUNION

Michael Jan Friedman

Captain Pickard's
past and present
collide on board the
U.S.S. *Enterprise*™

POCKET
BOOKS

Available in Hardcover
from Pocket Books

444-01